Bridge Over Calm Water

Jan Kendall

Strategic Book Group

Copyright © 2011

All rights reserved – Jan Kendall

No part of this book may be reproduced or transmitted in any form or by any means, graphic, electronic, or mechanical, including photocopying, recording, taping, or by any information storage retrieval system, without the permission, in writing, from the publisher.

Strategic Book Group
P.O. Box 333
Durham CT 06422
www.StrategicBookClub.com

ISBN: 978-1-60911-732-0

Book Design: Suzanne Kelly

In Memory of Mrs. Clara Collier

Acknowledgment

To God be the Glory, "I can do all things through Him who strengthens me." Philippians 4:13

Contents

Introduction		ix
ONE	The Nightmare	1
TWO	Collin	21
THREE	On the Bridge	33
FOUR	Facing the Truth	46
FIVE	Unexpected Kindness	57
SIX	A Heavy Load	69
SEVEN	Doubts, Fears, and Trials	89
EIGHT	Lilly's True Mother	105
NINE	Starting Over	121
TEN	Jinx	137
ELEVEN	Sorrow	152
TWELVE	Home at Last	166
THIRTEEN	Grace Arrives	180
FOURTEEN	A Hard Truth	199
FIFTEEN	A New Beginning	219

Introduction

I would love to believe that my daughter and her generation realize they stand on the shoulders of those who have gone before them. When I watch them make life-altering decisions in a frivolous manner and insist on acting like children into their twenties, I have to wonder. Do they understand the importance of building for the future? By living only for themselves, do they not realize they are destroying the foundations on which their lives are built? Countless selfless acts have gone into building our nation. Is it possible for one generation to dismantle all that has been accomplished by so many people?

The story of Rea grew out of my frustrations. Born a child of the Great Depression, by the time she was in her mid to late teens, Rea was expected to take on the responsibilities of an adult. The young men and women of her time stepped from difficult childhoods headlong into a world torn by war. Even though thousands of the brightest and bravest were killed on foreign battlefields, the ingenuity and hard work of those left pulled our nation with them into a promising future.

Rea's wisdom and sense of responsibility were common traits among her peers. Accustomed to a life swamped with tribulation, she was more than prepared to face the heartache and pain that beset her in the summer of 1941. Her advantage over the young women of today was that she did not have great material wealth that weighed her down with the desire for the next best thing.

Jan Kendall

I fear for us when I look into the future; I suppose my fears are deeply embedded within this story. A nation mirrors the characteristics of its citizens. Will we continue to be a great nation throughout the generations to come?

CHAPTER ONE

The Nightmare

I'd had this nightmare so many times I could visualize every moment in my waking hours. I stood cold and shivering on the rough wooden boards that paved Rock Island's one-lane bridge. The iron trusses above me were silver grey in the moonlight. As I watched, they began to shiver. I felt the vibrations in my feet. Looking out toward the lake, I saw that the surface of the water was as smooth as glass and reflected a full moon. The trees along the bank stood sentinel, still as death. My attention returned to the bridge. The shiver became more violent in nature. The trusses turned and twisted, groaning in complaint. The bridge began to undulate, and it was difficult to keep my balance. It occurred to me that I should run to one end and find safety on the quiet shoreline. The option to run was quickly lost as the convulsing bridge knocked me to my knees. Grasping for the side railing, I barely kept myself from rolling off into the lake below. Had I been thinking clearly, I would have realized the water offered a safe refuge from the horrific creature the bridge had become. Petrified with fear, however, I could not think. Desperate to control my fate, I refused to release the railing. This would be my final decision. Suddenly the structure heaved upward with an unseen force toward the heavens, rendering it no longer recognizable as a bridge. I felt myself falling, trapped among the broken and dismembered metal and wood. The dream always ended there.

Waking in a cold sweat, my heart raced and the blood pounded in my ears. I fought to control the fear that had followed me through to reality. For years, this nightmare had found its way to live among the more pleasant dreams of my childhood. Fantasies I had read in books during the day took on a life and were relived in my sleep. However, I never called forth the nightmare. It came unbidden and unwanted from the recesses of my mind. Enslaving me in uncontrollable mutilation and agony, it destroyed the bridge and, eventually, me along with it.

As I grew up, I thought the nightmare would go the way of all things youthful. Maturity, I reasoned, would purge its fiendish hold on me. To my utter dismay, it clung with a vicious tenacity somewhere in the darkest reaches of my being. It sucked at the very thing that made me human. It wanted to weary and then destroy the peace of my soul.

Waking once again from the struggle, I could feel the warmth of the sun on my face. Startled by the brightness in my room, I rose to my feet quickly. The nightmare had held me in its grip too long. Stumbling to the wardrobe to grab my work clothes, I jerked them on as I made my way out of the room.

I hoped I had not slept beyond the point of redemption with Pa. A strong coffee smell washed over me as I descended the stairs and ran headlong out the front door. By sleeping late, I had burdened Ma with cooking breakfast alone. Stopping in the kitchen would have resulted in a tongue lashing. My reprieve would be short-lived; she would find ample opportunity to make her displeasure known later.

The morning was cool. Each breath I took turned to a cold fog and clung to my eyelashes as I slipped and slid across the dew-covered grass. Pa's voice rose above the noise of the animals as he gave Jinx, our field hand, instructions inside the milk barn. I couldn't afford to delay my arrival. The tone in Pa's voice was harsh. He often took his displeasure out on the person in his path at the time of his anger, even when they were innocent of any wrongdoing. Jinx did not deserve to suffer for my sin.

"I'm here, Pa."

"Get over here, Rea, and take my place. I should already be out in the field."

"Sorry I was late, Pa. I didn't hear Ma knock on my door this morning."

"You been up reading again?"

"No, you took my lamp out of the room the last time I was late for chores."

"Oh, yeah. Well, being late again will still cost you those precious books and earn you a good whoppin' with my belt."

To add emphasis to his statement, Pa threw the cleaning rag into the bucket of soapy water at my feet. Cold water splattered up, wetting one side of my clothes and the Jersey cow beside me. She cared as little for the dousing as I did and kicked at the air, narrowly missing my leg. I had already suffered one broken bone because of these ornery creatures; I did not want to endure another.

Jinx remained intent on his work with his head down. He would never comment about my shortcomings. Had my brothers been there that morning, they would have jumped at the opportunity to go into a tirade about the inferiority of females, especially me.

The men in our family shared the same view of women. We were to be silent, obedient, and preferably ignorant. Adjectives such as weak and slow always found their way into the verbal battering I endured for their entertainment. The fact most often driven home was that having been born a girl, I had inherited responsibility for the original sin from Mother Eve. All women were cursed because we were responsible for man's fall from God's good graces.

Once, when I was younger and didn't fully comprehend my place in the world, I had tried to defend poor Eve. Very carefully, I explained that since women were so weak, she couldn't have forced Adam to eat the fruit. It was obvious he chose to eat it just as she did, making his sin equally as bad. I suffered a good licking from Pa for my insolence. I never again questioned my father's religious convictions, but I later imagined that the curse adhered to me like a second skin.

Now my brothers were gone. They had left the farm to pursue other ways of making a living. Pa intended for both of his sons to be well educated. To his credit, he wanted a better life for them than the one he had endured on the farm. My older brother, Steve, worked at a feed mill near Nashville and was studying to become a minister, God help us all. Jeff, who was two years older than me, worked as a hired hand on a farm near Knoxville while he attended the University of Tennessee. Pa sent them every extra dime we were able to make beyond what was necessary for our survival. We often went without food so that they could finish their educations.

That left me, his only daughter and youngest child, to work in the place of my brothers. Pa had determined it was my duty to marry and provide him with permanent cheap labor for the farm. He expected this to be acceptable to me and the unfortunate man I would marry. We were to work the farm; however, my brothers would inherit the land. It seemed that my choices for a husband would be limited to men of little intelligence and ambition. Only a man of such character would sacrifice himself for so little in return.

To my dismay, several men in the area around our farm fit the necessary qualifications. Although I was only fifteen, Pa had already begun sizing up the candidates. Occasionally, one would appear at our front door. It was obvious that the potential suitor came to look me over like a heifer at the local sale. To my advantage, they had little to see. For at my very best, I was plain. This would be my saving grace, I hoped. Evidently, all men preferred their wives pretty even though they might be the most pitiful of male specimens themselves.

Realizing that freed me from making any effort at improving my appearance. It suited the fancy of my mother that I continued to follow that course of action. Her paternal aunts were of dubious reputation, and she lived in the fear that I might have inherited their tendencies. It was far better in her mind that I was plain to look at than for any shame to be visited on the family because of me.

While the hunt continued for my future husband, Pa still allowed me to attend school. He did understand that time moved the world away from the life he was accustomed to on the farm. My education would be beneficial in helping the farm make the transition into an uncertain future. Because Pa had not gone beyond the third grade, he saw the opportunity to advance his education through me. Since I would forever be tied to the farm, he would always have my knowledge at his disposal. High school was as far as he intended to let me go. He considered anything beyond that level to be a waste on a mere girl.

Pa left me no option other than to aspire to growing old alone. Even if I had beauty at my disposal, I had nothing else to offer a man of high consequence. I had seen many well educated and beautiful young women in Rock Island during the summer. They came to stay at their family camps, and it was not hard to recognize the difference between us. I was, if nothing else, realistic about my options. The very best I could hope for was to be an old maid. To accomplish this goal, I would have to walk a thin line over the next few years. Convincing the selected suitors that I was not worth the effort might take some maneuvering on my part.

"Rea, are you going to talk to me at all this morning?" I had completely forgotten about Jinx who was not ten feet away. Normally, he would not even speak unless I spoke first.

"Sorry, I've been thinking about some personal stuff. I can't believe I overslept again this morning. I thought I had that problem solved when I moved my bed closer to the door. Ma doesn't knock very loudly."

"My ma yells at me every morning. Why can't yours just open your door and yell at you?"

"She's afraid she'll wake Pa up too early. He doesn't get up until breakfast is ready. This morning, I was in the middle of the nightmare when she knocked, so I didn't hear her."

"That the same nightmare you always have?"

"Afraid so. I didn't get up in time to help with breakfast, so now I'll get it from Ma when I get back to the house."

"Life's awful tough ain't it, Rea?"

"Yep."

I'd known Jinx Cummings most of my life. He'd been helping us on the farm since he was a small boy. His family was very large, eleven children in all, and very poor. Their father hired all of his sons out as soon as possible to supplement the family income. I knew we were close to the same age although I was not certain how close. Jinx had attended grammar school for a while, and we were in the same class. His grades were always high even though he had no time to study. His mind was quick, his memory flawless, and his loyalty unquestionable.

In all the years we worked side by side, he had saved me from many thrashings by taking credit for my mistakes. As a result, my Pa thought he was simple minded and not capable of being responsible for complicated tasks. Pa wasted many hours each day explaining over and over directions to jobs my friend could do blindfolded in his sleep. Pa considered it his Christian duty to help Jinx, who accepted his humbling treatment without complaint. I knew not why. Maybe the meager pay he received helped his family more than I could imagine. I thanked God in my prayers every night that Jinx and my pa could tolerate each other. Jinx's presence on the farm was necessary for me to maintain my sanity. Beyond that, the farm could not have operated without him.

Milking the twenty cows that my father called his herd took some time, even at a steady pace. I helped Jinx as long as I dared before heading back to the house. He would finish my part for me. This was an arrangement we had used often in the past. Entering the kitchen was a sobering prospect, but I had no choice. Ma had already cleaned away what was left of breakfast and had begun her daily chores. I knew nothing would be left of the morning meal. In general, Pa's hogs ate better than me on days I failed to help Ma in the kitchen.

"Ma, I didn't hear you at the door this morning. I did not skip out on my chores on purpose."

"Rea, I could hear you mumbling to yourself, probably reading one of those books."

"It was a nightmare, Ma."

"You use that excuse a lot. Now get cleaned up and head out, or you'll miss your ride to school. Oh, and I expect I'll have quite a bit of work for you when you get home today, so don't waste time getting here."

Bridge Over Calm Water

"Yes, Ma."

Once again, I rushed to change clothes. With few choices, it did not take long. Only three dresses hung on the hooks in my room, two for school, the other one strictly for church. Each had been made by Ma to ensure that they showed no hint of my figure. This was an unnecessary effort on her part because I had no figure. If Ma would have agreed to let me wear my overalls to school, the only thing that would have betrayed me as a girl was my long, dark hair. I received many snide remarks from the other students at school about my lack of wardrobe. However, my skin had grown tough over time, and I barely noticed the comments anymore. I had no time for my morning bath. I only hoped that the smell of the milk barn, so evident on my work clothes, had not settled into my hair and on my skin. Dressing took only a few minutes, and I once more ran down the stairs and out the door.

The ride that had become so important was waiting on me in Rock Island, over two miles from our farm. I would have to run to make it on time. Dr. McKinney owned the only car in the area. He drove every day to McMinnville to the hospital and returned at night to his home near our farm. On Saturdays, he operated a clinic out of his house for the local residents, many of whom would never be able to travel the long distance to town. In addition to supplying me with a way to school, he also paid me to clean the clinic for him on Saturday afternoons. I would have preferred to work for free, but Pa would never allow me to "waste" so much time without something to show for it.

Dr. McKinney was also the source of my reading materials. Every Saturday, he had a new book for me at the clinic to replace the one I returned from the week before. Pa had no idea the doctor lent me the books. He thought they came from a traveling library that stopped in Rock Island on every third Friday of each month. I worried about Pa not approving of my borrowing the books, but Dr. McKinney said that what Pa didn't know wouldn't hurt him.

I guess things were just about as good as they could be at that time in my life—except for one thing. The accursed bridge stood between me and the McKinney home. I had to cross it twice every day. Knowing the demon of my nightmare lay ahead of me was grating at my nerves already, and I had just left the house.

Running shortened the trip to the bridge considerably. Most days, other people were coming and going on horseback, by wagon, walking, or sometimes in a car. Rarely though was the bridge deserted as it was in my nightmare. Those were the hard days. When it was just my imagination to keep me company, terror followed as my shadow across that short span of timber and steel. Coming around the curve that brought the bridge into view revealed that it was empty of traffic. I stopped and considered waiting to see if someone would show up before I crossed. But that would only add to my lateness and increase the risk that Dr. McKinney would leave without me. Forcing myself to walk in a direct path, I tried to push aside the fears that were rising in my mind. My legs began to shake and grow weak. Eventually, I dropped to my knees. My heart raced as it did when I awoke each time from the nightmare. Frantically, I tried to catch my breath and calm my nerves. It would be very unfortunate if someone came along at that moment to see me kneeling before the bridge in terror. Finally, a small amount of calm eased into my legs, and I slowly began to stand up.

It was then that I recognized the sound of an approaching horse and its rider very close behind me. There was no doubt that the rider saw me kneeling in the road. The person could not have seen my face and probably assumed I fell. Making the effort to stand and step aside from the road took a great deal of my energy. My legs began to quiver as each step became more difficult. Having made the decision not to look at the rider directly, I acted as normally as possible and kept my eyes on the ground in front of me.

"Rea, you all right?" Relief flooded over me. Jinx's familiar voice swept the panic out of my body. I slowly turned and faced the one person who would never judge me harshly for my fears.

"What are you doing here?"

Bridge Over Calm Water

"You didn't answer my question."

"Oh, I just needed to rest for a second. I ran all the way from the house."

"Wouldn't your face be red and not white as a ghost if that were the truth?"

"Well, if you must know, I was having a hard time making myself cross to the other side."

"You looked like you were praying to me. I don't think God will pick you up and set you down on the other side. Give me your hand, and I'll take you across."

God might not have put me on the other side miraculously, but He was going to get the credit for sending Jinx. I reached up to take the strong arm extended toward me. Jinx easily pulled me up to sit behind him. As I wrapped my arms around his waist, it was not hard to notice that Jinx had grown and that his boyish build had been replaced by that of a man. I had been so obsessed with my own life and misery that my best friend had changed, and I had failed to notice. With confidence, he took the reins and urged the horse into a canter. It did not take long to reach the safety of the other side. I had been holding my breath even with the comfort of my prince on an old plow horse. Heaving a sigh and relaxing my body, I lay my forehead against Jinx's back.

"It's just a bridge Rea, not a monster."

"I know that Jinx, but the nightmare has been coming more often than usual. It's just this bad on the days after I have one."

We rode in silence the rest of the way to the clinic. Jinx took my arm and eased me down to the ground with the same effortless motion he had used to pull me up.

"Thanks, you never did say why you are here," I commented.

"Come to pick up supplies for your Pa at the store."

"I'm glad you showed up. I might not have made it across without you."

Jinx broke into a smile and turned the horse around. He left me watching him ride away. Dr. McKinney's car was parked by his gate. Apparently, I had arrived in ample time. The stone wall that edged his front yard looked like an inviting place to rest and wait. The air had begun to warm up, making the stones feel cool to the touch. I was listening to the song of a robin in a small tree beside me when my name floated across the breeze from the house.

"Rea, come into the house. Robert has a patient, and it will be a while before he can leave."

Sarah McKinney stood framed in her kitchen door. She was the most beautiful woman I had ever seen. Taller than most, her chestnut colored hair hung in loose curls across her shoulders. She had soft features and crystal blue eyes. More impressive in my mind was her determination and self-assurance. She never appeared to be intimidated and approached life with casual ease.

It was not surprising to me that Pa cared little for the doctor's wife. When given the opportunity, he raved about her lack of humility and called her arrogant and self-serving. On the few occasions in which they had been close enough to speak to each other, it was evident that Sarah was not the least bit impressed with my pa. She appeared to live life as her own, not at the will of her husband. I had heard her say that she took full responsibility for her own mistakes. I was sure she did not like my pa, but she was too much of a lady to mention it.

Walking up the path toward her, I felt very small and unimportant in the world. To add to my discomfort, the wonderful smell of bacon drifted out onto the morning air, and my stomach protested its emptiness just as I passed her going into the house. The rumbling was too loud not to be heard.

"Rea, did you eat anything at all this morning? You look a little pale."

"Well, I slept through breakfast, and after I finished the chores, I didn't have time to eat. I'm not hungry though," I added hastily to the end of my defense.

"Slept through breakfast you say? Well, sit down and I'll make you a bacon sandwich. I just took this bread out of the oven and milk is in the pitcher. Pour yourself a glass. By the way, does your father ever sleep through breakfast?"

"No ma'am. Ma wakes him up when it's ready. I usually help her cook and eat as I walk to the barn to start helping Jinx with the milking. Pa comes down to the barn after he finishes eating." The expression on her face made me realize that she didn't understand the way things worked on a farm.

"Just so that I'm sure I understand, you and your mother get up first and cook the breakfast. Then she wakes your father up after you have already gone to the barn?"

"Yes ma'am, you see, I have to get my chores done early so that I can go to school. Pa has all day to finish his work, though sometimes he does not come in from the fields until after dark. When my older brothers were home, I didn't have to help with the milking, but now there is only me and Jinx."

"Is Jinx your brother?"

"No, he has been our farmhand since we were in grammar school together. I suppose this will sound bad, but Jinx is more important to me than my own brothers."

"Was he the one who helped you down from the horse? The way he was looking at you, I'd say you're important to him too."

"Yes, that was Jinx. He and I have spent so much time together working that we know what the other one is thinking without having to ask."

"It makes me happy that you have such a good friend. Now eat, Robert will be ready to leave in a little while."

Sarah left me in the kitchen to enjoy my sandwich. Talking to her about Jinx made me start to think about that morning. Obviously, I had ignored the fact that Jinx was really more of a man than a boy. I had never asked him his age, but I would at the next opportunity. Considering how much I depended on him, it would be wise of me to prepare myself for the day when he would surely leave. Pa might think Jinx was not smart, but I knew better. Someday soon, he would have the chance to do better for himself, and he would take it. The prospect of life without Jinx produced a queasy feeling in my stomach. I chewed the last bite of the sandwich excessively to make sure it stayed down. I was still chewing when Sarah returned to the kitchen.

"Robert's finished and ready to leave. Looks like you enjoyed the sandwich." She could tell I was struggling to swallow and speak at the same time. "It's all right, Rea. I know you appreciate the meal. Go on before you choke."

Flashing a grin in her direction and waving, I ran out the door and down the path toward the gate. Dr. McKinney stood by the car talking to a man with his arm in a sling. I slid to a stop on the grassy slope, not wanting to disturb their conversation. I could only see the back of the stranger. But even from this direction, I had to force myself not to stare. He was about the same height as the doctor, several inches taller than Jinx I guessed. His frame seemed too lean for the clothes he wore. Nothing about him screamed for attention except his hair. I knew of no words to describe the color. Somewhere between blond and silver, it literally shimmered in the sunlight reaching down through the trees. As if the color was not enough, his hair fell in perfect curls. Try as I might, I could not get the word halo out of my head. The memory of Ma talking about entertaining angels unaware beat at the sides of my skull. No doubt my mouth was opened because just as Dr. McKinney looked up in my direction, some disgusting bug flew in and landed on the back of my tongue. I turned to face away and tried to dislodge the bug without losing my breakfast. By the time I regained some sense of dignity and looked up, the stranger was walking by me up the hill. Very deliberately, he ran his free hand through his hair as if he knew what I'd been thinking.

"Are you ready to go, Rea?"

"Yes, sir." I couldn't resist one last look in the stranger's direction. Then I turned and ran down the hill and got into the car.

"So I gather you enjoyed some of my wife's wonderful cooking this morning?"

"Yes, she made me a bacon sandwich. I'm grateful because I missed breakfast."

"She told me that. So you're still helping with the milking?"

"Yes, sir. I imagine I'll be milking for a long time to come." I did not have to go into detail. He knew my pa and ma relied on me to pick up the slack since my brothers had left. Once I heard the doctor talking to Pa about the fact that it was not good for a girl to do the amount of heavy work that he expected of me. Pa had not been hateful, but he had been firm in his assertion that I was his daughter and under his authority. It was my obligation to do as he deemed necessary. The kind doctor never questioned Pa again. He did, however, offer me the ride into town so that I could continue on to high school. I imagine he was trying to spare me some of the hard work at home by doing so.

That morning, the trip progressed without further conversation. Dr. McKinney seemed lost in thought, and I was thankful for the silence. On many mornings, he would drill me on the book I was reading at the time. Soon we came to a stop at the corner two blocks from the front door of the high school. It was my request that he always let me off at least that distance away.

At first, he was reluctant to put me out on the street so far from my destination. After a long discussion, I finally had to give him my reason. Like the social hierarchy that existed in our county, one the doctor was very familiar with, the high school had its own. As a farm girl from the country, with only two dresses, my status fell at the very lowest level. It would have caused all kinds of needless gossip and questioning were I dropped off by a car at the front door. Dr. McKinney insisted gallantly to be allowed to do the gentlemanly thing. It took a few unbidden tears on my cheeks to make him understand my need to be as invisible as possible. He conceded to my wishes, and even during the worst of weather, he did not press the point.

Walking down the street toward the school, I started to prepare my mind for the multitude of finals that I would face on this last day of the school year. They would give proof I had mastered the information presented to me by each teacher. My poor night's sleep and stress-ridden morning had made me feel sluggish. I could only hope that it had not spread to my brain. When I came to the school two years ago, I was required to take a placement test. The teachers feared my education at the country school might have put me at a disadvantage. To their surprise, I surpassed most of the students in the grade above me. Unfortunately for me, they placed me as a sophomore, not a freshman. The students my age were not receptive to me. By putting me in with students who were at least a year older and often two years older, I became an outcast on every level. My teachers seemed blind to the hostility toward me in their classes. They took every opportunity to comment on my abilities while pointing out the obvious lack of advantages in my life. This was the environment I was about to walk into as I climbed the steps one more time.

Pushing through the front door, I was hit hard by the smell and noise of the mass of bodies pressed together in the hall. It appeared that every student in the school had managed to find their way to the main hallway at the same time. I could hear our principal directing students into the auditorium for the senior awards ceremony. Thankfully, I was not required to attend. Underclassmen could choose to study in the library. By looking at the crowd, I might have the entire library to myself. Awards were very important to the socially minded of this school. The more recognition, the more important a student became. Slowly, I made my way around and through one group of students after another. For the most part, I was unnoticed until I reached the main office door. The principal's secretary saw me and yelled, "Rea Wilson, come in here immediately."

The irritating woman knew every student by name and face. I should have walked down the other side of the hallway. Students stopped to stare at the sound of her voice. By her tone, it appeared I had committed some offense of which I was not aware. Several of my classmates exchanged grins. The sheer joy that these people seemed to experience at another's suffering never ceased to amaze me. Their joy had no foundation with me for I had already overcome the worst my day could offer. No matter what I found waiting for me in that office, it was of little consequence to my life. Suddenly, I smiled back in their direction. This pretty much wiped their faces clean of expression. I turned from them to walk into the office, which freed me of the chaos in the hall.

"You need me I assume?" My voice sounded more disrespectful than I intended, but the day was wearing on me.

Bridge Over Calm Water

"Miss Delton wanted me to send you to her office as soon as you got here. Hurry on up there; she has to be in the auditorium in a few minutes."

The conversation ended there, so I stepped back into the hallway. Most of the students were seated in the auditorium ready for the ceremony. It took very little time to travel up the stairs and into the guidance counselor's office. I could not imagine why she needed to see me. We had set my schedule for next year several weeks before. Whatever it was, she would not have long to explain. She was to give the awards out in less than ten minutes according to the clock on her wall. Miss Delton motioned for me to sit down in the chair and began to shuffle through the papers on her desk.

"Rea, I have some wonderful news for you. I sent your scores to several colleges. One women's college from out of state has offered you a full scholarship. You only have to finish the rest of your required classes by the end of next year." She smiled brightly and waited for my reaction.

Saying that I was speechless really didn't cover the stupor that grasped my mind in a stranglehold. The silence in the room stretched to an uncomfortable level.

"Rea, you don't look pleased by this news. I thought you would be as excited as I am for you. It's not often any student gets an offer for a full scholarship at the end of their junior year, especially a female student. Aren't you even interested in which college made the offer?"

"No ma'am, I don't want to know where the offer came from. I just assumed you knew that college is not an option for me. I am the only one left at home to help my pa and ma. With both of my brothers gone, the workload is too much even with our hired help. It's not that I don't appreciate the effort you put into getting this for me, but Pa has my life pretty much mapped out and college is not part of his plan."

Miss Delton sat very still. I saw her struggling with what she was going to say next. "Neither of your brothers received offers for scholarships, Rea. Your father should be proud of you. He should not punish you for being the only one left at home."

15

"Besides the fact that I'm the youngest, my pa doesn't believe women should go to college. He has definite ideas about the place of women in the world. Honestly, I'm happy he has agreed to let me finish high school."

"Will you at least talk to him over the summer about the scholarship? He might change his mind."

"Yes, I promise I will. But please don't expect him to give his permission."

"You have until the middle of the next school year to make up your mind. Hopefully, by then, your pa will come to his senses. Now, I have to go to the awards banquet. Are you coming?"

"No ma'am, I am going to the library to study."

As Miss Delton nodded, I quickly retreated from her office. The disappointment written on her face was heartbreaking and flooded me with remorse. She saw me as weak of spirit and downtrodden. I was neither. Now I faced the rest of that day and all those that followed realizing that there were other opportunities for me outside the narrow scope of my present existence. Looking at what could have been only made living with what had to be seem almost impossible. A weighted heart made the rest of the day long and tiresome.

Once my tests had been completed and the school day came to a close, the fresh air outside did little to relieve my exhausted mind and body. Placing one foot in front of the other took great effort and concentration. My body ached as if it were wracked with fever. Walking to the park in the downtown square took longer than usual.

Dr. McKinney's schedule varied each day. I could have waited at the hospital, but I preferred the park. It offered a variety of sights and sounds to occupy my thoughts. Only very inclement weather forced me to continue on to the hospital waiting room. The warm weather had coaxed an assortment of older men onto the many benches spread out among the trees. Most held small pieces of wood in their hands. Whittling with their pocket knives produced little piles of shavings between their feet. Their language was colorful; their stories deep in character. Pa would have been furious to know that I positioned myself close enough to eavesdrop on their lively tales and proficient cussing. Their accounts of days long past fascinated me, and I relished the time I spent on the fringes of their informal gatherings. That day was no different. Losing myself in one story after another allowed me to clear out the abundance of confusion that had my mind twisted in knots.

While I listened to the old men, one of my hardest-learned lessons came barreling out of the depths of my memory. When all dreams and fantasies fail, reality will land a crippling blow right between your eyes. Remembering the reality of my situation forced me to dwell on the concrete evidence before me. In life, unfounded hopes pose great danger. As much as I wished that my life could somehow be different, that wish had no solid foundation on which to stand. Unlike childhood dreams, reality is anchored by the facts of family and financial considerations. Most would call me a coward for not demanding that I be given the chance before me. Most do not understand truth. A coward would take any road out of a hard life, no matter the cost to those left behind. I would tell Pa about the scholarship to remain good to my word. However, college would remain a fantasy. Something to be worked into my dreams at night, but it had no place to put down roots in my life. It was simply an unnecessary consideration.

Eventually, the passage of time became obvious as the men made their farewells and set out in search of an early supper. Without a watch to be certain, I could only guess that the doctor was well over an hour later than normal. With Ma's promise of extra chores from that morning, a late arrival home would only make my afternoon harder than usual. Depending on the time of year, sickness would sometimes delay Dr. McKinney's arrival. One day last fall, it had been nearly dark before his appearance due to some sort of terrible accident. Waiting now, I wished for the tiniest amount of patience. Exhaustion from the day tempered my urge to pace. Instead I began shifting my gaze between my tapping feet and the street leading toward the clinic. This useless waste of energy was thankfully interrupted by his car coming toward me down the street. Something seemed different about the driver at the steering wheel. The closer it drew toward me, the more certain I became that this was the doctor's car but not the doctor driving.

After pulling to a stop by the curb in front of me, a stranger turned to gaze at me with a rather bored look on his face. Although I had never seen the face clearly, I had not forgotten the hair framing it.

"I assume you're Rea. I have been sent to take you home. Get in the car please."

Orders were a fairly constant occurrence in my life. This wasn't even an order; it was more like a request. My years of training in obedience should have made me follow the request without hesitation. However, I just couldn't make myself rise to my feet and comply. I had too many questions; the most prevalent being, who was this man and how did he get the doctor's car?

"Are you deaf and dumb? Get in the car."

Now it was an order and an insult. By standing my ground, I ran the risk of insulting someone that Dr. McKinney knew. It had been a long and hard day; I had completely used up my ability to overlook the rudeness in others.

"I mean no offense, but I don't ride in cars with people I do not know."

"I can't imagine you having the opportunity to ride in very many cars other than this one. You saw me this morning at the clinic. I'm Collin, Sarah's brother. Now will you get in the car?"

Having provided the answer to my objection, I reluctantly climbed in the back seat. It seemed best to avoid any further conversation considering he was compelled to insult me every time he spoke. To prevent my temptation to ask about the cause of Dr. McKinney's absence, I fixed my gaze on the passing scenery. My curiosity was short lived.

"There was an accident down on the river bluff today. I helped with the recovery and rode back with Robert to the hospital. He insisted I tell you this so you could relay the message to your parents. It's beyond me why he feels the need to burden himself with being your chauffeur every day, much less transferring that burden to me."

Bridge Over Calm Water

"Thank you for telling me. To be honest, I don't understand why Dr. McKinney is so nice to me either. I am truly sorry that you are being forced to take me home." A truer statement I had never uttered.

"I have no idea where you live. You'll have to give me directions from my sister's house."

The tone in his voice had changed but not enough that I cared to continue the conversation. My answer to this last question would fulfill my obligation to be civil. "I will walk from Rock Island. It is not my intention to be more of a burden than is absolutely necessary."

"You sure use big words for such a little country girl. Robert said you were smart. It would be fine with me if you walked, but I promised Robert I would take you all the way home. I prefer not to go against his instructions."

"Fine, just take the main road past the house and across the bridge. The farm is two miles from the bridge on the left."

Turning my head back to the window, I tried to rest for the short time left in the car. Soon the big, blue house belonging to the McKinneys came into view, and not long after, the bridge. Having never crossed the bridge in a car, it took me by surprise how quickly we reached the other side. As the farm grew closer, the thought of explaining why a strange man was driving me up the lane grew more unpleasant.

"Please let me out at the bottom of the next lane. There is not enough room to turn around up at the house." It was a lie, but he would never know.

"Does your farm come all the way down to the main road?"

"Yes, so you won't be breaking your word to Dr. McKinney."

Collin pulled the car into the lane and stopped. I wasted no time climbing out, thanking him as I stepped onto the packed ground. The sun was already sinking below the tops of the trees. I did not look back after beginning the climb up the hill. Collin did not back out of the lane until I took the turn into the trees and disappeared from his sight. The strangest sensation began to spread up my back once I knew he could no longer see me.

Ma met me at the door, a stern expression boring out from her eyes. She gazed suspiciously down the lane behind me. The arrival of the car had not gone unnoticed. "What was that noise I heard?"

"There was an accident at the river bluff today. Dr. McKinney made his brother-in-law bring me all the way back to the farm so I wouldn't get home so late."

"His brother-in-law! Was anyone else in the car?"

"No, ma'am, but I rode in the seat behind him and tried not to be a bother."

"It ain't fittin', you riding around in a car by yourself with a man we don't know."

"Yes, ma'am, you're right. If I have to walk all the way home next time, it won't happen again."

"Get to the barn and help finish the milking. Then come back here and start on those extra chores."

I didn't bother changing clothes. Turning around, it was hard to make myself head to the barn. Pa met me on the way and didn't acknowledge me in passing. He seemed not to even notice me; his eyes were downcast and his body was weary. Jinx, ever faithful, had the milking well underway by the time I got there. Although he made no mention of my late arrival, he did seem a little amused by my dress. In a strange sort of way, I felt more at ease there than anywhere else. The day's trials slowly vanished as I worked and talked with Jinx.

CHAPTER TWO

Collin

During the summer months, my life settled into a routine of chores and church. Pa's demands were not unreasonable, and Jinx was still around every day. Ma became easier to please as I was always available to help with gardening and canning. Any thought of the college scholarship was lost in the million moments of simple everyday life. Two weeks after school finished, Pa walked into the barn one morning earlier than usual. He spoke briefly to Jinx, repeating the same instructions he issued every day. Poor Jinx just stood and smiled. When Pa finished, he turned to speak in the direction of the cow I stood behind.

"Rea, starting this Saturday, you will be working in Dr. McKinney's clinic all day. They expect you there as soon as you finish your chores on Saturday morning. When the milking is done this morning, go see Mrs. McKinney. She needs to fit you to a uniform."

Pa strode out of the barn whistling without giving me a chance to comment. I heard Jinx snicker from somewhere farther up in the barn. The humorous point of this whole situation must have slipped by me.

"Want to tell me why this is funny? All I can get out of this is more work while Pa gets more money to send off to my brothers."

"Well, I reckon your Pa is happy about the extra pay, but I don't think that's the reason he's gonna let you work there all day."

"Oh really, what would be the reason then?"

"Think about all the people that come to that clinic every Saturday. They come from everywhere, at least three different counties."

"So, I fail to see how this is funny."

"Rea, for someone so smart, you sure are dumb sometimes. Think about all the single men and their families that will get the chance to see you working in there. I bet that uniform ain't like them dresses your ma makes neither."

My face grew hot, and I hid behind the cow as I tried to control my temper. No doubt he was right. Pa was setting me up so that everyone could see what he had to offer. Under normal conditions, working at the clinic would have been a nice way to escape the drudgery of the farm. Now Pa would make sure the word got out. If anyone wanted to look over the merchandise, all they had to do was stop by and take a gander. Pa was smarter than I had given him credit for. He had me right where he wanted me. I was trapped with no way out. Tears streamed down my face as I halfheartedly saw to the rest of the milking. Jinx must have heard me sniffling; he didn't say anything else.

Pa evidently told my ma about ordering me to visit the clinic. She had a list ready for me to take to the store. Handing me the piece of paper, she said nothing as I walked out the front door. Anger still seethed beneath the surface of my otherwise bewildered emotions. Living with Pa's opinions, each one a combination of human tradition and his religion, had never been easy. I didn't have to guess where he stood on any given subject. He was more than confident enough to override any opposing view—if you were brave enough to voice one. To him, I was his property, just like the cows in the field. He seemed to have decided to step up his efforts to find me a husband. More than likely, he too was aware that Jinx was fast approaching the age when he would feel free to find his own way. Replacing him through me would be the best possible solution from Pa's point of view.

Bridge Over Calm Water

Women have held a very small place in the world where my Pa existed. Mothers, aunts, sisters, or grandmothers: they simply took what was given to them—good and bad. Each started out young and freehearted. Most ended up old, bitter, and often cruel. Because Pa followed the example of the men before him, he never noticed the irritation in Ma's eyes. His ears never heard the defeat in her voice. Considerations of his life did not include the feelings of Ma or me. This did not make him a bad man, just a sadly misguided one. Knowing what motivated his decisions made understanding them so much easier. I was having no trouble understanding this decision to put me up for common display at the clinic. The problem, however, was accepting it as an unavoidable condition of my continued existence. Pa always reminded me that he had brought me into the world and he could take me out. Refusing the path he had chosen for my life might give him reason to back up that promise.

Walking at a brisk pace away from the farm did little to temper the fury that was slowly building up inside me. Preoccupied with my musing over Pa, I crossed the bridge without noticing and had almost reached the McKinney home before I realized it. I had begun to wonder if the doctor and his wife were aware of Pa's real motives behind my increased hours at the clinic. More than likely, they had no idea. It would lower my estimation of their intelligence and kindness if they willingly went along with Pa's plan.

Movement off to the side of the road caught my attention as I passed the small community cemetery not far from the clinic at the top of the river hill. Slowing my pace, I saw Sarah McKinney carrying clusters of flowers toward the back of the cemetery. Like almost everyone else in this tightly knit community, I was aware of the two small graves underneath a cluster of dogwood trees nestled up against the hardwood forest. The doctor had been the salvation of many desperately ill people since coming to Rock Island. However, twice he had been unable to save the frail premature babies his wife and he had so wanted. Grief stricken, they placed the graves as close to their home as the cemetery would allow. Many times before that day, I had seen her clean the graves of leaves and debris. Once, she swept away snow as if she could ward off the cold. Seeing her then reminded me we all carry burdens that cannot be removed this side of death. Ma's list gave me a purpose to delay my arrival at the doctor's house. Redirecting my steps toward the store, I glanced back and saw Mrs. McKinney bending down to lay the flowers on one of the graves.

Shopping for Ma did little to improve my mood. Canning supplies that were heavy and awkward would not make the walk back to the farm pleasant. Simply making it to the counter with my arms loaded with Ma's requested goods was a trial. Mrs. Mitchell, the store owner, offered no help since she was otherwise occupied with a man I had never seen. By the time she was finished, I had arranged the supplies on the counter for her inspection.

"That's quite a load for you, Rea."

"Ma really has no idea how hard this stuff is to carry long distances. I imagine I'll have to stop several times on the way back."

"I heard about you starting to work in the clinic on Saturdays. Bet you're excited about that."

"Yes, ma'am."

I sincerely hoped Mrs. Mitchell had gotten her information from someone at the clinic and not from some gossip started by Pa in an effort to attract possible suitors. Before the store clerk could question me further, I grabbed the box she had piled Ma's supplies in and left. The distance to the McKinney home seemed twice as long carrying the heavy box and a serious case of melancholy. I tried to leave both of these loads at the gate before walking up the hill to the porch.

Sarah answered the door rather quickly. She led me into her sitting room and showed me a white dress. Jinx had been correct in his assumption that it would be nothing like the dresses Ma insisted I wear. Once I had put it on, Sarah made me stand very still while she measured and pinned at various places on the garment. When her alterations were finished, she took me into her bedroom where there was a large mirror. Sarah explained that there would be an apron to wear over the dress made out of pink ticking.

"Mrs. McKinney, I was just wondering if you showed Pa this uniform before he said I could wear it?"

"Please, call me Sarah. No, the only thing he asked was if people would be able to tell you are a girl when you have it on. That seemed like an odd question at the time."

"It would not seem odd if you knew my pa better." Undoubtedly, Pa expected this uniform to make me prettier. Oh, he was so wrong. I couldn't have looked worse had I tried. Even with Sarah's effort at taking it in, I looked like someone's shrunken old granny. I couldn't help but smile at the thought of any man thinking I would be a good catch.

"That's a nice smile, Rae. Do you like the uniform?"

"I think it's perfect, and I know my ma will think so too."

Sarah told me the uniform would be ready by Saturday, and I thanked her again for the job with a much lighter heart. Stopping at the gate, I retrieved the box for Ma but not the melancholy of the morning. The walk back toward the bridge was slow and tiring. In less than one-half mile, I had to stop twice to rest. At that rate, I didn't make it back before dark and that was just fine with me.

The rest of the week offered little in the way of variety. Because life on a farm falls into such a routine, it becomes difficult to distinguish one day from the next. We had no visitors, and the days were so long that it was a relief to fall into bed at night. Thankfully, the nightmare did not return. Not walking across the bridge twice every day helped. There was no time to read even if Ma hadn't taken my book.

On Saturday morning, thick grey clouds smothered the sunlight. Pa seemed in high spirits, laughing with Jinx while we finished up in the milk barn. I left them enjoying some private joke and ran to the house to clean up. It was evident by the tempting smells floating out of the kitchen where Ma was at that moment. After changing, I could not resist stopping in the kitchen to seek out a snack. Ma heard me coming down the stairs and turned to look in my direction. Her face, once lovely and soft, now was covered in layers of thin wrinkles.

"I'm leaving for the clinic, Ma. It may be dark before I get back."

Ma began to walk toward me across the kitchen, pulling something from her apron pocket. She raised her hand toward me, turning her palm up. Lying in her hand was a worn and tattered envelope. Her eyes gazed at me with a puzzled expression as I searched my mind to find information that might remind me of what the envelope represented. She pushed her hand in my direction without speaking. I took the envelope, turning it to see that it was addressed to my parents and had come from the high school. Ma took very little interest in my activities at the school. The fact that she had obviously had this envelope for some time did not make sense.

"I have not told your pa about this because I have been waiting on you to say something."

"Ma, I don't know what you're talking about."

"The school did not tell you about the scholarship you have been offered?"

"Yes, ma'am, the last day of school, but I forgot to tell you about it. Besides, there is no way Pa will ever agree to this. I told Miss Delton that it was not possible for me to leave with Steve and Jeff both away at school."

"You owe your pa enough respect to tell him about this and let him make the decision."

"I meant no disrespect. Will telling him tonight be all right, since I need to go on to work?"

"Tell him as soon as you get back."

She turned away and went back to her cooking. Pa had total control over our lives. His word was law, and I had gone around his authority by making this decision without him. Sometimes it felt like my body was dissolving away. Every time the forces at work in my life shifted direction, it was as if I left part of my solid substance behind. It would not surprise me if one day I simply disappeared. That thought held my attention as I walked through the door to the outside where unexpectedly Jinx sat on the porch, holding the horse's reins.

"Hey, Jinx, what are you waiting on?"

"Your pa wants me to take you over to Rock Island. He says you're moving slowly this morning."

We boarded Max from the porch, and Jinx spurred the old horse into a gentle trot down the hill and onto the main road. My conversation with Ma left me feeling weary and dejected. The day had not begun on the best of terms. I could only hope that my experiences in the clinic would not follow the same course. Looking for a distraction, I focused my attention on the sounds of summer around me. Birds, bees, and dragonflies swirled in and around the trees as we passed. The air had grown thick with moisture, forecasting a hot and muggy day. I felt the heat radiating off of the animal beneath me, which brought to notice his smell. The combination of the two made my head spin and stomach lurch. For just a second, darkness passed before my eyes and sent me into a panic. I grabbed at Jinx's shirt just as I felt myself begin to slide off the side of Max.

"Something wrong, Rea?"

It required some concentration to soak in his question, and by the time I did, he had drawn the horse to a stop and turned to face me.

"Rea, you don't look too good."

"I don't feel well. Just keep going, Jinx. Sitting on this stinking horse is part of the problem."

Always striving to please, he quickly turned back to the duty of delivering me to the fate that awaited me at the clinic. Swaying with the horse's stride did nothing to improve my equilibrium. Thankfully, only a few minutes passed before we stopped in front of the McKinney home.

Jinx dismounted before I could even consider climbing off. He gently lifted me down to the ground and set me squarely on my feet. Placing his hands on my shoulders, he looked me in the eyes. "Don't know, Rea. You're still kind of peaked."

"I'll be fine. Anyway, if I am getting sick what better place to be?"

"Want me to come and get you later?"

"No, I really have no idea when I will be finished, but thanks for the offer."

"I'm taking my little brother fishing after work. Look for us when you go home. We'll be around the bridge somewhere."

"Okay, thanks."

He easily swung himself back up on the horse and rode off toward the farm. It was then that I became aware that someone was sitting on the porch of the house humming. Bushes blocked the view of the person in one of the rockers, but I could see the very top of the chair as it moved back and forth in a slow deliberate motion. As the clinic entrance opened on the side of the house, I would be forced to walk by the porch to reach it. Common sense told me that whoever sat there was paying no attention to me, yet an uneasy feeling crept into my chest. Walking up the hill, my head felt funny again and my ears were ringing. Just as I drew even with the porch, a male voice spoke to me through the bushes.

"Hey, farmer girl, is that your sweetheart?"

The tone of the voice rang with a demeaning quality that I had heard before. Sarah's brother, Collin, was speaking to me from the porch. At the risk of being rude, I continued walking toward the clinic entrance and disregarded him and his comment entirely. Just as I reached the door, a strong hand latched onto my shoulder and jerked me around. Collin stood very close to me, just inches from my face.

"I don't like being ignored. Answer the question. Is he your sweetheart or not?"

I stepped back to increase the distance between us, but he closed it immediately and leaned in even closer. I was unaccustomed to having anyone that close to me, especially a complete stranger. Ma and Pa were not physically affectionate people. In our family, personal contact only came in the form of corporal punishment. This situation held the same sort of intimidation and hostile nature. I could have just answered the question, but, at that moment, it felt like a cowardly thing to do. I seethed inside at his boldness and arrogance. Years of taking the unreasonable demands dished out by my Pa boiled to the surface. Taking a deep breath, I braced myself for what might be the result of what I was about to say.

"That is none of your business. Now let me go. I am going to be late."

Before I could move, he shifted his hand from my shoulder to grip my upper arm. The haughty expression on his face quickly dissolved into fury as the blood rose up from his neck. Very slowly, he increased the pressure on my arm, which caused it to ache.

"You're not going anywhere until you answer my question. As I said, I don't like being ignored, especially by the hired help."

To emphasize his determination to receive an answer, he dug his nails into my arm. He seemed to think pain would produce the results he wanted. He didn't know I'd been raised on physical pain. Any little misstep in my life had been corrected with a sound thrashing. I may have had to accept what Pa dished out to me, but I didn't have to take this.

Thinking quickly, I used the element of surprise to my advantage. I flashed my most joyful of smiles to distract him before ramming my right hand into the base of his nose and upward. I was stronger than I looked; it was one of the few benefits of working on a farm. Collin released my arm instantly to raise his hands to his face. Blood ran down his chin and dripped onto his pristine shirt as I turned and walked through the clinic door. I had felt the bone give and was confident that his nose was broken. As I reached the reception desk, Sarah looked up and started to speak until she saw Collin who had followed me in. Her eyes darted from me to the bloody mess behind me.

"Collin, what happened?"

He ignored the question and continued on through the waiting room toward the examination room in the back. Several people were already in the office, but they paid little attention. Injuries were just a normal fact of life on farms. Sarah followed her brother but ordered me to stay at the desk until she returned.

The gravity of what I had done slowly began dawn on me. I had just inflicted bodily harm on my employer's brother-in-law. Sarah had been very kind to me, and to repay her, I had broken her brother's nose. This was not good. I would lose the job, and Pa would be so furious that he'd take a belt to me for sure. I should have just answered Collin's question. From behind the door that swallowed up Collin and his sister, I heard the sounds of muted voices. Although their words were not understandable, the conversation seemed to be quite animated. Minutes ticked by as more and more people came in and joined the growing crowd of waiting patients. Most did not know me, but I noticed two women and one man from our church. When Sarah returned to dismiss me, we would have quite an audience.

I've always heard that the consequences of our misdeeds are the devil to deal with. That statement made sense to me in light of the situation. A burning panic started to rise up out of my stomach. My breath grew short, and my skin began to tingle. Gasping for air, my lungs felt as though they were stuffed full of the bile that slowly spread up my throat. Ma told me almost every day that I had inherited Pa's terrible temper. Apparently she was right. Just as I broke into a nervous sweat, Sarah walked back into the room followed by her brother with a murderous look frozen on his face. His nose was covered in tape and blood was splattered across his shirt. He stalked across the room and out the door without looking in my direction. This seemed odd to me. You would have thought he would want to stay while his sister fired me. Turning my attention from Collin to Sarah to accept whatever punishment they had decided I deserved, I heard Sarah calling in the next patient to see Dr. McKinney. She glanced in my direction as I held my breath waiting for her to begin.

"Rea, go in and put on the uniform. You'll find it in the storage room. Hurry, we have a lot to do today."

This command stunned me, considering it was not what I had expected, and I was slow to rise to my feet.

"Rea! Did you hear me?"

"Yes, ma'am, sorry."

Jumping up quickly, I forced myself not to run out of the room. The uniform lay in its appointed place. My hands shook, which made it difficult to wrap myself in yards of white cotton and get the apron on straight. When I returned to the front desk, the room had grown even more crowded. Sarah was busy with a patient. I caught a couple of the women with amused expressions as they looked me over from head to toe. If I hadn't been so upset at that moment, I would probably have been worrying about how ridiculous I must have looked in the mountain of material Sarah called a uniform. I failed to notice Dr. McKinney standing with his back to me, so it startled me when he turned around and looked me in the eye.

"Rea, could you come with me, please?"

"Yes, sir."

From the tone of his voice, it was hard to tell if he was angry with me, but the request had been made with a smile on his face. I was beginning to wonder if Collin told them what happened to his nose. It then occurred to me that he might be embarrassed by the fact that a girl could claim responsibility for his injuries.

The knot in my stomach began to loosen as Dr. McKinney led me into his office. Mounds of papers and folders were strewn across a table to one side of the room. He headed toward the table without pausing. "Rea, these are patient charts and the papers need to be sorted and filed in the appropriate chart. Each paper has a patient name and number on it. You will find a chart for every patient in these piles, which are in alphabetical order already. Once you finish with the chart, please put them in the shelves over on the other wall. If you get confused or need to ask a question, just catch the nurse between patients. One last thing, what do you think about your uniform? It looks a little cumbersome to me."

"Well, seems like a waste to put this much material into one dress. I don't mind it though, and Ma will like it if she ever sees me in it."

"Well, just know that you don't have to wear it if you don't want to."

"Thank you, I'll keep that in mind." Dr. McKinney left me as I stood mulling over his instructions. Apparently, this morning's confrontation with Collin was not going to affect my job here. Thinking back on his expression as he left the clinic, a chill ran down my spine. Collin did not seem like the type of person to let me get by without some sort of retaliation. Deep down in my soul, I knew he would never let me escape judgment for what I'd done. Now I wished that I had not rejected Jinx's offer to come and walk me home. Right then, with so much work before me, however, was not the time to dwell on what he might do. The nurse returned to the office and I began my appointed duties, eventually forgetting about Collin and his nose.

CHAPTER THREE

On the Bridge

Once Dr. McKinney finished seeing his patients, I still had to clean the clinic. I worked as quickly as possible. However, darkness replaced daylight before I prepared to leave. The only bright consolation to the long walk home hung in the sky just over the trees. Large and brilliant, the moon cast a silvery light that lay softly on the landscape. I have never been especially fond of night. After the disturbing beginning to my day, the prospect of going home alone was not a pleasant one. With no other option available to me, I gathered up what little courage I could muster and walked slowly down the hill from the clinic and out the gate.

The two miles of road leading to my room loomed before me like a long, narrow corridor. Large trees lined each side of the way. Draped lazily and intertwined above, they blocked out the majority of the moonlight. Added to this gloomy effect was the presence of the dreaded bridge. It was not surprising that my heart rate began to increase. Strange noises echoed from among the twigs and vegetation on the ground. The hairs on my arms rose up at each unfamiliar sound. Although it appeared I walked alone, I had an uneasy feeling that someone or something was traveling in the same direction but out of sight.

To block out the unnerving cadence of the night air, I began to hum softly. That helped to slow my heart rate, but the feeling of an unwelcomed guest close by did not dissipate. Just before

Jan Kendall

stepping onto the bridge deck, I paused and listened closely to my surroundings. I heard only the water below. It was too quiet now. Frogs and crickets should have been battling for notice in the night air. Instead, only the simple song of the water's waves colliding with the shoreline greeted my attentive ears. It was as though the world had stopped to hold its breath.

I could not avoid the thoughts connected to my nightmare. The moonlight shining against the bridge's supporting beams drew my eyes upward as I slowly began to walk across to the opposite shore. Trying not to let my imagination get the best of me, I chose to ignore the shudder that my eyes caught running along the beam's length. I felt no vibration in the planks beneath me as I did in my nightmare, but I could still see the beams dancing. I stopped to stand in the middle of the bridge, straining to focus my eyes and make the metal still its quivering. My concentration was focused above me and not on what might be behind me.

Suddenly, I was shoved and began stumbling toward the railing. I tried to grab at the metal coming toward my face, but I could not prevent the front of my head from slamming into the sharp edge of the rail. My sight blurred and pains shot down my neck into my back. Grasping at the bridge supports, I tried to stand up. My efforts were useless because my feet were jerked from beneath me. I was losing my strength and becoming numb. A violent ringing had invaded the space behind my ears, and blackness slowly took away my sight. I felt my body being roughly thrown to the bridge decking. I was living the nightmare that had haunted my sleep for so long.

Warmth and pain mixed with fear and an unexplained sense of grief brought me back into reality. The sun's rays slowly spread up my arms. The warmth I felt there did not ease the cold shivers that had overtaken my body. My eyelids would not open; pain racked me from deep within. Before I could stifle it, a violent scream ripped out of my throat. My eyes were matted shut by blood oozing from a cut on my forehead. My legs fought me as I tried to stand. I was tangled in the undergrowth along the bank, making me realize I was no longer on the bridge. Using the slope, I felt my way down to the water's edge, which allowed me to clear my eyes so that I could open them. My dress was torn and hung in shreds around my legs. My hair was matted to my head, which felt heavy and unbalanced, making me woozy. Turning to face the bridge required too much effort, and I slid down the bank into the murky water. I heard someone call my name but nothing else.

Time lost significance as hours passed unnoticed. Life returned to my conscious mind in small increments—first light and then sounds. Muffled noises slowly became voices that were deliberately hushed. At first, my surroundings were unfamiliar due to my lack of focus. The smell of antiseptic made me aware of where I lay. My face reeked of it, strongly suggesting that it saturated the bandage I felt pressed against the skin of my forehead. Somehow, I had found my way to the clinic. As hard as I tried, I could retrieve no memory of how I had arrived there. That presented the probability that someone had delivered me into Dr. McKinney's care. Realizing that made me very interested in the voices I heard across the room.

"Robert, has she come around yet?"

"No, is he still sitting out there?"

"He hasn't left. At least he seems to care. Her parents sent word that they would be here after church. Apparently, they've gone to ask the church to pray for her."

"Sarah, praying for her recovery is a very caring thing."

"Not for her recovery, for her deliverance. It seems strange to me they are not here."

The conversation ended and someone left the room. People were praying for me. Obviously, I was in bad shape. Was I about to die? I felt the urge to leave the bed and maybe escape to a place not ridden in pain. Moving brought agony to my insides. I bit my lip but whimpered anyway. That drew the attention of Dr. McKinney who came quickly to stand over me.

"Rea, don't move please. I had to do some stitching on you, and you need to lay as still as possible. Your parents will be here shortly, and your friend, Jinx, is outside. We'll have plenty of time to discuss your injuries when you are stronger. They are fairly severe in nature, so you'll have to stay here a few days. Now rest and I'll go tell Jinx that you're awake. I'm going to restrict your visitors for a while though, so he'll have to come back later to see you."

"Dr. McKinney, how did I get here?"

"Jinx found you and carried you here. He hasn't left since he brought you in just after sunrise. Now, no more talking. Even when your parents come, I don't want you to say anything. You just let me do all the explaining for the time being." He left the room without another word.

The nurse returned and administered a shot to my already sore arm. A warm and pleasant feeling spread along my limbs and up toward my head. The pain began to ease, and I slipped out of reality into a profound darkness on the precipice of nothingness. A void so vast and bottomless that it pulled at me to leave the safety of my perch and plunge headlong into an eternity of pure black. The attraction to leap grew stronger, and I felt my strength to resist it fading. Pain stopped me just short of my leap into the void. Ever increasing in intensity, the sharp jabs began to creep up from places that were foreign in nature to me. Lying still became increasingly hard to do, and I could feel hands restraining my movements as my senses began to acknowledge more and more of my surroundings. Words such as "infection" and "fever" danced within the agony my senses were subjected to. I struggled to remember what brought me to that horrible place, but the memories were not within my reach. The void, ever beckoning, drew me time and again to the edge, and then the pain jerked me back. My body and spirit were at war. That much I was sure of. One wanted to live, the other to die. I knew it was my spirit longing for the void, but my body kept reaching to pull it away.

Finally, the struggle ended. I was left dumbstruck by the realization the body had been victorious. Opening my eyes brought only shadows and darkness. At first, I feared my sight had been forfeited in the battle. But eventually, I became aware that it was night, and only one, low light in the corner illuminated the room. My body felt disconnected in some places and shattered in others. Sitting up seemed impossible, but I tried anyway. Nausea flooded through me, and I fell back to the bed panting. It was not long before Dr. McKinney's face was only inches from mine.

"You've come back to us, Rea. I know that you're not feeling great, but, in time, you'll recover. I am going to send Sarah in with some broth, and I need you to drink it all. Will you please try to do that without too much of a fuss?"

Nodding my head once answered his question and sent my senses into a tailspin.

"Good girl, try to sleep after you finish. I'll be back to check on you later." Sarah brought in the broth as promised and sat patiently at my side, holding the cup in the long spaces between each sup. Her kindness toward me in this simple act infused me with a peaceful calm. A caring spirit radiated from her soul, and I sucked at it as a starving baby would cling to its mother's breast. Lying there accepting her help and encouragement brought me to a place that was alien to my world. I had been nursed before but never with compassion. I could visualize Ma sitting here now, but I knew without doubt that it would not be the same. Blame and consequence would be bound up with any form of healing aid. My soul would be made to suffer right along with my body.

Something took root in me at that moment and grew over the next several weeks within the nourishing attention of Sarah's care. I began to understand the concept of compassionate care. Dr. McKinney refused to allow me to return home; my parents made little effort to be involved in my recovery. Ma never came to visit me and Pa only once. His visit resulted in a very heated conversation with Dr. McKinney, which I could hear through the walls but could not understand. In general, my days were silent and peaceful, a calm before the storm.

Once my strength returned and I was able to sit for long periods, Sarah allowed me to go out onto the porch to enjoy the cool afternoon breezes. Dr. McKinney came to sit with me one afternoon. "Rea, would you mind telling me what you remember about that night before Jinx brought you to the clinic?"

"I don't mind, Dr. McKinney. I don't remember much though."

"That's all right, Rea. Just tell me what you can remember."

"Well, I remember feeling funny as I walked from here down to the bridge. Kind of like someone in the woods was watching me. When I was on the bridge, the beams started to quiver, and I stopped to look up at them. Something knocked me down from behind, and I hit the railing with my head. I tried to get to my feet, but they kept getting knocked out from under me. Then everything went black. The next thing I knew I was on the riverbank in the brush. I couldn't open my eyes because of the dried blood, so I felt my way down to the water to wash. When I turned to see if the bridge was still there, I got dizzy and slid down into the lake. I don't remember anything else until I woke up here."

"Why would you look to see if the bridge was still there?"

"I've had a dream all my life that the bridge falls while I'm on it. At night, with a full moon, just like the night I got hurt. Didn't the bridge fall?"

"No, it's still standing."

"I don't understand. What happened to me if the bridge didn't fall?"

Dr. McKinney looked down at the floor of the porch for several minutes. When he raised his head to face me, his eyes were no longer warm, but cold and dark. He hesitated a few seconds longer before he began to speak. "Someone followed you onto that bridge, Rea. Did you see anyone there at all?"

"No, sir, once I hit the railing, blood started running into my eyes and everything went black. Don't you know who was there on the bridge with me?"

"No one saw what happened that night, Rea."

"So you are telling me someone did this to me?"

"I'm afraid so."

"How can you be so sure? I could have just fallen and hit my head on the railing. Maybe it addled me, and I just wandered down to the bank by myself."

Bridge Over Calm Water

"I know you didn't do that because you were very violently assaulted. You were raped, Rea. I'm so sorry, but there is no doubt as to what was done."

"Is that why Ma and Pa have not been here to see me?"

"Actually, I would not allow them to come. They have some absurd idea that you brought this on yourself. They would not even allow me to contact the sheriff. You were having such a hard time fighting off the infection from lying in the river water that I thought having them around with these notions would be bad for you. Unfortunately, your pa has seen you sitting out on the porch and is demanding that you be sent back home immediately. I can postpone it for a while, but eventually you'll have to go back."

I had only heard the word rape once in my life. Once had been enough to know that even though it was an act against my will, I was now no longer pure in the sight of God or man. Ma and Pa would see this as a horrendous mark against our family. They felt women were the cause of all such bad behavior.

Dr. McKinney interrupted my thoughts before my mind could carry me any further into despair. "Rea, your attacker was unusually brutal with you. Can you think of anyone who would want to hurt you for any reason?"

I lowered my head as one name flashed blindingly across my mind. He had a reason to want to return hurt for hurt, especially for wounded pride. Saying the name out loud would have brought sorrow to the two people who had been most kind. I could not bring myself to do it. The image of Sarah's compassion easily forced the other face to the back of my thoughts. I made the decision then never to voice any accusations. I had no proof. If I were wrong, the hurt could never be undone. The only recourse was to face the truth and accept whatever reprisals arose from what had happened to me. My temper had overcome me, and now there was a debt to pay. Sarah had shown me that God could love me through the worst. She had known all along what had happened and had not once shown anything but kindness. Because she chose to care so willingly for me, I chose to show the same care for her. If I were right, it was best she never knew. The suspicion of Collin would die with me.

"I did not see a face, Dr. McKinney. It would be wrong to accuse someone without proof."

He did not press me further, and I vowed never to mention it to him again. Within the next few days, Pa came in the wagon to take me home. The moment did not call for celebration or condemnation. My return brought about little change in the routines of the farm. Pa had promised Dr. McKinney that he would keep me from heavy labor until the end of September. To my surprise, he was good to his word. I joined Jinx every morning to help with the milking, but he would not allow me to lift or pull even though it seemed to make life harder on him.

We had not returned to the easy friendship we shared before that night on the bridge. Jinx would not talk to me about how he came to find me in the river. I did learn that several neighbors had searched the woods along the road for many hours without success. Jinx only said that he heard me scream, which led him to where I lay far down the riverbank and away from the road. Apparently, everyone else had given up on finding me; only Jinx continued to look.

Standing in the barn one morning, I glanced up and caught Jinx watching me with sorrow etched across his face. This was not the first time he had cast a look of pity in my direction, and I had grown weary of having him feel sorry for me.

"Jinx, I wish you wouldn't look at me like that."

"What are you talking about, Rea?" His face grew bright red, and he turned to fix his gaze on the task in front of him.

This was dangerous on my part. Jinx had a tender heart. I ran the risk of destroying our already-strained friendship by pushing him to face the demons between us. I didn't remember much, but I did remember the pitiful state of my dress. Jinx saw more of me than he would think proper. It was apparent that he felt as though he violated my privacy in his effort to help me. We had only talked once before about this subject when I thanked him for taking me to the clinic. He believed I was never fully conscious, and I had continued to allow him to think that. However, the pity had to stop if we were to move beyond our shared discomfort; I could bear it no longer.

"Jinx, I need to ask you to do something for me. If I could go back and change what has happened, I would. However, it's not possible to do that, so I must go on from here. You did all you could to help me that morning. Now I need you not to feel sorry for me."

He stood perfectly still for a long time. The silence became almost unbearable as I watched emotions play across his face. Finally, in a very low voice, he found the words he would lay at my feet. "Believe it or not, I have tried very hard not to think about that night. Your pa was convinced you had run off to keep from getting married. They had all given up on finding you, but I just couldn't. Dr. McKinney told me you could not have survived much longer once you ended up in the water. If I had been fishing, like I told you I would be, this never would have happened. Truth is, Rea, I can't forgive myself for not sticking around 'til you came along. My brother got hungry, and I took him home right before dark. What you see in my face is guilt. I failed you as a friend."

"That's ridiculous; it is not your responsibility to watch over me."

"I wish I didn't feel this way, but I do. I can't take it much more either. I made a decision while you were staying with the McKinneys. I will be leaving next week. I joined the navy right before you came back to the farm. I leave for basic training next Friday. That will solve both of our problems." Jinx turned and walked out of the barn, leaving me devastated.

That he would not be staying on the farm forever was something I knew as fact. I had hoped all along that he would put it off for a while. Now the inevitable was happening and caught me unprepared. The news did not help my already-weak system. My body began to shake, and I collapsed into a heap on the barn floor. Pa came in search of me not long after Jinx left. He helped me to my feet and into the house. At his orders, Ma put me to bed where I spent the rest of the day. Until that day, crying had not come easily to me. When it did, I could not make myself stop. In my ignorance, I did not think things could get any worse. My innocence and only friend were lost to me. What more could I lose?

Jinx left the farm that afternoon. His younger brother came to take his place the next morning; life continued as it had every other day. The crying fit, as my ma called my day spent in bed, seemed to suck the very life out of me. I felt more exhausted each day, and the nausea had returned that I had fought during the time of the infection and fever. My output at the farm became less and less, and I caught Ma and Pa talking in quiet whispers more than once over the next week. School was scheduled to start in ten days, and I struggled just to get out of bed each day when the sun came up. One morning was especially trying as rising from bed brought on a severe attack of queasiness. That afternoon Pa walked into the kitchen and informed me and Ma to get ready to make a trip to see Dr. McKinney. I was too sick to wonder at Ma's involvement in this situation. She had never once visited me in all the weeks I had spent at the clinic. Pa did tell me she spent many hours on her knees praying for my deliverance. I never understood what she thought she could deliver me from. Today would answer that question.

I had not seen Robert or Sarah McKinney since Pa picked me up to take me home. The thought of me walking across the bridge to go to work in the clinic was repulsive to them and my parents. The nightmare had ceased after my attack. I no longer feared the bridge as I once had, but they would not listen to my pleas to be allowed to return.

Dr. McKinney had just arrived home when Pa pulled the wagon up to the gate. Pa quickly lifted me out of the wagon and carried me up the path and in through the clinic door. My father had never been especially kind toward me; his concern and care of me in that moment confused me. Ma acted even stranger. She barely spoke and would not look me in the eye. Dr. McKinney told Pa to lay me on the table and wait outside. He did not seem the least bit surprised at our unexpected appearance or at the state of my health. Sarah and Ma both stayed in the room, and I experienced another of the many embarrassing examinations

I had been subjected to for my injuries. When he finished, Dr. McKinney nodded at Ma and Sarah and asked them to leave us alone.

The doctor sat with his back to me, writing on what I knew to be my medical chart. I did not have the strength to sit up and face him. When he turned, I was still laying on my back staring at the ceiling. Dr. McKinney pulled his chair up to the bed and took my hand. "Rea, do you remember us talking about the fact that you were raped on the bridge?"

I could not find my voice, so I just nodded without looking in his direction.

"Then you understand what happened during the rape?"

This time the nod brought tears to my eyes.

"It breaks my heart to tell you this, Rea. It is so unfair. You are not feeling well because you are expecting a baby. By my calculations, it should arrive in early March."

Tears streamed down my face, but I never looked in Dr. McKinney's direction. I thought back over the summer to my mother's never-ceasing prayers. I heard her pleading every night and morning. Now I knew why she was so persistent. She was trying to get heaven to intervene and spare me this. Heaven had not seen fit to prevent this child's existence. As I lay there, I thought of the small graves that Sarah tended so lovingly and knew that not every child was brought to life. That thought vanished immediately, and I was confident the child would not only survive but thrive. I felt numbness in my heart and a repulsion toward what now grew within me. My thoughts turned to my parents and the embarrassment they would suffer because of this.

It was then that I realized Dr. McKinney was still holding my hand. Turning to face him, I wiped away my tears for they would do me no good. "It's all right, Dr. McKinney. Thank you for telling me in such a kind way. I assume that my parents already knew before they brought me here?"

"They feared this outcome all along. I had hoped the severity of your injuries and the fevers would prevent a pregnancy. Honestly, for many days, I did not know if you would even survive. I think your parents, faced with the possibility that they would lose you, decided to accept whatever followed and be grateful you were alive. Now they are only concerned about you and how you will handle it."

"Right now, I would just be happy not to be so sick at my stomach."

Dr. McKinney smiled and patted my hand. He called Sarah from the other room and asked her to lay a wet cloth across my forehead. While she fussed over me, Dr. McKinney left the room to talk to my parents. Under Sarah's tender care, I fell into a heavy sleep. Only slightly aware of being lifted up and carried to the wagon, I barely noticed the ride home.

I awakened late the next day with the sun shining through my window. Ma came into the room carrying a plate of food. She crept toward the bed to see if I still slept. I rolled over to face her as she reached the bureau.

"Ma, why did you let me sleep so late? I missed the milking."

"There's food here if you can eat it. Are you still sick?"

"It's not so bad this morning. I'll come downstairs and eat. You don't have to bring it to me."

Ma's face began to tremble, and tears shimmered in her eyes. I had rarely seen her cry and never for me. It broke my heart to watch her fighting for control. She wanted to be strong, but this was more than even my ma could bear.

"I am so sorry, Rea. I should have never let you go to work at that clinic."

"First, Jinx blamed himself and now you are blaming yourself. Ma, sometimes things just happen in life beyond our control. You should know that. This is just one of those things. I'm tired of wishing it never happened. I don't have any choice but to accept that in the spring I am going to have a baby. I'm just sorry that you and Pa have to go through this with me."

I understood then that talking about the pregnancy was much harder than just dealing with it. Rolling over, I placed both feet on the floor and slowly stood up. Ma hovered near me in case my balance failed to land me in an upright position. Smiling weakly, she took my hand and led me down the stairs and into the kitchen.

There are times in life when you crave the everyday normal things. For me, that morning was one of those times. I wanted Ma and Pa to go back to treating me in the same sort of detached way that was so familiar and comforting. I decided my only choice was to turn my back on worries bound up in the future. I would not walk in fear of what lay ahead; the bridge had taught me that. Living for each day as it came would free my soul to enjoy the tiny miracles of life. As Ma and I entered the kitchen, a beautiful little bluebird sat perched on the kitchen window sill. Most days, I would have missed the way it turned and peered at me through the window. On that day, it felt like a gift from a loving and gracious God.

CHAPTER FOUR

Facing the Truth

In the days that followed my visit to Dr. McKinney, I learned many things about the worth of family. In all the hours of my life, I had seldom felt as though my parents truly loved me. We weren't a family of expressed emotions or affection. During those days, we were even more reserved in some ways if that was possible. We each lived a relatively solitary life, crossing paths on occasion, never interacting more than necessary. Add to that the seclusion of farm life, and I existed in a bubble, shielded from the outside world. Even my brothers had avoided us since that night in June. No visitors came to our home; our only trips were to the small church a little more than a mile from our house. The people who attended our church were kind and gentle souls. Even so, I still wondered how they would react to my condition once it became evident. Lately, most of them had been more apt to avoid me. They did not know what to say concerning the attack. In all of this, Ma and Pa wasted few words, but their silent support was ever present. And so we waited, each caught up in thoughts too difficult to discuss.

Returning to finish high school was no longer an option. Pa would never need to know about the scholarship. I continued to take my days with complacent resignation. Actually, it literally had become a minute-to-minute existence for me. Focusing on each single motion that was required to complete any task helped keep me from worrying. Nights offered the only escape from the heaviness that blanketed my mind and body. The month of September passed almost unnoticed until early one morning when I walked into the kitchen to help with breakfast. Ma pulled another letter out of her apron. This one was not worn and was addressed specifically to me. She looked in my direction briefly but said nothing and continued with her cooking. The return address and name were unfamiliar. SN Jackson Cummings did not, at first glance, register as someone I knew. Ma noticed my hesitation and stopped cooking to speak.

"I told your pa you would not recognize the name. I also told him that you would be hearing from that boy, and I was right."

She turned back to the stove without another word. Sometimes, I had to drag information out of her. Lately, my mind had been foggy, so instead of trying to figure it out, I just asked. "Who is Jackson Cummings?"

"It's Jinx, Rea."

It felt as though she had drawn back and punched me in the stomach. It had been difficult, but I had managed not to think about Jinx very much since he left that summer day. Actually, no one mentioned him ever, not even his own brother. It was a situation that could not be helped or altered. Jinx made the decision to break any ties he had with this family abruptly, and for me, he did it at a very bad time. The letter I held not only baffled me, it was disconcerting. My hands trembled enough to shake the paper as I removed the letter from the envelope. Ma noticed my agitation. She noticed everything during those days.

"Sit down at the table, and I'll get you a cup of coffee."

Once I had braced myself in the chair, reading the letter seemed a little less unnerving. Jinx had never been one for many words, and, at one glance, I knew his letter followed suit.

> *Dear Rea,*
>
> *I am called by my given name here. My nickname is not well thought of by the men on my ship. I guess it is not hard to understand them not liking it. I am sorry about leaving without talking to you again. Please forgive me. You will never know how hard it was to walk away that day. I hope we can still be friends. It may*

be too much to ask of you considering the way I left, but it would be nice to hear from you. I am stationed in Hawaii. You can write to the address on the front of the envelope. I hope you are well. I have gotten no news from home. My family is not much for writing letters. I was kind of hoping you could catch me up on what's been going on there since I left.
    Sincerely,
    Jackson (that sounds funny doesn't it)

    Instantly, I hated that he felt as though I might not consider him my friend. Next, the reality of my present situation came crashing in to make me wonder if being my friend would be good for him considering the situation. His guilt over not being there to stop the attack would only be compounded by the knowledge that it brought on the pregnancy. This was even more heartbreaking than not hearing from him at all. Try as I might, I could not prevent tears from streaming down my face. My back was turned to Ma, but she came to warm up my coffee and waited on me to say something. Instead I handed her the letter.

    "Oh, Ma! What am I going to do? I don't want him to know about the baby, but I want him to know that we are still friends."

    "Write him back, Rea. You don't have to mention the baby for the time being."

    She didn't say it, but I knew Ma still hoped that the baby wouldn't survive to be born. She was wise though and not telling Jinx was the wise thing to do. I owed him that much as his friend. Ma handed the letter back, and I slid it into the envelope. Climbing the stairs once more to place it in my room took more energy than I could spare. I found myself sinking onto the bed in a daze. Several minutes passed before I made my way back downstairs to help Ma with the daily chores.

    The letter lay by my bed and in the back of my mind for days. During the next few weeks, each time an opportunity to answer occurred, I found an excuse not to attempt it. With the passage of time, the urge to reply to Jinx felt less pressing—until one late October afternoon.

Pa had summoned the vet for help with a sick cow, and the two men talked by our back door. The weather had been especially warm, and Ma had opened the kitchen window. Standing at the sink beneath the window and peeling potatoes, I could easily hear what my pa and Dr. Johnson were discussing. Apparently, the war raging in Europe had grown only worse since last spring. Having been secluded on the farm, I had almost completely forgotten the war. At school, our teachers had often discussed the progression of Hitler's Axis Alliance and their quest for more territory. The vet informed Pa that the United States was slowly becoming involved in the war in an effort to help Great Britain. He called it an undeclared war against Germany and felt it was only a matter of time before we sent troops to aid in the conflict.

It suddenly occurred to me that Jinx was one of those troops. My friend could easily find himself in combat before long. I had been a coward by not writing him back, and it made me feel less than human. Suddenly, with our country on the brink of war, my life and struggles seemed insignificant. As the sun slowly set, I sat down to the task of correspondence.

Dear Jackson,

Using your name makes you seem older somehow. Things at the farm are pretty much the same. Jim has been a great help to us, but he could never replace you. Pa has taken a break from husband hunting. I am very thankful not to be constantly on display. I did not return to school this fall. An unexpected situation arose, and I am needed here right now. Being stuck on the farm most of the time, I hear very little about the war in Europe. I hope we are not drawn into the conflict and that you are forced to fight. It is comforting to know that you are so far away from the war in Hawaii. I will keep you in my prayers, and when you write back, I will relay any information to your family that you want to send. Keep safe, and keep in touch.

Rea

Once the letter was completed, I felt relieved and apprehensive. I had not lied to Jinx about what was going on, but he was very smart and might press me for more information the next time he wrote. Every day, I reaffirmed my trust in God and hoped that I would be able to walk in the path He had chosen for me. Otherwise, I was doomed to fail myself, my family, and the new life within me. Writing this letter was just one of the many things that I did in the next months that made me step outside of myself for someone else. I sealed the letter and took it down to give to Ma. She accepted it with a questioning look on her face.

"It's okay, Ma. I was very vague. Jinx will have no idea what is happening here. Ma, can you do one thing for me? When it becomes obvious that I am going to have a baby, please insist to Jim that he ask his family not to relay the information to Jinx."

"Are you sure that is what you want to do?"

"It will make it easier for Jinx."

Ma did not push the subject further, placing the letter where Pa would pick it up and take it down to the mailbox. Pa did not mention the letter just as he never mentioned Jinx. His tendency to shy away from any talk of his former employee brought an uneasy feeling to my chest. The only explanation could be his total misconception of Jinx's value as a person. He truly felt that Jim was a much more intelligent and responsible worker than his brother. Pa failed to realize that Jim did not cover up or take the blame for my mistakes. I found myself tempted to come to Jinx's defense, but Pa would never believe me even if I did. He had no idea a friendship existed between Jinx and me.

As October painted the hardwoods on the farm in a brilliant display of color, the air grew cooler with each passing day. The cold, clean weather seemed to sweep away the cobwebs that had grown thick and sticky in my brain. As the haze lifted, which had clouded my thoughts since June, I realized I had been waiting for a revelation. Not that I expected God to speak to me directly, but I was hoping that something would trigger an understanding of the events that had put me on this unexpected road in my life. One Sunday morning, I found myself ready for church earlier than usual. I sat at the kitchen table waiting on my parents. The bright sunshine called to me from the window, and I rose and stared at the beautiful view stretching out into the woods that led from the farm toward the road below. Very suddenly, my body yearned to be surrounded by the warm colors literally dripping from the trees.

"Pa, would you mind very much if I walk through the woods to church this morning?"

"No, but don't be late."

I needed no further encouragement, and soon I was breathing in the magical smell that can be found only in the forest during the fall. A gentle breeze tickled my skin, lulling me into a pleasant state of calm. A sense of the new life growing within me tugged at my thoughts. I forced myself to acknowledge it was not fair to define this baby by the source of its beginning. It was not difficult to see from my life how very singular we are as human beings. We are born a combination of the past through our parents, but we are not bound to it as the people we will become. If the child came to life the next spring, it entered the world in God's sight a truly unique and precious soul. It should not be punished for the sins committed by its parents, not the father's nor mine. Knowing that to be true, I still could not find the least bit of mental connection to this child.

It had always seemed to me that expectant mothers shared a blissful sort of enthusiasm toward their developing children. Taking into consideration that all of the pregnant women I had known were married, I tried to blame my apathy on the rape and forced acceptance of this condition. But I feared that maybe it had more to do with my inability to feel love. This poor child was to be born both bastard and unloved by its mother. I could do my best to treat it in a loving way, but how could I rid myself of the loathing I felt every time I thought of this baby? Surely God would understand that this was too much to expect of me.

Just thinking about my responsibilities made my head spin and my stomach twist. I gazed around in search of a place to sit before I fell on my face. A nearby barren rock offered a safe resting place. I lowered myself to the hard surface and stared in silence at the multicolored trees that stood silent around me. The magnitude of the task before me brought back the nausea and soon I retched up my breakfast to spoil the soft, green moss surrounding the rock. In that moment, I lost all sense of connection to my surroundings. My heart all but dissolved within my chest, and I couldn't stop the tears that streamed in torrents down my checks. My body shook uncontrollably, and I curled up on the rock clutching my knees trying to keep myself from coming apart in jagged pieces. As time passed, I cried out the frustration and bitterness. Eventually, I sat up feeling complacent. Oddly, the panic had been replaced by resolve.

Voices softly drifted through the trees, and I realized that the church was over the next rise. Wiping my face and cleaning the debris off my dress, I began to climb the hill that would lead me to the back of the building. Just as I reached the crest of the hill, a conversation taking place nearby caught my attention.

"My Aunt Wilma says she's positive the Wilson girl is pregnant. She says that she has seen her parents sneaking her into Dr. McKinney's office almost every month. You know my aunt lives right across from the McKinney house. She doesn't miss much that goes on over there."

"Anna, you don't know that's true. They could just be taking her in for treatment. She was hurt pretty badly in the attack."

"Aunt Wilma says that whole story about an attack was just a cover up."

"That's enough, Anna, you're just spreading rumors. I'm not going to listen to this anymore, and the rest of you need to ignore this too."

"Well, you'll see I'm right, Lois and it won't be long according to Aunt Wilma."

As I came around the corner of the building, I could make out several of the women involved in the conversation as they walked through the front door. They were all young, some still in their teens. Apparently, I had become a subject of much discussion around the area. Keeping me cloistered on the farm had not been as effective as my parents had hoped. The late afternoon visits to Dr. McKinney had not gone unnoticed either.

Bridge Over Calm Water

If tongues were wagging in the church, I could only imagine how much worse it was within the general population. Very little excitement occurred in Rock Island. The incident on the bridge had been a variation from the boredom of everyday life for many people. They were obviously not going to let it go. Something had to be done before it all could fester into a sore that would not heal. It was painfully obvious that since I was the source of the gossip, it was my responsibility to literally cleanse the wound of the decay that had begun to build. I had never been especially brave or confrontational. But now, I began to feel the seeds of both growing deep roots within me.

The walk around the building gave the roots time to spread and cluster. When I reached the front door, my mind had wrapped itself around a course of action. My parents stood outside waiting on me and seemed more than relieved that I had actually shown up. The undisguised stares in my direction appeared more numerous than usual, but I could have been paranoid because of the remarks I had overheard. Taking our customary seats and settling in for the service tempted me to gaze around at the crowd, but I resisted the urge. My resolve could waver if I thought too much about the people who sat on the pews. Instead of concentrating on the sermon, I went over and over in my head what I planned to do and how to accomplish my objective.

The singing startled me back into the moment, and I stood with the rest of the congregation. The time for all sinners to approach the front had come. What better time to address the sin that had smothered me in its embrace for so many months? My pulse rate rose with my fear as I pushed my way out of the pew, past my pitifully confused parents.

The second Sunday after the attack while I lay wracked with fever and delirium, my parents had felt compelled to have the elders announce to the congregation that I was obviously a sin-ridden creature in need of their prayer. This one act had placed the blame of what happened on the bridge squarely on my shoulders. I knew that some of the responsibility was mine, so I let the people here believe I brought it all on myself. In retrospect, it was not a wise thing to do. However stupid it had been in refusing to face the truth about the nature of the attack, the deed was already done and gone. I could only deal with the effect of it, and so I made my way toward the pulpit. It took only a few seconds to reach the front pew, which was saved for those in need of salvation. I sat down and waited for the minister to come and receive my confession.

It didn't take him long to make his way to where I sat. The expression on his face did nothing to expel the knot that had formed in my stomach. I knew instantly that he was very uneasy about even talking to me. He could tell that I was not in a remorseful state and that I was not sitting in this pew to confess or ask for forgiveness. I was about to put him in a bad position, and I knew it, but I really had no choice.

"So, Rea, what can we do for you today? Are you here to request prayers for some reason?"

"Brother Tim, more than enough prayers have been directed toward heaven for me."

"There can never be too much prayer said on our behalf, Rea."

"Maybe you're right, but this is not going to be taken care of by prayer. I need to speak directly to the congregation. I know this is not what we normally do in this church, but believe me, it is the only way."

"Rea, what are you going to say?"

"I do not want to say this twice. Will you let me speak or not?"

"All right, but let me prepare them before you get up there."

"Whatever you think," I replied.

As the congregation completed the invitation hymn, our minister rose from his seat and walked to the podium. He stated my desire to speak and stepped to the side of the podium, giving me room to join him. Unexpectedly, he remained close to my side as though he wanted to support me in this rather strange request. I smiled and nodded in his direction before I turned to face the people in the pews. I slowly scanned the audience made up of people I had known all my life. As I did so, their expressions varied from shock to obvious confusion. In some faces, I saw pity, and that spurred me into my speech.

"I'm sure that since last June there has been much speculation and ah . . . conversation about what happened to me on the bridge. I would gladly give you a detailed description if I could remember it all, but I can't. I know some people here will doubt that as a truthful statement. I overheard some of you discussing me outside the church this morning. However hard it may be to believe, what the doctor told me after he treated me is that I was brutally attacked. Yes . . . that was the word, brutally. I know that this is an uncomfortable situation for many, and I don't want to scare or frighten the children, but this is the only time I can speak to you all in one place. As I heard this morning, it has been speculated that I will become a mother soon. Unfortunately for me, the speculations are true."

I heard several gasps from different areas in the church, but I kept my eyes on the back for fear of losing my nerve.

"I stand before you today to ask you for one thing. No, in truth, I'm here to beg you to please accept this child as precious in God's sight and to treat it as such. If you feel the need to be less than Christian about this, please direct your unkind talk and actions toward me. I will gladly bear the burden of this whole terrible mess. The baby's only hope of a normal life lies directly in your hands. If, as a church, you do not accept this child and show it love, then the community as a whole will have no reason to be kind. Try to remember that it is just an innocent child, and as pathetic as this is, it is not wanted by its mother."

Here I had to pause and take a deep breath.

"So you see that it enters the world without much hope of the love most children would experience. I am placing this at your feet and hoping that you can be strong where I am weak and make up for what this child will not get from me."

My voice cracked, and I felt it best to end the humiliation that I was experiencing at that moment.

"I guess that's all I have to say."

I walked between the pews and out the door without looking at anyone directly. I was aware that most heads were down.

Jan Kendall

Few people watched as I left. The trees once again offered a safe refuge from the world that was falling into chaos around me. My spirit felt less weighed down now, and the walk home seemed much more pleasant. Ma and Pa returned shortly after I arrived home and said nothing about my speech at the church. This was a pleasant surprise. I thought Pa would be very angry at me for my unexpected behavior. Maybe they were relieved that I took the responsibility of telling everyone out of their hands. But it could have been just wishful thinking on my part. We were all fully aware that by this evening the majority of our community would have heard various versions of my confession from the members of our church. I could only hope that they could glean truth from whatever they were told.

CHAPTER FIVE

Unexpected Kindness

The conviction of spirit that gave me the nerve to stand before the gathered members of my church on Sunday withered during a restless night's sleep. As the sun rose, I finally wearied of tossing and turning. Dragging myself out of bed and dressing in a slow stupor, I began to second guess my decision to be so candid about my condition. Even though the members were men and women of faith, they were still only human. Sins of the flesh always brought the worst sort of condemnation. Some people would choose not to believe the truth of the attack and saddle me with responsibility for the sin.

I heard Ma make her way down the stairs to the kitchen, calling me as she went. I quickly descended the steps to join her in her labors. She had already begun to gather the ingredients for our breakfast. Cooking had become such a routine for her over the years that she barely noticed what she was doing. Without the need to pay close attention to the task at hand, she launched in on me just as I walked out of the hall and into the kitchen.

"Rea, I think you were very brave yesterday, but I fear you have only made things harder for yourself."

"After worrying about it all night, I will agree that you are probably right, but I overheard some of the women talking about me as I came up from the woods. It appears someone had noticed all the trips we've made to the clinic and had already started a rumor about the baby. If people are talking about it at church, it's probably all over the community by now. The church members deserve the truth, and I gave them the truth."

"Your pa thinks you've pushed them into taking a stand. If you had left it alone, they might have just overlooked all of this a lot longer."

"Overlooked what, Ma? Overlook the fact that I was attacked and am paying a heavy price for that happening? Sure, it would be easier for all of you to not even talk about this. Apparently, you would prefer to let the whispers and sideway glances continue unchecked. You have lived here long enough to know that gossip just gets worse the longer it is allowed to be passed along. By being honest with everyone, maybe I can stop it before it spreads outside of Rock Island—at least for the immediate future."

Ma didn't press the subject any further, but I knew she had a point. Now that the truth about the matter was public knowledge, the feelings and opinions produced by it would definitely bring about all sorts of reactions. It could be bad for my family's honor. Family honor was one of Pa's favorite rallying cries when he was trying to keep us all in line. In my mind, the family honor pretty much sunk to the bottom of the lake beneath the bridge that June night.

After not sleeping all night and rehashing the whole thing with Ma, it became clear to me that I had been idle for too long. Work would push all the useless worries out of my mind. I needed to return to a set schedule of chores on the farm. I would have to visit Dr. McKinney and convince him to lift the restrictions he had my parents put into place. I intended to do it that day if I could get Pa's permission. I knew he was probably not happy about the episode in the church the morning before. Facing him would be tough. Unfortunately for Pa, the attack had changed my whole perspective of my place in the world and his authority over me. I no longer quaked at the thought of confronting him. Well, I still shook inside a wee bit, but it definitely was not a quake.

As if the powers that be wanted to test my resolve, Pa stalked into the kitchen and sat down to wait on Ma to serve him break-

Bridge Over Calm Water

fast. My family had always run on a very smooth schedule. At times, my parents gave the impression that they could read each other's mind. After years of living and working together, they wasted no energy on unnecessary conversation. Since June, my life had landed one shattering blow after another to disrupt the serenity of their lives. They would not appreciate my attempt to make my own decisions after all we had been through.

"Pa, if it is all right with you, I want to start doing my chores again. I thought I might go and see Dr. McKinney this afternoon to get his permission. Also, I want to ask if maybe he would let me return to work at the clinic on Saturdays. If I am about to bring another mouth to feed into this house, I need to do my part to help. I want to be as little burden to you as I can be for as long as I am here. I know that you want to marry me off as quickly as possible, but I doubt anyone will have me before this baby is born. I feel like I need to take some of the responsibility for myself and what is going to happen between now and the delivery. After that, I'm not sure how things might work out."

"Can't say that I think any of this makes sense. You're getting awful high-handed in your attitude if you ask me. I'm still head of this house, and you'll do as I say. That little show you put on in church yesterday didn't help either. You forget that we are just as worried as you are. We've been doing the best for you that we know how; it seems to me that you're mighty unappreciative."

"You misunderstand me, Pa. I feel so bad for putting you through this. I really can't explain what it feels like to be me. The attack was bad enough but to be pregnant because of it . . . . Well, it all makes me feel so loathsome. You need to let me do this if for no other reason than to allow me some control over what is happening. I may make a lot of mistakes, but at least I will make them and they won't be forced on me by someone else. Please, Pa, give me a chance to face this on my terms."

Tears began to run slowly down my father's face. He stared out the window until the silence became almost unbearable. Ma kept her back to both of us. Busy cleaning up dishes in the sink, her head and shoulders slumped forward in a dejected manner.

To know that my parents were suffering right along with me did not make anything better. Their obvious pain added to my already soul-crushing burden.

Pa sighed heavily and turned to look in my direction with his hands planted firmly on the table. I could see a change in his eyes. It gave me the hope that he would allow me the freedom to choose. Ma came to the table to pour more coffee in his cup and took the seat beside him. She would never voice an opinion before him or fail to show him support for whatever decision he made. So I stood patiently across the kitchen from my parents and waited for Pa to say his piece.

"With your determination and strength, I often wished you were born a boy instead of a girl. Why God chose to bless you instead of my sons is beyond me. It seems such a waste for a girl to be hankering for so much knowledge and so envious of man's God-given right to authority. You ain't willing to accept your rightful place in this world, Rea. You spoke out-of-turn at church and opened a can of worms. You overstepped your place in my household. I wash my hands of the whole thing.

"Do whatever you want. I will let you stay here as long as you don't cause no more trouble and don't make no more speeches. You best be figuring out in all this what you are gonna do with this baby once it gets here. Don't you forget whose house this is you're living in while you're doing all this deciding! Do you hear me girl?"

"Yes, Pa. I hear you."

He rose immediately from his chair and stalked out the back door, leaving Ma and me to stare down at the table in cold silence. I have no idea how long it was before Ma pushed herself to her feet and began to finish cleaning up from breakfast. I should have moved to help her, but I was mesmerized by Pa's words. I had no idea he felt that way about me, and I realized that he would have never told me under any other circumstances. I would have lived my entire life oblivious to the fact that he considered me, in some ways, superior to my brothers. This was truly a life-changing revelation for me. By letting me know he saw strengths in me, not present in Steve and Jeff, he unwittingly gave me confidence in my ability to overcome the problems ahead of me. Pa might be right. I had a place in the world, and maybe I had refused to accept the conditions that would bind me to that place. With his confession, he set in stone my determination to make my own decisions. If I settled for less than what I believed to be possible, I would dishonor myself.

The rest of the morning passed quickly. Since breakfast, I had obsessed over Pa's words, and try as I might, I could not clear them out. Pa had freed me to make my own choices. I could see a glimmer of light down the long, dark tunnel that was my life. Freedom of choice, even when the choices available are not that great, is a soul-lifting experience. With it came a courage I did not know I had. When Pa returned to the house for lunch, I drew on that courage to face him and asked him to allow me to ride Max to Rock Island. To my surprise, he saddled the stinky animal and helped me up. He eyed me wearily as I swayed uneasily from side to side trying to get in a comfortable position.

He surprised me again by speaking in a gentle and caring voice. "Are you sure you can make it on this ol' horse? Remember when Jinx took you the last day you worked there? I sure would feel better if he was here now to take you. If you wait until tomorrow, I will take you in the wagon."

Pa was a man of contradictions. He had a good heart wrapped up in all that temper and bullying. I could see the concern in his eyes and almost wavered in my decision so that I would not disappoint him further. Somehow, I managed to force myself to look at him confidently—although I did not feel very confident sitting on Max. "You won't have time tomorrow either. I need to do this on my own. Besides Max will barely trot; all I have to do is hold on to the saddle."

I gently nudged the animal to start him off in the right direction and made sure I held myself up straight. I rode away looking like I had conquered my fear of horses. Pa's words and the smell of the horse reminded me of Jinx, which made my heart a little heavier and brought to the surface dark memories I preferred to leave in the past. The slow ride did nothing to improve my mood. With every clip-clop, the tension in my back built. By the time we reached the bridge, I felt as though someone had kicked me between my shoulder blades. The bridge no longer terrified me, but I didn't relish the thought of riding across it either. Pa was right about my poor riding habits, it had never been easy for me.

I pulled the cumbersome animal to the side of the road and climbed down to lead it over the wooden planking toward the far bank. Halfway across, I felt drawn to the side and stopped to peer down into the deep, green water. The water was calm and reflective. Oddly, it was not memories of the attack that rose up to greet me from the water but thoughts of Jinx. Overcome by the recollection that he was gone, a world away from me, my heart ached for my friend. It was then that I understood that over the years I had grown to love him as more than a friend. Had I been wiser, I might have seen the possible answer to my problems with Pa standing right there in front of me in the barn every morning. I knew Jinx cared for me, but how much had he cared? Whatever might have happened had been washed away that horrific night by the water under this bridge, making my thoughts that afternoon only an empty daydream.

The horse pulled at the reins, eager to reach solid ground, and tugged me back from the railing. The sun was sinking slowly toward the horizon, and I needed to be back at the farm by dark. Once I led Max off the bridge, it was a real effort to heave myself back up into the saddle. That was the first time I became aware of the added burden within me. It was apparent I would become more uncoordinated as the child increased my girth.

Dr. McKinney sat in a rocking chair on his front porch as I rode up to the gate. He quickly came to my aid and helped me to the ground before I could climb off on my own. He began to speak before I explained the purpose of my visit. "Rea, you do not need to be riding a horse. Your injuries make this pregnancy dangerous. Being bounced around on that horse could break open the repairs I made during surgery. You could start to bleed and die before we could stop it. I should have told your parents this. I am sorry for not warning them."

"As a matter of fact, that's why I'm here today. From now on, could you tell me, not my parents, what is necessary? I want to take as much of the burden off of them as I can. Also, I want to go back to helping Pa more with the work around the farm. Up until now, they have barely let me out of the house. He won't let me help until I get your permission."

"Well, as long as you don't do any lifting—the work will help you build up your strength."

"There isn't much I can do on a farm without lifting, how about in the kitchen?"

"No heavy skillets or pots. I don't want you lifting anything heavier than a dozen eggs."

"All right, but I need you to write this down so that my parents don't worry. Also, I was wondering if you would let me come back to work in the clinic on Saturdays? I need to help out with our money situation."

At my request, the strangest look crossed Dr. McKinney's face. He stood very still for the longest time. It was obvious he was struggling with the answer.

"Rea, would you please come and sit on the porch for a few minutes while I go talk to Sarah? She has struggled through each of her pregnancies and suffered so greatly after each loss that I want to make sure having you around won't upset her. I hope you understand."

"Yes, sir, I would never want to do anything to hurt Mrs. Sarah."

It was Sarah McKinney who came out of the house a few minutes later to stand beside me on the porch. She simply put her arm around my shoulder and quietly told me she would be delighted to have me come back to help her in the clinic. Dr. McKinney returned shortly and insisted on driving me back to the farm. He assured me that Pa would not mind riding back with him to retrieve the horse and that would give them a chance to talk about my chores. The trip back was shorter and much more pleasant in the car. Pa appeared relieved to see me back at our door without Max and left immediately with the doctor to fetch him.

Jan Kendall

The day had been a balm to my shattered spirit, but the truly surprising part awaited me on the kitchen table. Ma was not in the house when I returned, but I made my way straight to the kitchen in search of food. Since the nausea had abated, I was constantly hungry. Very thoughtfully, she always had some sort of snack sitting in view on the stove.

The food was soon forgotten. As I walked into the room, I spotted a soft pile of cloth in front of me. Lying neatly folded on the table was a beautiful quilt of soft delicate colors. I knew where the quilt had come from instantly. The ladies of the community gathered the first Sunday afternoon of every month to quilt. They always kept extras to give as gifts for marriages, births, and tragedies. This was one of their baby quilts. I had seen many in my life; all were given as gifts at showers that would precede the birth of any child in the community.

I knew there would be no shower for my baby. However, the quilt said much about the kindness of the women who had spent hours making it. The mothers, daughters, aunts, and grandmothers who worked on these quilts represented almost every family in the area. Ma had never been involved in this joyous group of women. Pa felt it was not proper to do such socializing on a Sunday. On many first Sundays, I would sneak off from the house while Pa napped and watched them turn small pieces of scrap fabric into wonderful creations. Ma knew where I went because the women mentioned it to her, but she never stopped my trips. She seemed to go to a great effort on those first Sundays to fix Pa's favorite food, so that he would overeat and quickly fall into a deep sleep.

As I held the quilt obviously meant for my unborn baby and fingered the material, which was flawlessly assembled and stitched, I felt hope for this child as it grew within me. Ma returned to find me staring at the colors that were dancing and swimming before my eyes.

"Mrs. Casey dropped that by not long ago. She said to tell you she was sorry you were not here. The ladies discussed this after church Sunday, and they wanted this to be the first gift your baby got. She said that they checked today with the other quilters in the community before she brought it over, and they all agreed that you should get the prettiest quilt they had. It appears they think quite a bit of you, Rea. I must say that this surprises me."

Ma waited for me to speak, but I could only rub the quilt and smile. Knowing these women felt that way made me very happy, and I didn't want to ruin the feeling by talking.

November passed as the weather went from wonderfully cool to often cold and rainy. The first Sunday in December, the seventh, started pretty much as any other. The day passed pleasantly even though I could no longer sneak away from the house to watch the women quilt. I spent the afternoon in my room going through a treasure trove of gifts. The quilt had only been the beginning of many gifts that followed. Most simply appeared on the porch—delivered by swift and silent feet. Ma grew more amazed at each unexpected arrival. Pa never acknowledged the gifts. Most people were pleasant enough when forced to be in my company, but it was apparent that I made them uncomfortable. The fact that so many reached out in this manner was heartwarming. Only a few things delivered to the porch included a note. Most were simply left there, no one taking responsibility for the generosity demonstrated toward the baby. I spent many free hours looking at each piece trying to imagine who might have been the giver. It was a useless endeavor, but it helped fill the time spent indoors because of the bad weather.

The afternoon had grown late without me noticing when I heard the radio come on in the living room below. It was not unusual for Pa to have the radio on, but something sounded different. The volume had been turned up, and the voice coming over the speakers was unfamiliar. So I climbed out of the pile surrounding me on the bed and descended the stairs to investigate. My parents sat in the semi-dark room listening, but the looks on their faces made fear rise up to grip my heart. Something very bad had happened.

The radio announcer soon gave words to the sheer terror on their faces. The Japanese had attacked our base at Pearl Harbor. The many warships anchored in the harbor had been caught by surprise. The destruction was unbelievable in scope. Instantly, I knew Jinx was somewhere in the carnage—alive or dead. He had not mentioned on which ship he was stationed. We had no way of knowing if he had survived. I had once thought that the worst had already occurred in my life. Oh, I had been so wrong. My problems became very small and unimportant in less than a heartbeat.

The next few weeks would be so much harder than all of those that had gone before. Not knowing what had happened to Jinx brought new meaning to pain. I prayed and cried into the early morning hours almost every night. The loss of sleep made me more and more emotional.

One Saturday morning, Dr. McKinney called me into his office to investigate the cause of my severe sadness. "Rea, I know the fact that we are now at war is worrisome and your condition does not help with your feelings, but you are abnormal in your mood and response to this situation."

"I am sorry that I have not been pleasant, Dr. McKinney, but Jinx was stationed in Pearl Harbor. No one has heard whether he lived or died, not even his family."

"Jinx? Was he the young man that helped your father on the farm and brought you to the clinic that morning of the attack?"

"Yes, sir, I have known him most of my life. I just wish I knew either way. It's the not knowing that's so hard."

"Seems to me you have a lot of emotion invested in this young man, energy you need to keep your health from deteriorating. Sarah and I have been discussing you quite a bit lately. We think, considering all the factors, you should come and stay here for the final couple of months before the baby is born. I am telling you this before I talk to your parents. The damage to your body during the rape was extensive. I honestly don't know how you will do with the birth. You need to be close when the labor starts so that we can cope quickly with any problems. It may be necessary to bring you here sooner if anything unexpected happens.

"As for the matter of Jinx, I know several people who work for the government. One of them might be able to get the information you want. But you have to promise not to dwell on this any longer. Do you understand how important it is that you keep your spirits and strength up from now until time for the baby to come?"

"Yes, I understand. Thank you for offering to check on Jinx. I will think about what you have said and try to do better. I think I will be okay at home though."

"Understand, Rea, coming here is not up for discussion. If we have to lock you in our spare bedroom, that's exactly what we intend to do."

Dr. McKinney rose from his chair and returned to examining patients. He had never been so blunt with me. It was rather unnerving. Returning home that afternoon, I tried to think in a more positive manner. The fact that there had been no news about Jinx might actually mean he was still alive. I determined to wait and see what Dr. McKinney could find out. Concerning his declaration about my future living arrangements, well, I would let him break that to Ma and Pa.

I didn't have to wait long for news concerning Jinx. The next Saturday, Dr. McKinney told me that Jinx was not listed among the dead or missing. He did stress that the list could be wrong, but there was a very good chance that he was still alive, though no one knew where at the moment. The news inflated my spirits. To add to my joy, more gifts continued to arrive in greater numbers as the Christmas holiday neared.

Every church and family in the area had their own traditions for celebrating the Christmas season. The war put a damper on the festivities, but it did not hinder them completely. Families with sons and fathers near or at the age to serve in the military who were still at home filled every moment with love and hope. Ma and Pa didn't speak of my brothers often, but they wondered how long it would be before one or both volunteered to fight. There was not much to celebrate in our home that year beyond the fact that we were still intact as a family, and for that, we were very thankful.

On Christmas Eve, most everyone in the area congregated at the local community center for the annual Christmas pageant.

Jan Kendall

Children dressed as shepherds, angels, and wise men ran amuck among live sheep and cows. It was a solemn occasion but could quickly become comical in the endeavor to pull it off. That year was no exception. An angel managed to fall from his perch above the manger with no significant injury other than the loss of one wing. A shepherd, standing to one side holding onto the rope attached to an unfortunate lamb, practically strangled the poor creature before anyone could notice and loosen the noose. The baby lay quietly in the manger until the final song began. At that point, he joined the heavenly chorus with a scream that more than drowned out the best effort of the singers. Even with all the commotion, it was a wonderful evening, and joy abounded in every heart even if just for a while.

    The year ended with the hope that the war would not last long and the losses would not be devastating. I was not very optimistic for the long term. We still had not heard anything from Jinx. Like everyone around me, I prayed the New Year into existence. It was the least I could do for the ones I loved and those I did not know who fought for our country.

CHAPTER SIX

A Heavy Load

What little joy the residents of Rock Island could squeeze out of the Christmas holiday dissipated quickly after the New Year. The weather turned bitterly cold and wet. On many days, ice clung to the tree limbs and covered every surface on the farm. Merely walking back and forth to the barn was treacherous. More and more of the men from surrounding farms and homes volunteered for service in the armed forces. Both of my brothers joined up without giving my parents prior notice. Steve enlisted in the air force; Jeff signed up with the army. Pa was proud of his sons but disheartened that they had to leave the pursuit of their educations and put their lives at risk. The tension in our house was high before the boys shipped out. After they left, we began to avoid each other as much as possible. Ma would burst into tears if we looked in her direction. I'm sure she believed that the family could not have been in any worse shape, and honestly, I could not have disagreed.

It became increasingly more difficult to accomplish any simple task. As the baby's weight put pressure on my insides, I endured pain most of the time. In general, I managed to hide my discomfort, but I noticed Jim staring at me early one morning as we worked to finish the milking as quickly as our frozen fingers would allow us.

"Something wrong, Jim?"

"You look really sick this morning."

"I don't feel well. Maybe I'm catching a cold."

"Why don't you go back to the house and let me finish?"

"I'll be all right. Let's not waste any more time talking."

"Jinx always said you were stubborn as a mule. Ya know, he wrote Ma and asked why you didn't go back to school. Wanted to know what was wrong."

I quickly stood up from a stooped position to look Jim in the face, a motion that almost made me pass out. He knew by the look on my face that I was in a panic, and he had been responsible.

"Ma didn't write him back. She told me that if you wanted him to know about the baby you would tell him. Was Ma right? Have you not told Jinx?"

"Your Ma is a very smart woman. What good would telling Jinx do now? He felt bad enough about the attack. Telling him now would only make all this worse. I don't want Jinx worrying about things that are out of his control."

Jim didn't say anything else. Instead, he turned his back to me and continued his work. Even though he was only one year younger than me, at that moment I felt so much older than him. Something about the way he made an effort not to look at me gave me an uneasy feeling. He was right about my health; it was going from bad to worse and very quickly. By the time we completed the milking, I was shivering violently, and every part of my body burned. Any energy I had left evaporated as I made my way back to the house. Ma did not acknowledge my entrance into the kitchen, and I just kept going toward the stairs and up to my room. Whatever else needed to be done that day would not be done by me.

I am not sure, but I think several hours passed before Ma came into my room to check on me. I was on my back prostrate across my bed. All of my clothes were drenched in sweat, and I was having a hard time focusing on any one object. She took one brief look in my direction and ran back down the stairs yelling for Pa as she went. They returned to assess the state of my well-being and determined that they must get me to the doctor immediately. After much discussion, most of which sounded like gibberish to me, Pa disappeared and left Ma applying cool cloths to my forehead and cheeks. Considering I thought my skin was burning off in layers, the cold water should have been a welcomed relief. Unfortunately, it only added to my misery, and I began to push Ma's hands aside, trying to get her to stop. To my horror, she ceased only long enough to enlist Jim's help in holding me down.

Jim's strength was well known throughout the community, but he did not hurt me as he kept me pinned to the bed. Ma not only wiped down my face, she also began to work on my arms and legs. If I hadn't been so very sick, this situation would have been embarrassing. Eventually, every male member of the Cummings clan who worked on our farm would witness me at one time or another in a compromising position. Trying not to think about how Ma had me exposed, I turned my attention to their conversation.

"I told her to come back to the house this morning and let me finish the milking, but she wouldn't do it."

"My daughter inherited her stubborn ways from her father. She never knows when to give up on anything. It has gotten her into more than one mess. I wish her Pa would hurry—the fever seems to be getting worse."

I had no idea what Pa might be doing, but it mattered little. I remembered nothing after that short exchange between Ma and Jim. The nightmare of the bridge returned with a vengeance as I slipped from reality. Mixed with the pain from the fever, it grew to be more visually clear and physically tormenting. Eventually, my mind tired of the chaos, and I slipped into oblivion. Once again, I stood at the edge of the dark unending void, but this time something was different. Beyond what my body felt, there was something calm and inviting and just a pinpoint of light. A small beacon in the darkness, it was intense enough to catch my attention and hold it. Within that very tiny illumination, hope and redemption lived—just out of reach. To get there meant stepping into a cold and hard blackness, soul crushing and frigid. I tried to make myself go, but I lacked the courage. For what seemed like an eternity, I tried to force myself to leave the safety of the cliff on which I stood. Finally, I knew that I was too cowardly to make the leap. With that decision, time and distance vanished; I awoke in unfamiliar surroundings.

"She's been in a semiconscious state for almost two weeks. Dr. McKinney says she might be able to hear us, but I doubt it. I think the fever melted her brain. He says there is still hope for the baby, but what will happen to the poor little thing? Her ma won't even talk about it, and her pa hasn't been to visit her since they brought her here."

"Nurse, I've told you not to talk about her in this room. Now get out and stay out if you can't keep your mouth shut."

"Dr. McKinney! I'm sorry. It won't happen again."

"No, it won't. If I hear of you in this room again, you can find another place to work. Have I made myself clear?"

"Yes, sir."

The good news gleaned out of this conversation was that I understood them and that my brain had not melted into a glob. The bad news was that I couldn't summon the energy to talk. But I felt tears traveling slowly down my cheeks. It did not take long for the doctor to notice. Very quickly, he stood over me in the bed.

"Rea, don't try to talk, and don't pay any attention to anything that stupid woman said about you. It seems you are at my mercy once again though. Right now, we have you in McMinnville, but as soon as you get your strength back, I'll be taking you to stay at our house. If you understand me, would you please try to squeeze my hand?"

I tried with all I had to squeeze, but I failed miserably. I did manage a sort of smile, which seemed to satisfy the kind man leaning over me. He was good to his word, for I never heard the nurse's voice in my room again. My strength came back in small measures, but not completely. After the doctor's rough treatment of the nurse, no one would speak inside my room or to me. One nurse was willing to tell me, only after I promised not to mention a word of it to Dr. McKinney, that I had been overcome by pneumonia.

Through it all, the baby continued to develop and seemed to thrive. Late one afternoon, just before they loaded me into the doctor's car for the trip back to Rock Island, Ma came into my room to sit and wait to make the trip with me. After several minutes of silence, she turned in my direction and a rather sad and forlorn expression filled her face. "It would seem that this child is so determined to enter the world that it would sacrifice the only person with any interest in its welfare. It may rid itself of a mother and me of a daughter before this is all over."

That was the only comment Ma made concerning the baby in all the months from June to March. It was a cruel thing to say about an unborn child, yet I understood how she might have felt. Weariness lay heavy on my shoulders, and in truth, life held very little appeal for me after my return to Dr. McKinney's. At that moment, I no longer cared to live and had no idea how I would make it through a birth if it was nearly as difficult as I had heard described by other women. My fears of what lay ahead took my mind back to the dark void. Many times, I wished that my courage to leap had been stronger.

Up until the pneumonia, I had tried to keep a positive attitude about everything. After the fever, I could no longer find the strength to do so and fell into a constant state of sour spirits. However, my time spent with the McKinneys was a true luxury for me. I was free of chores, and Sarah was always there to care for my every need. To fill my empty time, she began to distract me with tales of her childhood and family. Eventually, she got around to the story of Joseph and Collin.

Sarah's mother had given birth to two sons. Joseph was two years younger than Collin and four years younger than Sarah. Her family loved nature and spent many hours hiking the trails around her home in Chattanooga. One early spring afternoon, Collin, who was eighteen at the time, gave in to his brother's begging. He agreed to take him hiking along an especially difficult and dangerous path that ran along the top ridge of Lookout Mountain. Their mother pleaded with her sons to wait until their father could accompany them, but they were impatient to be out in the warm, spring air.

As was their normal practice, Collin took the lead. Joseph followed his brother's steps in and around the boulders that lined the path. As they approached the top, Collin heard a noise and looked back just in time to watch his brother fall from the cliff one hundred or so feet to his death. According to his sister, Collin became a different person after that day. Blaming himself for his brother's death, he grew bitter and hardhearted.

I wondered why she chose to go into such detail about the effect the accident had on Collin. She spent a great deal of time describing the child Collin use to be and the man he became after Joseph died. On that particular day, she was working in her kitchen and I sat in a chair at the table. Sarah had tried to coax me to eat by setting several sweet treats in front of me. What little appetite I had completely vanished the minute she mentioned Collin's name. She made a statement that hit way too close for comfort.

"Rea, I couldn't help but notice that the last time Collin was here, it seemed that you did not like him. Most women find him quite endearing, even with his bad temper."

What could I say? I was the one who broke his nose? That I was pretty sure he is the father of this baby? Nope, that wouldn't do, but she had turned to look at me and was expecting an answer.

"When I first saw your brother from the back, I thought he looked very much like an angel. He has the most beautiful hair I have ever seen. Beyond that, I really didn't notice much. He was not part of my world, and honestly, with Pa trying to find me someone to marry, I had enough to think about besides Collin."

"What do you mean your father was trying to find you a husband?"

"That's why he let me work in the clinic on Saturdays—so everyone could see me. Do you remember him asking you if I would look like a girl in the uniform?"

At first, I didn't think she understood. Then she burst into laughter. It took several minutes before she could compose herself enough to talk.

"That's the most absurd thing I have ever heard. He put you on display at the clinic so that he could find you a husband?" Suddenly she became very somber and sucked in her breath in a great rush of air. "Do you think it was one of these prospective husbands that attacked you on the bridge?"

"I doubt it. Remember it was just my first day to work inside the clinic. I don't think anyone around here was responsible for this. More than likely, it was someone just passing through."

"You know, I've talked to Collin several times lately on the telephone. He has enlisted in the army and is about ready to be shipped out. He never fails to ask me how you are doing. He seems to have taken quite an interest in you since I told him about the baby. I think you and Collin might actually become friends if you had the chance to get to know him."

"I don't think we have enough in common to ever be friends, but I'm flattered you think that might have been possible."

"Maybe you'll feel differently after he comes for a visit next weekend. He had been refusing to make the trip over until he knew you were staying with us. He became quite excited at the idea of helping me keep you company for a while."

Until now, I had not noticed the similarity between Sarah and her brother. Their facial features were almost identical; the only difference was the hair. I could tell she assumed his eminent arrival would be something I considered a wonderful prospect. In reality, it knocked the air right out of me. I literally had to make an effort not to let her see me gasp and fight for my breath. Sarah noticed my discomfort and misread it.

"Oh no, Robert will be very mad at me for exciting you so!" She picked up a glass of water and handed it to me saying, "Take a drink of water and try to calm down, and here I thought you didn't like my brother. I promise I won't bring it up again; you won't have long to wait though. He should be here by late Friday afternoon. Now let's get you into the bedroom so you can lie down and take a nap before Robert gets home."

Sarah fussed over me until she was confident I was comfortable before she left me alone. By the time she had me settled, my breathing had returned to a fairly normal rate. However, my pulse still raced, and my head was beginning to ache. Within a few minutes, I could not raise my head off the pillow. When Sarah returned to fetch me for dinner, I told her that I was too tired to eat. She didn't press me but sent Dr. McKinney in to check on me anyway. He took my temperature and blood pressure then left me to battle my fears.

I could not rest knowing that Collin and I would be in the same house all weekend. Panic began to grip me as I imagined all the horrible things he could do to me in such confined circumstances. Common sense argued that surely he would behave in his own sister's house. However, I would remember the attack and common sense would lose out to hysteria. These two emotions battled within me all night long. By morning, I could barely move from the bed. Trying to drag myself to my feet brought on the very first pain. Sharp as a knife, it sliced its way around my back, encircling my belly and knocking me to my knees.

Sarah heard me hit the floor and groan. She hurried into the room and found me bent double on the floor. She helped me back into bed and went in search of her husband. Up until this point, I had thought the pain I went through as my body healed from the attack was the worse I would ever know. Like so many other things, I was wrong about that too. I felt as though I was splitting open from the inside. Hard as I tried to stifle a scream, I couldn't, and that brought Dr. McKinney running—not even completely dressed for work.

Since that day, I often have tried to remember the specifics of the several hours that ensued. I can only recall the pain. I was consumed in it, buried alive. I heard words and phrases such as, "too much blood," "danger of infection," and "send for her family." Even then I didn't care. Just when I thought that I would surely die from the agony, I began to fall down a long tunnel into nothingness.

Then I heard a little noise, just a little, bitty, tiny noise. Not a cry, more like a mew, it latched onto my senses, and I began traveling back, being pulled along by the sound. Opening my eyes to a fuzzy, blurred world full of that irritating noise was very confusing. I made out the vague form of faces but couldn't tell who they belonged to. It took several minutes for my eyesight to clear as my head pounded out a rhythm behind my skull.

Bridge Over Calm Water

Finally, I focused enough to find Dr. McKinney in the crowd around my bed. He was smiling, and I found that very odd. Maybe he was pleased to have rid me of all the pain and replaced it with this headache. I would have to admit, it was much better than what had come before. Then I looked toward the foot of the bed and realized I could not see the bulge that had blocked the view of my feet for so very long.

I heard Dr. McKinney's voice. "Rea, we did it! She's here. You have a baby daughter. She's very small but quite a fighter. Sarah has already fallen in love with her. I must say she pulls at my heart strings too. Now tell me how you feel."

"My head hurts, and I'm sick at my stomach."

"The ether I used to put you to sleep would cause both of those problems, but I had no choice. We had to do some cutting and stitching. I'll explain everything later. Right now, I want you to rest. But can you tell us what you want to call the newest resident of Rock Island?"

"Lilly."

"Lilly suits her, but you'll have to take my word for that. We have her in an incubator since she's so small and a few days early. You go back to sleep. We'll introduce you to her later."

It did not bother me in the least not to have to face the child yet. I needed to be in better shape to control my emotions and at least seem pleased to see my newborn daughter for the first time. Right now, I felt overwhelmed. It took all my strength not to burst into tears while everyone watched me. I closed my eyes and felt someone give me a shot. Just before drifting off, I grabbed the nearest arm.

"What date is today?"

"Today is March third. Why?"

"Was she born today?"

"No, very late last night. Her birthday is the second of March."

Sleep came to me quickly, and it was a peaceful, dreamless sleep. The next time I awoke, I was back in the McKinney bedroom, but it looked more like a hospital room than I had remembered. The last day I could recall clearly was Sunday, but was this Monday, and why all the hospital equipment? Then the memory of Collin's impending visit exploded vividly in my mind, followed by the memory of the pain and a baby girl. But how many days had passed, and what had happened to the child? I didn't have to wonder very long because Sarah breezed into the room with a tray of food, humming happily.

"Wonderful—you're awake. Now let me help you sit up and see if you can eat some of this rather bland breakfast my husband has ordered me to feed you."

Complying with her wishes was difficult and somewhat painful, but I managed without much groaning and complaining. The food was bland, but I was very hungry; eating was not as hard as I first thought it would be. Sarah left me in peace to eat, but not for long. Soon she came back to retrieve the tray.

"Robert says you must get up and move around today. It's been three days since Lilly was born, and you have been still for too long. As soon as I take this back to the kitchen, I'll come back and help you walk around the room." Sarah was good to her word.

The rest of the week, I spent my time sleeping, eating, and very slowly moving about the house. She did not mention the baby often, and I never asked any questions. Even though Sarah didn't make me feel guilty about my lack of interest in Lilly, I felt guilty enough on my own.

One morning the sun came up behind a heavy mist, and Sarah came to fetch me and take me into the kitchen for breakfast. I had gone to sleep the night before determined to be a more concerned mother, although I still didn't feel like one.

"I was wondering how Lilly is doing and if I could see her anytime soon?"

"Oh, Robert felt like you needed some time to adjust to this whole situation since you haven't said anything much about her. She's actually doing so well that he will be bringing her home from the hospital today. We were hoping you would be happy about that."

"I won't lie to you, Sarah. I haven't been happy since that night on the bridge. I feel as though my life ended, and, since then, it has been one constant nightmare. Can you tell me how I'm supposed to feel about this baby? Ma and Pa have been so silent through all this. I have no idea if what I'm feeling is normal or if I'm just a horrible person. I've tried to feel love for her, but in truth, I don't feel anything except fear. I've pretty much lived in fear since Dr. McKinney told me I was pregnant."

"I'm so sorry, Rea. We have had such a hard time keeping you alive so that you could deliver Lilly, we completely ignored how you were handling the stress. I've wanted a baby for so long, I just got carried away with the fact that there was going to be one. I am sorry that I have not been considerate of your feelings. When Robert gets here, we will just put Lilly in another room until you're ready to meet her."

"I am as ready as I'll ever be to meet her. I'm just not sure I'm ready to be her ma."

"Would you mind if I helped you take care of her until you are ready to be her mother?"

"You wouldn't mind? Won't that be a lot of trouble?"

"Rea, it would make me so happy to have a baby in this house, even if it's just for a little while."

"All right, I owe you so much already. I don't know how I will ever repay you."

"Don't worry about that. I will be right back, and we'll get you out on the porch for some fresh air."

As I sat on the porch, I thought about Sarah and her brother. They seemed so different to be such close kin. Thinking of the brother and sister reminded me that Collin was due to arrive on Friday. I tried but could not remember what day of the week it was. Fear of Collin arriving while I sat out in the open prompted me to slowly make my way back to the bedroom. Lying down was the only thing I seemed to do well, so I eased onto the bed and stretched out to stare at the ceiling. Midday approached and through my open window, I heard a car come to a stop. I could not see the front gate from my room and had no way of knowing who was in the car. It could have been the doctor or Collin. It was not very long before someone came to my door and tapped lightly.

"Rea, are you awake? May I come in?"

"Sure, come on in, Sarah."

She stepped in the door and smiled. "Robert just got here. Do you want me to bring in Lilly?"

"Might as well, I want to get this over with."

Sarah left the room, which gave me a few minutes to mentally prepare myself to be strong and calm. Without a doubt, this was going to be the hardest thing I had ever done. I did not have long to wait on the task before me. Sarah slowly opened the door. Very quietly and softly, she walked into the room holding a small bundle of pink. She stopped by the bed and bent down to place the baby in my stiff arms.

"What if I break her or something?"

"She's tiny but not that fragile. Make sure you support her head and try not to squeeze her too tightly. Wait till you hear her cry. She has a very high voice."

I stared at Sarah until she finished speaking, then I forced myself to look at the little face surrounded by folds of pink material. To my complete astonishment, two eyes bored straight into my gaze.

"Can she see me clearly?"

"Not yet, but I imagine she recognizes the tone of your voice. Remember, she's been right there with you since June."

The baby never took her eyes off my face. It was as though she expected me to answer some unspoken question. For several minutes, we stared at each other. Apparently, my daughter was going to be as stubborn as her mother. Finally, I broke my stare with a sigh. Instantly, her face lit up. I knew it wasn't possible, but I thought she smiled. In less than a heartbeat, she filled the room with a high-pitched squeal. I jumped and Sarah laughed out loud.

"Unnerving, isn't it? I've never heard a newborn with such a loud cry."

"I hope it doesn't get any louder as she grows."

"She's probably hungry. Robert has put her on formula. I'll go and get her bottle ready."

Sarah abandoned me still holding Lilly and feeling awkward. Once the door closed, Lilly began to squirm and twist about inside the blanket as though she was unhappy about being wrapped up so tightly. I tried frantically to keep her covered. The more I fought her, the harder she worked to free herself. By the time Sarah returned with the bottle, Lilly had managed to dislodge herself from the blanket, and I was panting from wrestling with a baby so tiny she would fit easily into Ma's bread bowl.

"She doesn't like being confined. It's been a fight to keep a blanket on her. Unfortunately, she won't leave it on more than a few minutes."

Sarah offered me the bottle. But I shook my head in frustration and handed her the wiggling little creature that had already bested me in our first confrontation. This had done nothing to ease my fears of being totally incapable of handling motherhood. I watched as Sarah carefully and tenderly wrapped Lilly up and offered her the bottle that was enthusiastically accepted. Having never been around a newborn, I was fascinated by the sheer speed at which the bottle was emptied. Sarah showed me how to burp her. Minutes later, she showed me how to change a rather nasty diaper. The smell sent me gasping to the window for air. I turned to see the doctor standing in the door with a sympathetic smile on his face.

"Sarah should have warned you. That formula doesn't smell great before it goes in, but when it comes out, well, it's not very pleasant." The McKinneys fussed over Lilly for several minutes until Sarah declared it was time to put her down for a nap. To my relief, they left me in peace taking the baby with them. At the time, it seemed easier to let someone else take responsibility for her. I would later come to regret my cowardly behavior concerning my daughter. The fact that Collin was soon going to be in the house had left my mind in turmoil, and I could not concentrate on the baby.

Once I was alone in the quiet room, I tried to convince myself that Collin was not the attacker that night on the bridge. Why would he come back to see a person he had treated so viciously? Surely, I was mistaken. I had been too quick to assume he was guilty because of the damage to his nose. I even thought about Lilly and tried to see Collin in the tiny child. Sarah was such a kind person. How could her brother be so different? By the time I could see the sun begin to set through my window, I was no longer so sure that Collin was Lilly's father. It is strange how you can reason away fear if you try hard enough, and I tried very hard. Still when Sarah knocked on my door, my heart beat wildly against my chest wall.

"Yes?"

"Rea, dinner is almost ready. Do you feel like coming into the dining room to eat?"

"I'll be there in just a minute."

"Take your time, we'll wait."

It was not normal for Sarah to serve a meal in the dining room. I ate on a tray in my room. She and Dr. McKinney ate at the kitchen table. I couldn't go to the formal table in the ratty gown I was wearing. I also couldn't remember what I had on the day I came down with the fever, but I was sure that it wasn't appropriate for a meal at the McKinney dinner table. I opened the closet door expecting to find nothing. To my surprise, a very lovely cotton dress that I had never seen before hung in the closet. After inspecting it closely, I could tell that Sarah had taken one of her dresses and altered it to fit me. She must have kept the measurements she took earlier to make my clinic uniform. It only took me a few minutes to put the dress on, but I looked in the mirror for a very long time. The dress was the most beautiful color of blue. I had never had anything like it in my life. Looking at my reflection, it stunned me to realize that I looked older than I remembered. Then another knock interrupted my staring at myself.

"Rea, are you ready? I would like to serve dinner."

"Coming."

I stepped out of the room to find Sarah waiting on me. "You found the dress. Do you like it?"

"It's beautiful, but you shouldn't have done this."

"I enjoyed fixing it up for you. By the way, Collin is here. Now come on so dinner won't get cold."

In the time I spent worrying, Collin had arrived without my noticing it. I had the uneasy feeling that this dress might be

Sarah's attempt at making me more presentable for her brother. I followed her dutifully to the table and forced myself to take the seat she pointed out next to Collin. At that moment, my life took on the weird feeling of a horror story. Collin smiled in my direction, which forced me to return a polite nod in his.

Sitting only a few inches away from him made the hairs on my arm stand straight up and my skin ripple with nerves. The conversation started out slowly but gained momentum when the subject turned to Lilly. Dr. McKinney began to fill me in on all that had taken place since the day Lilly was born. Apparently, she spent most of her time in the incubator, but she still managed to charm all of the nurses and doctors. Everyone agreed that for one born so small, she seemed to be very aware of her surroundings. Sarah and Robert both swore that she had smiled at them, and I almost added my observations to theirs but was stopped by an interruption from Collin.

"When I was holding her, she looked right at my eyes. It was like she knew me and was waiting on me to recognize her. It gave me the weirdest feeling."

Sarah just laughed, but I almost choked on the bite of food I had been chewing. It took all my concentration to gain control and try to act normal. Collin had been holding Lilly and that made me very uncomfortable. The rest of our dinner conversation centered on the small baby in the other room, which only added to my confusion and misery. You would think Lilly had bewitched everyone at the table except me. My head began to spin trying to keep up with them as they talked and laughed. Suddenly, I could no longer bear being that close to Collin and feeling like an outsider because everyone knew more about my daughter than me. I excused myself, citing weariness. Once I made it back to my bedroom, I quickly removed the dress, grabbed my gown, and climbed into bed. It took some time to calm down, but I finally felt sleep coming and, for that, I was very thankful.

A violent headache woke me early the next morning. Dreams unfamiliar to me had haunted my sleep. The sadness I had been battling for so long returned and weighed heavy on my heart, pinning me to the bed. I had no desire to wake and face whatever unpleasantness the day would surely hold. The only escape I could concoct was to spend all day in the bedroom because of the pain in my head. I saw no other alternative that would keep me away from Collin.

Throughout the morning, I kept fighting myself concerning my suspicions of Collin. His behavior at the table during dinner was a compelling argument that he was innocent of my accusations. He had spent a great deal of time around Lilly yesterday and seemed quite taken with her. My experience with Pa did not prepare me for a man to be enamored by such a small child, especially a stranger's. Sarah had told me often how kindhearted and pleasant her brother had been before the accident. Her recent description matched the man I sat next to last night. The more I thought about it, the more my head ached.

I heard the sounds of people stirring in the house for several hours before anyone ventured to come to the bedroom door. It was rather a shock when the knock on my door was followed by the low, soft voice of Sarah's brother.

"Rea, I don't mean to bother you, but would you like to come and sit on the porch for a while? Sarah has made some fresh tea, and we are going to enjoy the warm weather."

"Thank you, but my head is aching, and I think I'll just stay in here away from the bright sun."

"Oh, please come out and get some fresh air. It will surely help your headache."

Some uneasy feeling kept nipping at me as I struggled to come up with a way to avoid leaving the bedroom. I could have been more forceful, but I did not want to be rude because of Sarah. "All right, I will be there in just a few minutes."

I took as long as possible to put on the same dress I wore the night before at dinner. It did not bother me to wear the same thing again. However, I would have preferred to wear my overalls or anything that didn't make me look like a girl.

Sarah and Collin were sitting on the porch swing when I arrived. I chose a chair as far from Collin as was possible without appearing to snub him. Once I had my tea, I turned my attention to the lovely springtime foliage in the McKinney yard. That gave Sarah the chance to excuse herself and return to help in the clinic. It seemed she had very skillfully manipulated me into an uncomfortable position. Tempted as I was to be angry at Sarah, I couldn't make myself feel any ill will toward her. Her brother wasted no time drawing me into a conversation.

"My sister is a very kind soul, is she not?"

"I have never met anyone kinder in all my life."

"Well, you aren't very old; but I doubt you ever will. She always thinks the best of people, no matter what they are actually like."

"I know that is true. She seems to think the best of me, and I can't imagine why."

"She says you are very smart, and she feels sorry for you because of your misfortunes, which is something I would like to talk to you about."

"I have no interest in discussing my misfortunes!" I turned and faced Collin with a rather hard look in his direction. If what I believed was true about him, he had a lot of nerve, and I was tired of being nice.

"Sorry, I don't want to upset you, but I saw some things that afternoon that might help you figure out who did this."

"I didn't see a face. It would only be speculation no matter what you saw."

"Please let me tell you anyway. It would make me feel better."

"It will make you feel better. Actually that makes no sense to me. Why would you need to feel better about something that happened to me?" Collin didn't even flinch.

"Actually, I feel very bad about what happened that night. Did you know that I was sitting on the porch when you left?"

"Really? I had no idea."

"You were in such a hurry when you left the clinic, you never even looked toward the porch. I had intended to try and talk to you about the little incident between us that morning. You do remember breaking my nose?"

"Sorry about that. I have a terrible temper and a real problem with people using force and pain to make me do what they want me to do."

"I apologize as well for being so overbearing. I just wanted to know if you had a boyfriend. Why wouldn't you just answer the question?"

"Well, I didn't think it was any of your business, and I still don't."

"You seem awfully defensive about such a simple, straightforward question."

"It wasn't the question as much as the tone and manner in which it was asked."

"Guilty as charged, but would you mind answering it now? I have a very good reason for asking it again."

"Okay, the guy you saw me with worked on our farm. His name is Jinx, and we've been friends for a very long time."

"So he wasn't your boyfriend?"

"No, if that had been true, I wouldn't have been here working at all. My pa was looking for a husband for me before all of this happened. That way he would have free labor for the farm. That is why I was here, so all the single men could have a chance to check out what he had to offer, so to speak. The baby kind of put a stop to all that. What man would want me after what happened on that bridge?"

Collin sat in silence for a few minutes, digesting all the pitiful aspects of my life's description. The expression on his face did not change, but his eyes seemed to cloud over ever so slightly.

"I wish you had told me this when I first asked you. After Robert finished setting my nose that day, I was pretty mad. I left and walked off most of the anger but not enough to come back and put myself close to you. Robert has fishing poles in the shed, and I took one. Then I went to the store to get some bait and walked down to the bridge to fish. I spent the day there, thinking over what had happened. I knew that I had spoken in a belittling way to you, and I probably deserved what I got. It's just that girls usually like me. I am so sorry for being unkind. I want to help you figure out who did this if I can."

"Like I said, it doesn't matter anymore."

"Will you please listen to what I have to say?"

Bridge Over Calm Water

I will never understand why I didn't just say no and leave the porch. Instead, I nodded at Collin, leaned back into the chair, and closed my eyes.

"I saw something while I was at the lake that afternoon. After I had been there for a while, your friend, Jinx, came down to the bridge with a younger boy. They fished on the other side. Jinx was drinking something while they were there; I kind of thought it was alcohol. When he left, he sort of stumbled up the bank. Anyway, I stayed on my side of the river longer. It was almost dark before I decided to return to the house. I knew you would be leaving soon, and I had decided to catch you before you left so I could apologize. Just before I stood up to walk back toward the house, I saw Jinx come back down the road on the far side of the bridge. I looked back before I rounded the curve at the top of the hill. Jinx had crossed the bridge and was just sitting down on the bank on this side. I didn't think anything about it at the time. When Sarah told me later about the attack and how Jinx was the one to find you, I knew he was there that night. They said you were so far off the road that all the searchers overlooked you the first time, but Jinx found you later. He was able to find you, Rea, because he knew where you were. I saw the way he had looked at you that morning. I'd bet anything he was the one who attacked you."

My brain froze, and my heart beat frantically against my ribs. How could this be true? Jinx had always been so kind and protective whenever I was around. I had never heard of Jinx drinking, but I suppose it could have been possible that he would drink after he left our farm. Still, how could my friend hurt me in such a horrible way?

"There's no way Jinx would hurt me like this."

"Sarah told me he left right after the attack. Said he joined the navy or something. It seems really strange to me that he would take off so quickly. She said that he gave you very little warning before he left. Looks to me like he skipped town before someone had a chance to figure out what he had done—someone like me maybe."

"Collin, I can't talk about this anymore. I just won't believe that he did this. It goes against everything I know about Jinx."

Collin stood as I rose to leave the porch. "Will I see you again before I leave tomorrow afternoon?"

"I don't know." It was a short dismissal toward someone leaving to fight in a war. But it was all I could manage at the moment. Maybe I would feel more like being polite later. Right then, I couldn't care less whether Collin thought me impolite or not. He had accused my best friend of being the reason for all my pain.

CHAPTER SEVEN

Doubts, Fears, and Trials

Ma and Pa suddenly appeared after Sunday's church service to take Lilly and me back to the farm. I knew by the look on Sarah's face their arrival was totally unexpected on her part. Dr. McKinney, however, seemed not the least bit surprised. I quickly began gathering up my few belongings and Lilly's. It suited me to be away from that house as soon as possible. Collin was still around somewhere, and I tried to avoid him. Thankfully, he never showed his face while my parents were there.

Dr. McKinney followed us to the wagon and helped Pa load our bags and get the baby settled. Just before I climbed aboard, he caught me on the arm. "Rea, I would not have minded you staying here longer, but Sarah was becoming too attached to Lilly. The longer you stayed, the more difficult it became for her. You have enough formula to last at least a week. Don't worry about getting more. Someone has offered to purchase the formula for Lilly to help you out. Your pa can pick it up for you until you feel like coming back to work at the clinic."

I began to protest against the idea that someone else would be buying Lilly's food. Dr. McKinney stopped me before I got the first word out. "Rea, you asked the people in this community for help by accepting Lilly. Once you told the church about her existence, word spread out across the entire area. This won't be the last generous favor to come your way. It's as important that you are willing to accept the help of these people as it is for them to give it. I know it can be humbling and humiliating at times to have to take help at all. Remember, it's Lilly's welfare that's important now and any help eases the burden on your parents."

"I understand. And can you thank whoever is being so kind for me, please?"

"I will relay your message as soon as possible. Now, if you have any trouble at all, you are to send your pa for me. Because Lilly is still quite small, she needs a little extra attention. I have given your ma a set of written instructions. She will be a great help to you. Try to remember she has raised three children of her own. Don't waste the chance to learn from her. One last thing—I need for you to bring Lilly back in two weeks for me to check her and you as well. We still haven't talked about the damage I had to repair on you after the birth."

"Yes, sir."

Robert McKinney was a very persuasive person. Looking back later, I could see so much wisdom in the words he spoke to me that day. Sarah did not really say good-bye as we left, and I never saw Collin again. The ride to the farm was quiet except for small odd little sounds that Lilly made during the slow journey. Having never been around a newborn, I had no idea if this was normal or not, but for some reason it seemed as though she was trying her best to communicate with us. I had heard the McKinneys talking about her constant movements and mewling. I supposed this was what they had been referring to. I watched Ma struggle to keep the blanket around her. I tried not to laugh, but finally she became so exasperated she let out a yelp and startled Lilly. For just one second, Lilly froze; her arms and legs stretched out as though she was trying to climb air. Then she returned Ma's yelp in the form of a screech and doubled her efforts to get out of the confines of the blanket.

"Dr. McKinney said to make sure and keep her warm, but this is ridiculous," Ma said. "We are going to have to dress her in warm clothes and let her squirm around all she wants to. Fighting with her will wear you out. Where does she get all this energy? What on earth is in that formula they've been feeding her?"

"Now, Faye, you're getting old and forgetful. Don't you remember how hard it was to keep Rea wrapped up when she was a baby?"

"It was hard, but not impossible. You're right about one thing. I'm too old to be foolin' with a newborn."

Ma turned around and handed Lilly to me where I sat cross-legged in the back of the wagon. I had already been down this road and didn't want to fight with her again. I laid her in the cradle formed by my legs and let her wave and kick herself to sleep. Once we reached the farm house, Pa found his favorite chair as Ma and I carried Lilly and our things up the stairs to my room. While I was gone, my parents had searched out my old cradle and placed it beside my bed. All of the gifts sent for Lilly were unpacked and arranged around the room. Ma had spent some time up there by the orderly look of things. Our old rocking chair had been brought up from the living room and was now sitting in the corner. Obviously Ma intended that Lilly remain in my room as much as possible. I'm sure Ma thought it would keep her out of sight and maybe out of mind for most of the day.

Once Ma was satisfied that we were situated, she left without even commenting on the day. Lilly lay very still in the cradle. It was an unnatural thing for me to see. I had never actually seen her at rest. She looked so peaceful and happy. As she slept, her lips formed a gentle smile. While she was still and quiet, I thought about the conversation with Collin and his suspicions of Jinx. How could a person I thought I knew so well be responsible for all of my heartache? I could not imagine Jinx doing such a horrible thing, and I couldn't bring myself to trust Collin. His words had put doubt in my mind though, and it grew the more I dwelled on his accusations. Lilly woke and interrupted my tormented thoughts. I decided to put all things concerning Lilly's father out of my mind and focus on the task of taking care of the very small child waving her arms and kicking her feet to her own rhythm.

So began my journey into a world totally alien to me. Lilly changed everything. Life no longer followed a set pattern at the farm. Her cries at all hours of the night kept all of us busy trying to calm her back into sleep. Ma said she had her nights and days confused and blamed Sarah for spoiling her. Once my lack of sleep made me clumsier and more apt to drop and break things, Ma was forced to relieve me of the responsibility of handling Lilly. To my surprise, she moved the cradle into their bedroom, and I could hear both her and Pa up during the night. I became aware of a side of my parents that I had never seen before. They were tender and loving with Lilly. Their voices took on a softer, gentler tone. They were quick to laugh and their faces seemed younger and less stressed. It was as though Lilly's constant motion infused them with energy. Watching them from a distance, I marveled at the change.

The farm, once so secluded and silent, became a virtual hub of community activity. The visits began the day after Lilly arrived. At all times of the day, people would appear, always bearing food or more gifts, each wanting to be introduced to Rock Island's newest resident. After the first week or so, various women rotated days and appeared at intervals to relieve us of the burden of caring for a newborn. Even old Mrs. Reel, well into her eighties, came often and spent several hours just rocking and singing softly to Lilly. Ma was tempted to complain that all the attention was only going to spoil the baby. But as Lilly grew, Ma could find no evidence to back up her accusations. In truth, Lilly seemed to bring out the best in everyone. Pa once remarked that he had overheard Beatrice Blankenship singing Lilly's praises to a group of ladies at the store one afternoon. To our knowledge, Beatrice Blankenship had never said a kind word about anyone.

Slowly but surely, I became only one of many caregivers in Lilly's life. At church, she was passed from family to family, another irritation to Ma, who believed that children should be quiet and pretty much unnoticed during worship. Lilly really didn't cause a disturbance, but you could always tell exactly where she was in the congregation. The people around her would always be smiling, and, in general, not really paying attention to the preacher. It was difficult not to watch the tiny baby kicking and squirming with such determination. Even resting quietly in someone's lap, Lilly exuded a joy that was contagious.

As spring drew to a close, I found myself settling into the web of activity surrounding Lilly but not really feeling like a mother. My pleas for help had been answered abundantly, and I had begun to feel left out. I was jealous of the affection lavished upon her by all of the people who had become part of her life.

My return to work in the clinic on Saturdays was of little consequence to the child's routine. Every day, someone came to aid in her care and take my place. It was almost surreal. Time and again, I found myself of little importance, just an afterthought. No one consulted me concerning any facet of Lilly's life. I suppose because I had no idea what needed to be done. I consoled myself with the thought that one day when I was wiser, God would bless me with another child and I would indeed be a mother to it.

However, the first week after returning to work at the clinic, Dr. McKinney called me into his office during an unusually slow afternoon and asked me sit down. It was then that I found out just how much I had given away when I had asked for help with Lilly.

"Rea, I should have talked to you two weeks ago, but to be honest, I have dreaded this conversation for some time. Do you remember me telling you that I had to do some repair work on you the night that Lilly was born?"

"Yes, sir."

"You do know that we had to deliver Lilly by cutting her out, but you don't know why. You began to hemorrhage, and we were forced to remove your uterus. I'm so sorry that we were left with no other choice, but I couldn't let you bleed to death."

"Oh." In less than a year, I had gone from young and pure straight to old and wasted. I would never have other children, ever. Lilly was destined to be my only child, and because of my decision to allow others in to care for her, she really did not recognize me as her mother.

"I wish you had said something about this right after she was born."

"I do, too, Rea, but your parents felt like you had enough to deal with and requested that I wait."

"I'm sure they meant well, Dr. McKinney. Is there anything else I need to know?"

"No, but you have healed nicely. I don't expect you will have any other problems because of what you've been through."

"Is that all? I need to get back to work if you don't mind?"

"Yes, that's everything."

"Thank you for treating me through all of this. I can never repay you and Sarah for your kindness." I turned quickly and left before the good doctor could see the tears poised on the edge of my lashes.

The fact that I was barely managing to hold back the tears frustrated me. Only a short time before, I had wished to grow old alone. Having the hope to never marry, children were not an option. Now that the ability to have children was no longer available to me, the sorrow that stifled my breath made me both sad and angry.

Spending the rest of the day at the clinic, pretending life was continuing in an unbroken manner, took a great deal of effort. By the end of the day, I felt as though I had no heart left and the walk home took more time than usual. Ma and Lilly were in the kitchen. Lilly was in a large wicker basket padded by quilts. Ma was in the process of heating formula on the stove.

"Rea, come and take my place so I can finish our dinner."

I could see Lilly's feet kicking above the edge of the basket. She was performing her air dance, babbling and bubbling contentedly, oblivious to us. Once Ma had second-tested the formula and deemed it the right temperature, I sat down by the basket to feed Lilly. Her arms and legs never slowed down. She latched onto the bottle and drank as though she had not been fed in days. While she worked to empty the bottle in my hand, I took the opportunity to gaze at the little face before me. I had not noticed until now, but Lilly's little bald head had a soft layer of fuzz covering it, making it look like the skin of a peach. It was hard to tell the color because it didn't appear to have any. Ma broke my concentration when she walked up to the basket and spoke my name.

"Rea, Jim told your pa that the family got a telegram yesterday from the navy. Jinx is missing in action. They presume he has been taken prisoner by the Japanese. They thought you would want to know."

"Are they sure he is not dead?"

"I don't know, but it sounds like they think maybe he is still alive."

Ma never looked back at me to see how her news had affected me. I maintained my composure, but it was difficult. Dinner was quieter than usual, even with Lilly's constant babbling. What could be said about the sorrow we all felt for Jinx?

After that day I began to see Lilly as that pinpoint of light so deep in that cold, dark void. She had been there all along, through all the heartache and misery. She was the light that came out of darkness; she brought that light into our lives. I grew to love everything about her. Her beauty took on a radiance that even my parents could see. They relished in her glow just as I did. During those early months, Lilly never really left the farm except on Sunday mornings. The world came to her and that seemed to suit her. Looking back now, I understand she drew out the best in all of us. It was a rare gift for such a small child.

One Saturday morning early I woke up with a terrible headache and fever. Ma took one look at me and sent Pa for Dr. McKinney. It didn't take him long to decide that I had contracted the measles from one of his patients. Ma hung a heavy quilt over the window to block out the light to my room. The pain in my head increased steadily and clouded my thoughts. It never occurred to me to worry about Lilly. Although I spent several days cloistered in the upstairs bedroom, I assumed that life was continuing normally in the house below me. During my confinement, Ma was my only visitor. After about a week, the spots covering almost every inch of my body began to fade. Dr. McKinney returned and deemed me no longer contagious. I had grown restless over the final two days and missed Lilly terribly. I dressed and made my way down the stairs listening for the familiar sounds of my daughter. The house was too quiet as I walked from room to room. I finally found Ma on the front porch.

"Where's Lilly, Ma?"

"We decided it was better that she stay at the doctor's until he was sure she hadn't caught the measles."

"She's been at the McKinney's all of the time I've been sick?"

"Yes, it was very kind of Sarah to take care of her for us. Your pa is going to hitch the wagon up and take you to get her in the morning. Have to say I'll be glad to have her back around here. Sure has been solemn since she's been gone."

I stood there frozen in my place. Even with the accusations that Collin made against Jinx, it had become more apparent every day that Collin was Lilly's father. As her hair thickened up and began to curl, it had the same texture and colorless sheen as Collin's. Her face had begun to fill out and her eyes were the same odd amber color as Sarah's brother. If the resemblance was so evident to me, I feared Sarah would see her brother in Lilly's face. I had gone to great lengths to keep Lilly on the farm and away from Sarah over the last several weeks.

"Something wrong, Rea? You look like your fever may be coming back."

"No, Ma. I'm fine. Do you need for me to do anything about dinner?"

"You just rest, Rea. You're going to need all your strength to keep up with Lilly when she comes back."

I spent the rest of the night dreading the trip to the McKinney's the next morning. Ma and Pa talked quietly about the return of their granddaughter during the entire evening. It was apparent that they were very attached to Lilly. Pa turned to me in a lull of their conversation and captured my attention with the mention of one name.

"I meant to tell you, Rea. I know that you have met Sarah's brother, Collin. I thought you might like to know that Sarah's family received word last week that he had been killed in combat in Europe."

"Killed? Are you sure?"

"Yes, Dr. McKinney told me when he came to pick up Lilly. He said that having Lilly around would be a godsend for Sarah.

She and her brother were very close, and this has been very hard on her."

"That's too bad for her." I tried to sound sympathetic. But to be honest, I didn't succeed. I expected my parents to comment, but they just sat and quietly stared in my direction. I knew that I had to give them some explanation for my callous attitude.

"I guess that didn't sound very sincere. I am sorry for Sarah, but I really didn't like Collin very much. When I first met him he wasn't a nice person, at least not to me anyway. He seemed to take great pleasure in belittling me. I tried to avoid him, but I still ran into him a couple of times while he was here. I never told Sarah about his mean behavior, and I don't want her to know, especially now."

"We thought you just knew who he was, not that you actually had ever talked to him."

"We did not talk much, but enough that I knew I didn't like the person that he was." I left the living room before they could continue their questioning. I vowed to never mention Collin's name after that night. It was the least I could do for Sarah, and it would benefit no one if what I believed Collin did actually became common knowledge.

For me, the truth about Lilly's father died on the battlefield with Collin. If I knew anything about Sarah McKinney, I knew she would never shame her brother now that he was gone. If she suspected he was Lilly's father, she would keep it to herself. In an odd sort of way, this news lifted the burden of fear I had been carrying. With Collin no longer around to defend his actions, there was no reason for the identity of Lilly's father to ever become public knowledge. She belonged to me now and only me. I did not have to fear his return and involvement on any level. I knew it was probably wrong of me, but I only felt relief at the news Pa had given me.

The next morning, we left very early to bring Lilly back to the farm. Dr. McKinney requested we pick her up before he left for work. Pa said very little on the way to Rock Island. He worried a great deal about my brothers who were fighting somewhere in that horrible war. Since Jinx's apparent capture and the report of Collin's death, Pa had become even more silent and reserved. I tried in vain to start a conversation to fill the minutes as the wagon slowly made its way down the road. He ignored all of my efforts.

As we rounded the last bend and came in view of the clinic, I could see the McKinneys standing in their front yard. Dr. McKinney held Lilly in his arms; Sarah faced away from me. However, I could tell even from a distance that they were having a disagreement. Sarah had never even raised her voice toward her husband in my presence. From where I sat, it was clear that she was practically screaming at him. Once she heard our wagon approach, she looked in our direction then instantly turned and went into the house. Dr. McKinney made his way down to the gate carrying Lilly in his arms. Once we came to a stop, Pa climbed down to load the basket holding Lilly's things into the back of the wagon. Dr. McKinney walked to my side and handed Lilly up to me.

"Thank you, but I wanted to thank Sarah for taking care of her."

"I'll tell her for you. This is difficult for her; she isn't having the best of mornings, and I know you're anxious to get Lilly back home."

Pa prevented me from asking anymore questions by thanking the doctor and turning the wagon immediately around and heading for home. I had a funny feeling all the way home that the fight I had witnessed had something to do with Lilly. I had plenty of time to think it over because Pa relieved me of Lilly almost instantly. Handing me the reins, he talked to her nonstop all the way back to the farm. The difference in my father when Lilly was anywhere close still amazed me.

Ma came running down the steps to greet us and took Lilly straight into the house. For the rest of the day, she and Pa seemed to spend every free minute playing with and caring for Lilly. It was as if they were afraid she was going to disappear at any moment.

Once again, life revolved around Lilly. The neighbors began reappearing to help, and Lilly continued to grow and blossom under the abundant attention lavished upon her. She grew more beautiful by the day. As I looked at her, I tried to find just one thing about her that reminded me of myself. I found no similarities, and it gave me comfort to know she would not be like me. Whatever she inherited from me must have been something long buried from generations back.

I became more comfortable with the idea of motherhood. As fall faded into winter, Lilly began to put on weight and she looked more like a cherub than a child. Her hair continued to thicken up and the curls were abundant, the color of silver blond, just like her father's. Collin's accusations toward Jinx came flooding back in my mind. He had caused me to doubt my friend. I would not ever be able to forgive myself for that.

December slowly inched its way toward Christmas. Once again, the holiday was more sober than merry for us and our neighbors. Too many people had family members fighting in the war. The rationing made it difficult to keep basic needs met, much less the ingredients that would make for a traditional Christmas. Everyone lived in fear of what might await them. Even with the lack of spirit, all agreed the Christmas pageant was an unavoidable necessity. The characters were chosen, and to my surprise, the unanimous decision was that Lilly, being the smallest child in the area, would portray the Christ child. This was truly out of character; a male child had always been selected to play the all-important part. When I voiced my objections, people just laughed and reminded me that no one would be able to tell Lilly was a girl lying in the manger. Reminding everyone that she was always in motion when awake and would be a distraction during the play had no effect on the final decision either.

Ma took this pageant in stride and gladly made the swaddling clothes for Lilly to wear, knowing all the time that swaddling Lilly was a futile endeavor. The night of the pageant arrived cold and damp. This was one of the few times that nearly all of the residents of Rock Island were in one place. The members of all the area congregations put their differences aside and gathered to enjoy the one thing they all had in common, the belief in the birth of their risen Savior.

Jan Kendall

The McKinneys stood just inside the front entrance as we brought Lilly into the building. Sarah shyly asked if she could hold her for just a minute before we took her back to the stage. I had no choice but to comply with her wishes, and in that same moment, it was so obvious to me that Lilly was the spitting image of her father. I had no doubt that giving her to Sarah was a mistake. Sarah had not seen her in several months. Her face began to turn pale, and the smile faded from her lips almost instantly when she took Lilly into her arms and gazed intently at her face. My parents and Dr. McKinney were distracted in conversation and did not notice the change in Sarah. Her body began to tremble, and tears hung on her lower lashes. I was just about to offer to take Lilly back when she suddenly handed her to me and ran out the front door of the church. Dr. McKinney apologized and hurried after her. I knew without a doubt that she could no longer deny Collin staring back at her from the child she had so often held in her arms. Ma and Pa seemed absolutely mystified but said nothing about her sudden departure.

The pageant started on schedule. Except for the little arms and legs waving above the edge of the manger, everything went off as planned. We did not see the McKinneys once the pageant was completed. Apparently, they did not come back in to watch the play.

Christmas came almost without notice, except for the piles of gifts that had accumulated under the cedar tree for Lilly. Every day, one or two gifts would appear on the porch. The generous nature of our friends and neighbors seemed boundless.

After the holidays, the winter settled in and our family kept close to home. Ma became obsessed with keeping Lilly warm. She would not allow me to take her out in the weather even for church on Sundays. Ma had never missed church that I could remember. She insisted on staying at home with Lilly and sent Pa and me to church. I suppose Ma figured I needed to be there more than she did. Pa didn't object to Ma's extreme measures. That was even more confusing, considering how he always had the last word in any decision. It was very odd behavior indeed.

Ma's drastic measures worked, and Lilly remained healthy throughout the worst of the winter. As her birthday approached, she began to crawl with authority and at a speed we all found bewildering. Pa said she reminded him of a windup toy. Her personality took on more dimensions, and her laugh sounded like crystal bells. Pa developed many ways to initiate the sound of those bells, and Ma never missed the chance to stop and listen.

Then on a cloudy February day, Lilly looked at my pa, pointed at me, and clearly said, "Rea." I was overwhelmed with surprise and heartbreak. Everyone else in the room was so focused on the fact that Lilly had uttered her first word they failed to grasp the significance of the word as it applied to me. I watched them fuss over Lilly, and she soaked up the praise like a sponge. I slowly left the room and Lilly in the capable hands of my parents.

The Sunday before Lilly's birthday, Ma decided the weather had improved sufficiently to allow Lilly to travel in the wagon to the church service. The sunshine drifted down through the bare branches and warmed my neck as I sat in the back of the wagon. We slowly made our way down the lane leading up to the church. More people seemed to be milling around the outside of the building than normal. That was probably due to the older folks coming back after being cloistered during the winter. Everyone seemed to be in an unusually good mood before service began, and, as had become the routine, Lilly was passed from one family to another up until the song leader took his place behind the podium.

On that day, the privilege of holding Lilly during the service fell to Mrs. Johnson. Georgia Johnson was big, soft, and perpetually happy. Even for her sixty some odd years, she seemed much younger. Lilly loved to bury her head in Georgia's massive bosom and sleep through the service. I could see my daughter from my position across the room. To my surprise, and Georgia's, Lilly remained awake and very alert. As the preacher droned on and on about redemption and repentance, I could tell Lilly was beginning to get restless, which was never a good thing. She could be quite distracting to the congregation when she began to seek forms of entertaining herself.

I always knew when our preacher was about ready to finish his prepared sermon. I thought I had acquired this ability from years of being subjected to the same sermon repeated over and over by a virtual army of men. These men seemed to know very little about the Bible, but they used their limited knowledge to manipulate their congregations with fear of eternal damnation. We were a pitiful lot as believers, beaten down and bedraggled by men who should have pointed us down the road of grace and salvation. It was not a life I wished for my daughter, but one of the many things that would be her birthright. Lilly surprised us all on that day. As the minister began to wind up, and give us all a chance to avoid the fire of hell, he used one of his most often repeated phrases.

"So brethren, take this opportunity before it is too late and you are condemned to burn for eternity. Come before God now in repentance to receive the forgiveness He is so willing to supply."

Before he could catch a breath and ask for the singing of the invitation hymn, Lilly clapped her hands once, something unheard of in our church. That got everyone's attention, even Brother Tim's. She followed the hand clap with a cheerful "Amen." The congregation vibrated, but no one actually laughed out loud. Everyone managed to recover their composure, but the laughing soon broke out once everyone had left the building. To add to the merriment, the ladies had planned a surprise birthday party for Lilly and had invited every family in Rock Island to join us.

The crowd was so immense that I saw Lilly very little. Each family took their turn playing with her. It was the one time that she slowly used up her abundant source of energy and sat quietly in one lap after another as the day wore on. I did not see Sarah McKinney, but Dr. McKinney made his rounds through the assortment of people present. He had treated almost everyone at one time or another since coming to our small, fairly isolated community. Eventually, he walked toward us where we sat beneath a large sugar maple. The weather was still quite cool, and Ma had become concerned for Lilly. Just as the doctor walked up, she left to fetch her granddaughter and add more layers of clothing. I knew she also intended to find Pa and encourage him to start toward home. This left me alone as Dr. McKinney took a seat beside me.

"How has Lilly been doing, Rea? We don't have the opportunity to see her often."

"Well, I'm no expert, but she seems awfully smart to me."

"I'm glad your mother left you alone. I need to talk to you about a rather sensitive subject. I have always had my suspicions about the identity of Lilly's father. You never want to think that anyone you know might be capable of the cruelty that was inflicted upon you, especially someone in your own family. However, it's hard to ignore the proof when it is staring you in the face. Forgive me, but I am sorry it is so obvious. I would have spared my wife the heartache that realizing the truth has caused her. Even she can't ignore the fact that Lilly is the spitting image of Collin. She has not been out of our house since the night of the Christmas play. I thought she might come today, but she just couldn't. I guess what I am wondering is did you know all along it was him on the bridge that night?"

"I was honest when I told you I never saw who attacked me. I guess deep down in my heart, I suspected him because of what I did to his nose."

"Now that the truth is so obvious, what are you going to do about it?"

"Exactly what do you think I can do about it? Accuse a war hero of rape and brand Sarah's family with this? No, Dr. McKinney, telling everyone the truth now would only cause more heartache. Sarah has always been so kind to me I could not do that to her."

"Collin's family is quite wealthy, Rea. They could help support Lilly. Have you considered that?"

"It's kind of you to tell me this, but I would really prefer that Lilly never find out how she came to be. The more people who know Collin is her father, the greater the risk of her being told the circumstances surrounding her conception."

"Sarah and I have talked about this a great deal. We thought we might tell Collin's parents that he was in love with you and that he intended to marry you after the war."

"That still makes Lilly a bastard and me a tramp."

"They are all so devastated by Collin's death that they would be thrilled to have Lilly as a family member under any circumstance."

I could see Ma making her way in our direction carrying Lilly. "Dr. McKinney, you will never know how much I appreciate your offer to do this, but I still think we should just let sleeping dogs lie."

Ma walked up, which prevented the doctor from saying anything further. In that moment, it seemed a blessing that the whole subject had to be dropped. I had no doubt the McKinneys did not want the truth spread throughout the area. It was especially important to all of us that my parents not know who fathered Lilly. I had overheard whispers and knew that everyone believed the man on the bridge that night had been someone just passing through the area. No one wanted to even consider it could have been someone they knew. Very few people had actually seen Collin on his visits, and he made no effort to get acquainted with anyone he met. Most of the residents believed Collin considered himself too high class for the simple folk here. Everyone chose to ignore his rudeness out of respect for the McKinneys.

At least I knew that Sarah could no longer ignore the truth in front of her eyes. However, I had not counted on the offer made by Dr. McKinney. It was unnerving. At first, I felt that my initial reaction was in Lilly's best interest. The more I thought about it, I began to waver. Was my pride depriving her of resources and chances that I could never offer my daughter? Having grown more attached to her over the long and isolated winter, I suppose that my reaction to Dr. McKinney could have been self-centered. Beyond what I wanted, Lilly's presence in our family had totally changed my parents. They were simply very different people since her birth. The ride back to the farm that evening was long enough to give me reason to doubt my refusal of his offer and the motives behind my decision.

CHAPTER EIGHT

Lilly's True Mother

As the summer of 1943 drew in the heat, my real lessons in what constitutes human existence began to pile up like the prodigious number of leaves that rotted under our sugar maples every fall. As children, my brothers and I were taught by our parents that our actions alone brought about the rewards or punishments of our lives. I learned that was not true. They never took into account how their decisions influenced the people we would become. Beyond that it was obvious our lives had been encroached upon by the decisions of possibly thousands of people, many long dead. Into this knowledge I stepped that dreadfully torrid summer.

I thought that the birth of Lilly elevated me to the role of an adult. I was wrong about that. Adulthood came when I realized what was found in that cold deep abyss. That darkness, as thick as molasses, contained the careless decisions of countless generations and the souls of the people who suffered as a result. Lilly was my chance to deliberately back away from the void. With her as my beacon, I could see consequences to every course of action I might adopt. I understood that all the things we do in this life, whether great or small, could lead to misery and be swept into the pit by those who will follow us to the grave.

I was tortured that summer by the knowledge that we never have enough information at our disposal to assure any decision is the right one. I reconciled myself to the fact that I was being pushed along in the great tide of humanity. One more helpless soul at the mercy of the waves created by others; all of us headed toward the whirlpool that ends in the abyss. Standing there in that hard place of understanding, the only warmth and peace I was offered came from God's grace.

And so that summer, the girl I had been, one of little confidence and uncertain steps, became an apparition not recognizable to me or anyone else. Life as I had always known it lost meaning and purpose, and something foreign grew to replace it. I withered away almost without notice. The being of Rea was sucked out of me decision by decision. I once heard that there is no real truth. Considering our species and the sorry pathway we have carved in our history, it is not a hard concept to consider noteworthy. As summer stretched out before me it became obvious there is always truth. It is our stubborn refusal to acknowledge that it will never be found in us that sets us on a course of destruction. We elevate ourselves to a position we are not worthy to assume as we profess that truth is somehow contained in human actions or thoughts.

That is where my steps took me as June wore away toward July. I turned to walk away from the abyss only to find that its pull on me increased with each step I took. I began to fall backward, scratching and grabbing to regain my balance and preserve my life. It is not difficult to understand how I ended up writhing and convulsing at the feet of a Savior. The hard part for me has been to grasp how and why He saved me at all. The reality is that truth does exist, but only outside of the world we know, beyond the everyday complaints and frustrations of our pitiful mixed-up existence. If we expect to find it in our fellow man, we will always be disappointed. It is beyond human comprehension; it can lie only in the realm of the Divine.

The transformation of my soul began slowly as the work on the farm picked up speed. There is never enough time or energy during the summer to keep the burden of chores at bay. Even with Jim working from sunrise to sunset, we barely staved off complete chaos. The help of neighbors with Lilly began to dribble and finally stopped as they too had no time to spare.

The only two people not completely enslaved by work were the McKinneys. I had heard the doctor discuss on more than one occasion the dramatic drop of visitors to his clinic during the summer. He often remarked that the people in and around Rock Island did not have time to be sick during the warmer months. Because our farm was no different, we found ourselves struggling to keep up with Lilly, often allowing her to run amuck.

One sticky airless morning, Sarah McKinney appeared at our door. Ma and I had already engaged in one disagreement that morning over my lack of control and discipline where Lilly was concerned. Ma would never admit to herself that she made little effort to rein in Lilly's youthful exuberance. I was not in the house when Sarah arrived and probably would not have known she was there if not for Jim. As he passed the garden where I was crouched pulling weeds, he asked me why the doctor's wife was at the farm. Stunned that she had come at all, I sat frozen in place. Jim did not wait for an answer but proceeded on toward the barn. Sarah could only be there for one reason—Lilly. I found Ma and Sarah in the kitchen, sitting at the table drinking coffee. Lilly was on the floor enthralled by some elaborate toy that was obviously a gift from Sarah.

"Hello, Rea. You already look hot and worn out."

I had hardly heard a word she said. I kept thinking of something I had read along the lines of, "Beware of Greeks bearing gifts."

"Rea, don't be rude to Sarah, answer her question."

"Sorry, my mind was on something else. Hello, Sarah. What brings you out so early in the morning?"

"Well, Robert was talking to your father the other day about how busy you were out here. I decided I could help since I have plenty of spare time."

"Really, have you suddenly decided to become a farmer?" The remark sounded snide, and I knew it. I felt myself slip back toward the darkness. Why would Sarah be here today after avoiding Lilly since Christmas? She had not once even asked me about Lilly at the clinic. She acted as though she didn't exist when I was around. Yet now, she sat before me in my ma's kitchen looking very calm and sophisticated. Ma eyed me suspiciously as I stood hovering over Lilly.

"Rea, she has come and offered to take care of Lilly this summer while we work. Isn't it such a sweet thing for her to do?"

"I'm speechless." Not a lie under the circumstances. At least I managed to sound impressed.

"I know I haven't been as much help as the other women since Lilly was born, but I would like to try and make up for my lack of effort. Remember, you did ask for help."

Ahh . . . my plea for help, something I would never be able to take back or forget. It kept returning to me wrapped up in well-meaning advice and instructions. It was a hard lesson to learn that words should be uttered softly and sparingly. They are powerful and can turn on you with no warning. Now they had been thrown back in my face by the one person who could claim a right to Lilly beyond my family. She waited, relishing in the fact that she had me cornered with nowhere to go. I had no choice but to thank her and return to the garden. I left her and Ma to work out the particulars. It was a mistake to walk out of the room that day, but it was only one of many I would make and come to regret.

I woke the next morning to the voices of Ma and Sarah filtering up from the kitchen. To my surprise, Sarah was already busy taking over the care of Lilly. Watching her with my daughter, it was painfully obvious that she grasped the finer points of mothering that completely stumped me. Ma had told me that a child craved the security of a confident parent. As much as children might rail against rules and limitations, they did not feel secure without them. Sarah was kind with Lilly, but she was also firm in her handling of the child's effervescent spirit.

Within the week, Ma began to sing the praises of Sarah and the blessing of having her around. Any objection I made was pointed out as sour grapes or my lack of wisdom where children were concerned. I began spending as much time as possible away from the scenes playing out around my daughter. In general, I felt deficient anytime I saw Sarah replacing me with such ease and success. The one advantage to having Sarah around to help was that we began to catch up on the work. On rare afternoons, we had enough time to have Lilly to ourselves.

The cherub child rewarded us splendidly with laughter and joy. She had learned to walk on steady legs while I had been elsewhere. Once again, I was the only one unaware of her progress. Yet another mark against me as Lilly's mother. Unlike me, Lilly was comfortable in herself and confident in her decisions. Stubborn to a fault, she added spice to our dull lives. I would remember those summer afternoons for the rest of my life; although at the time, I truly took it all for granted.

The Fourth of July dawned bright and clear, offering us a break in the work always before us. As the war still raged on two fronts, the holiday held even more significance for our country and community. The area-wide picnic began early and ran into the late evening hours. Pa and Ma threw themselves into the fray of workers and volunteers responsible for the festivities. This left me to wander with Lilly at our leisure through the crowd that had gathered to celebrate. Lilly was the queen of the day. She even looked the part in her red, white, and blue play dress brought to her the day before by Sarah. All of the women who had been so much a part of her life took turns marveling at the changes in the child before them. It was on this day that I began to notice the hidden meaning behind the remarks made to my face and the whispers people were unaware I heard.

"Rea, I can't believe how this child has blossomed in the last few weeks!" Olivia Campbell cooed as she lifted Lilly up for a hug.

"It's such a blessing for Sarah to be able to take care of Lilly. You know she was just born to be a mother," Frannie Harding announced to everyone within earshot while Lilly romped around her feet.

The comments continued all afternoon, all of them true. What could I say to defend my feeble attempts at being Lilly's mother? I stood before the sheer cliff I saw as motherhood, shaking in fear and looking for the easiest way up. At every opportunity, I had grabbed for hands offered as help. I would like to think that I had Lilly's best interest at heart in my choices to let others care for her. But in truth, I knew the decisions were self-centered.

As the sun set below the tree line, I began preparing to return to the farm. The celebration would continue, but I was worn out from self-loathing, and Lilly was exhausted from all of the attention lavished upon her. As I sat waiting in the back of the wagon, the child, so totally different from me, lay sleeping in my lap. I did not see Sarah approach me from behind, and she startled me as she walked up.

"Sorry, Rea, I didn't mean to frighten you. I've not been able to catch you away from other people until now. I asked your parents if it was all right to talk to you alone, and they agreed to give me time. I am going to ask you to listen to all I have to say before you speak. Would that be all right with you?"

All the hours this woman had cared for me before and after Lilly's birth lay heavy on my mind as I struggled with the feeling now creeping around inside me. To refuse her request was not an option although every inch of me wanted to. "Okay," a simple word, filled with the power to bring your life into shambles as it did to me that day.

"Robert wanted to come with me, but I wouldn't let him. This is something that I need to say to you alone. For one thing, I want this to be just between you and me. There is no reason for anyone else to ever know we had this conversation. I know now that Collin was the one who attacked you that night on the bridge. I also must confess that if I could undo what was done to you, God forgive me, I wouldn't. Now that Lilly is here, well, she is such a true treasure. I can only believe that she is worth all the pain that you endured. What my brother did was wrong in every way, but I have to cling to the knowledge that only the combination of the two of you could produce such a precious soul. Maybe it's just that I want to believe so badly that she makes all the wrong somehow justifiable. I am asking that you try to understand how much she means to me because of losing Collin, and please forgive me for feeling this way. I wish I could ask for my brother's forgiveness, but that is something even I cannot bring myself to do."

Sarah paused, raising her hand slightly to prevent me from speaking. I doubt I could have managed to say anything. At that moment, I literally felt myself filtering out and mingling in with the mist rising from the ground below. I felt no anger toward her. Her kind of honesty was rare. Had I said anything at all, I believe she would have been surprised to know I actually agreed with her. Lilly had shown me a side of my parents I never knew existed and would have never seen without her.

Sarah continued as I stared into the thickening mist. "Now I want to ask you to consider something. Lilly is the only connection to Collin my family has left. I have not told my parents about her. But I fear how they will react were they someday to see her on one of their visits. There can be no doubt about her father's identity; she is his mirror image. You know that I loved my brother very much. I've tried to convince myself that what he did on the bridge was in a moment of insanity. I never told you this, but he seemed to be quite taken with you. He had already quizzed me at length about you and your family before you started to work at the clinic. Apparently, the first day he saw you, he felt that you were destined to be together. Collin was always a romantic, and I just assumed he was attracted to you because of the vast differences in your backgrounds and ages. I think the fact that you were so much younger and still in school prevented him from being more open to you about his feelings.

"I have gone over and over in my mind all of our conversations, trying to figure out if he gave me any hint of what possessed him that night. After Robert told me you were responsible for the break in Collin's nose, I knew his temper had bested him. I think he was extremely jealous of your friend Jinx. He assumed too much when he saw you riding behind him that morning. My brother had many good qualities, but he was spoiled and unaccustomed to not having everything fall at his feet. You hurt his ego; he hurt you in return. Looking back now on the visit he made right after Lilly's birth, the attachment he showed toward her makes perfect sense. At the time, I thought he was just being supportive of you, but he knew without a doubt that Lilly was his daughter.

"Having explained all this to you, I pray that it will make it easier for you to accept what I am about to say. You are very young, Rea, and you have been through a great deal in the last year and a half. You confessed to me you were having a hard time accepting Lilly as your daughter and the position of motherhood. You and your family have very little to offer Lilly short of love. In this world, Rea, love is not always enough for children to thrive and reach their full potential. Considering the position you were in when this all came about, you should understand that better than most.

"What I am asking is that you allow Robert and me to adopt Lilly and raise her as our own. We can give her many things that you cannot, not to mention that she is actually family. Know that Robert would love to have her, but he would not pursue it at the expense of placing more pain on you. I want her whether it is painful for you or not. In return for Lilly, we are prepared to pay for you to continue your education, first at a private boarding school near Chattanooga and later at a college of your choosing. The only condition is that Lilly is never to have any contact with you or know you as her natural mother.

"I have discussed this with your parents. While they are very attached to her, they are willing to forfeit their claim as her grandparents. I know that the people in the community will be happy that you want the best for Lilly. Please think this over. The school term begins the first week of September, and we'd like your answer before then. As Lilly grows older, we run the risk of her remembering too much about you. I want her to know us as her true family. I only told your parents about the offer of adoption. They do not know about Collin. While you think about this, Rea, remember a good mother always wants what's best for her child, no matter the heartache to herself.

"One last thing, my parents will undoubtedly want to know the circumstances surrounding Lilly and the fact that she is Collin's child. His death has been devastating to them. To learn he could have been a rapist would destroy them. To prevent that from happening, I am also asking you to allow me to come up with an alternate story surrounding your relationship with him.

It will be detrimental to your reputation, and for that, I am sorry. It is the only way to end questions within our family pertaining to Lilly. I will keep the story as innocent as possible, but there will be talk since I plan to use it in this area with the people who knew Collin to explain her resemblance to my brother." Sarah hesitated briefly, which gave me the opportunity to ask something.

"What story would you tell?"

"It is best to stay as close to the truth as possible. We are simply going to say that you and Collin had become intimate, and your friend misunderstood the situation. He caught you with Collin that night and there was a fight. You attempted to stop it and became injured in the process. Collin was knocked out, and when he came to, you and Jinx were gone. He left to prevent any gossip about you. He and Jinx were both trying to protect your honor by letting the idea of a rape continue. With Collin dead and Jinx missing in action there is no one to dispute this version. The only one to suffer will be you, but it will be worth it for Lilly in the end."

"So let me see if I understand this correctly. My honor and life will be the sacrifice in all of this. In exchange, I give you Lilly and you send me off in hopes of bigger and better things never to return."

"You make it sound so heartless, Rea. Really think about the opportunity it gives you. You would never get the chance to go to college otherwise. Actually, this is a blessing for you if you will be honest with yourself."

Sarah waited for me to say something, and really I tried. But I was so confused and hurt that I could not think of one word. I just shook my head and stared into the rising mist. Sarah reminded me of the deadline for my decision and left me and Lilly in silence. Ma and Pa appeared shortly to leave for home, but no one mentioned the invisible burden now present in the back of the wagon. We could all feel the weight, and none of us wanted to lift it up and carry it. As we drove silently through the night, I watched as more of the girl that was Rea drifted out behind me into an ever-growing mist. I realized that night that against all the odds, I had fallen in love with this beautiful child that had been thrust so violently upon me. As she lay completely still in my lap, she felt such a part of me. I knew to give her away would cost me myself even if it was the right and best thing to do.

In the weeks, days, hours, and minutes that followed, the burden of the decision came to life. It wrapped itself around my heart and squeezed until I would dizzily fall to my knees on the ground. It clouded my thoughts with self-doubt and filled my ears with the heartrending observations of friends and family. I tried to believe that Sarah had been telling the truth and that no one in the community was aware of her offer. It was a hard thing to do with the continued talk of her evident abilities as a mother and her love for Lilly. Ma and Pa never spoke to me of the burden that was choking the life out of me. To do so would mean they would also have to shoulder it. This was mine and mine alone to bear. They made that painfully clear.

I drew on what little knowledge I had of families and, especially, mothers. I watched other mothers closely, ones with few physical assets but lots of love. I saw children clinging to them with adoration and depending on them for protection. Thinking back on my childhood, I could not remember a great deal of affection from either of my parents—not a comforting thought. If I were to keep Lilly, I might deny her the affection and praise I had already seen her receive from the McKinneys in abundance.

Late on an August afternoon, I came across my parents sitting side by side on the porch. Lilly was sound asleep on a pallet at their feet. It was a rare moment, peaceful and cool in the shade. As I walked onto the porch they looked in my direction, but neither spoke.

"I have avoided this as long as possible. I need to talk to you about Lilly."

Ma silently dropped her eyes and nodded her head in acknowledgement. Pa stared out across the field toward something I could not see.

"I want to know how you feel about the McKinneys adopting Lilly. I don't want you to make the decision, but either way, your lives are never going to be the same. Please tell me what you think I should do."

Pa shifted in his seat and never broke his gaze. As Ma would never speak before him, we sat waiting for him. After several long moments, he turned in my direction. "I never thought that a small child could pull so mightily at my heart. I loved all my children. You have to know that, Rea. But Lilly, she's just . . . just been a gift from God in my old age. This is your decision, Rea, so I will not tell you what to do. Whatever you choose, you have my blessing." He rose quickly and made his way down the steps and out across the field as though he was trying to catch something that was moving away from him.

Ma didn't move. After a silence of several minutes, she spoke. "This is awful difficult. The offer from the McKinneys is so very wonderful in so many ways. Lilly ends up with a family that loves her and can give her the very best, and you get the opportunity to use that good brain God gave you for something other than milking cows and doing housework. I've thought about this a lot. Since you have asked, I am going to say what's on my mind. It breaks my heart to see you struggling with this decision, but to be honest, Rea, I can only see one way for you to go. If you keep Lilly, we will be able to do very little for her. You'll be condemning her to repeat your life at the very best. She is a smart and beautiful child. I believe God meant more for her. I know you care for her. I've seen the possessive look you get when Sarah is around. Don't let your feelings influence your decision; use your head and not your heart."

Ma slowly stood and left me sitting on the porch staring at Lilly. I could not help feeling betrayed and abandoned. It seemed everyone had already decided that for me to remain Lilly's mother was not the best choice. I felt as though I'd been manipulated into a position with no escape. This decision lay with me, and no one seemed to want to even come close to suggesting I might make a good mother for Lilly.

As I sat on the porch, I began to think about my ma and her ma. They were good women, not inclined to great cruelties or even deliberate acts of unkindness. They were hard working and obedient. I had often heard we were a God-fearing family. At that moment, my fear of God was overpowered by my desperation that He would give me wisdom—no matter how much trouble I had caused Him. So I began to pray. It started out simple enough. *Please help me choose what is best for Lilly.* It ended up with me facing how utterly disappointed He must be with me. Like the rest of my family, I had stayed in the safe harbor of the familiar. It had been easier to just hide behind the beliefs of my ancestors, never searching Him out on my own. This was the lesson in all this for me. With God, you can never play it by ear. He covets your heart and will accept nothing less. He had placed me in a position that forced me to make a very difficult decision and look Him directly in the eye as I made it. I needed to do some searching, and I didn't have long to work it all out.

I began that night, without the usual pressure from Ma, to study my Bible. I sat down and started with the New Testament. Many truths are hidden within its pages, but I needed the big picture. I did not have time for details. The answer was evident, even to me. The love of God is found in the sacrifice. He gave His only Son, and then the Son gave up His life willingly for ours. Therefore, during those long nights of study, I grew to believe He expects us to sacrifice also.

At first, the answer seemed simple. Sacrifice the small child I had grown to love so that she could have a better life. Then I began to wonder if the opportunity of college would cause my sacrifice to fall short of acceptance in God's sight. Would he consider any decision a sacrifice when I would benefit in return? The more I thought, the more confused I became. After many sleepless nights, I still clung to the edge of the void, thrashing and choking on self-doubt and fear that I would make the wrong decision.

Late one night, I left my sweat-soaked bed and walked out of the house and across the field toward the darkness of the woods. I went in search of relief from the heat and my torment. The forest can be an unforgiving place in the dark. It did not take long for me to become tangled in briars and vines that prevented me from advancing or retreating. So I sat down in misery and eventually fell asleep. I dreamed again that night—a dream of the bridge. No longer threatening, it lay across calm and peaceful waters leading into a landscape of vivid color and cool breezes. It was then I recognized that the bridge had provided me a passage to a different time and place. To reach the other side, I had to sacrifice more than Lilly and my family. It was what dwelled within me that had to be sacrificed. I must change and with that change would be the answer I so desperately sought.

As the sun rose above the trees that morning, I worked my way out of the woods and back to the farm house. Ma did not comment on my sudden appearance in the doorway, nor did she question the leaves and twigs that jutted out from my hair and clothing. I approached my chores with a lighter heart and with more peace than I thought possible. Then as unexpectedly as the dream, Dr. McKinney stood silent above me as I wrestled an old cow into position for milking.

"Good morning, Rea."

"Morning, Doctor. Let me guess—you've come to talk to me about Lilly."

"Yes, Rea, but not for the reason you think. I awoke this morning with the urge to face you one friend to another. Please believe me when I say that we are friends, Rea. I want what is best for you, whichever choice you make. I love my wife beyond life itself. For that reason, I have not become involved in her efforts to persuade you to let us have Lilly. She is a good person, but her losses and the desperate need to fill the void left by the babies in those graves behind the house have made her unable to see what this is doing to my friend. I cannot be as blinded to the toll this is taking on you. Your weight has dropped to an alarmingly low level, and I can no longer see that strong and vibrant young woman in the weary girl standing before me now. I do not want you to be destroyed by this obsession Sarah has developed over Lilly."

This was the first cool breeze of compassion I had felt in weeks. The man standing before me, so much wiser and kinder than me, considered himself my friend. I suddenly saw the person I wanted to become in spirit and human abilities.

"It's all right, Dr. McKinney. I never thought I would love Lilly this much. It is not hard to imagine how Sarah has suffered."

He didn't speak for several minutes, and I chose to continue with the cow rather than to make this easier on him.

"About Collin, I knew he was a tormented soul. But I never dreamed he could do anything as horrible as he did to you. I feel partly responsible for what happened on that bridge. I should have been more observant that morning in my office."

"It seems to me that the only person in the world not the least bit willing to take responsibility for what happened on that bridge was Collin. He felt no remorse; he even tried to blame the whole thing on Jinx. I think that maybe it wouldn't have mattered what anyone suspected or did to try to stop Collin from doing this to me. He would have found a way no matter what."

I had no way of knowing if whatever path I chose would be the right one. My decision would determine the person Lilly would become and would influence the lives of people she would have contact with throughout her life. This was the reason I had struggled for so long to try and choose wisely. I was worn out from it all, but I knew that in reality, it was only the beginning. I would never be completely free of Lilly, whether she remained with me or not.

"Do you mind if I ask when you might be ready to let Sarah know?"

"I have picked my path, Dr. McKinney. Taking the first step by telling Sarah will be the hardest. Does she know you are here this morning?"

"No, I came on my way to work."

"Would you mind telling her for me? I don't seem to have the strength to do it."

"It is the least I can do, considering all that's happened."

"Tell her that she's a mama now. Will you do that for me please, Dr. McKinney?"

"Call me Robert. I will be happy to give my wife the wonderful news."

"Do you mind waiting for a day or two? I haven't told Ma or Pa, but I will the first chance I get."

"We will keep the news to ourselves until we hear from you."

"One more thing—the story she plans to tell her parents about the circumstances of that night, I do not want her to tell it around Rock Island."

"You have my word that she won't."

"Thanks, it will make this easier on Ma and Pa."

Robert left without stopping to talk to my parents. I had turned to finish my work when I noticed Jim standing in the back entry to the barn.

"How long have you been there, Jim?"

"Not long, but I guess you've decided to give Lilly to the McKinneys."

"Yes, but please don't tell anyone yet."

"I won't. But giving away your own flesh and blood don't seem right to me."

"Don't seem right to me either, Jim. That is what makes it so hard."

Jim left me to the milking with the promise of silence on his part. I began dreading the moment when I would tell my parents. I knew it would not be wise to wait. Ma called me in for breakfast not long after Robert left. She and Pa sat quietly at the table when I came through the screen door. Neither spoke, but unasked questions crowded out the silence of the room.

"I guess you saw Dr. McKinney."

"He didn't stop at the house on his way out. Do you mind telling us what he wanted?"

"No, he was wondering if I had decided about Lilly. Actually, I had not made up my mind until last night, but I will be giving Lilly up." Before my parents could speak, I stopped them by shaking my head. "Please don't say anything one way or the other. I really don't want to carry more grief around with me over this. If you have opinions or feelings, please keep them to yourselves. Up until now, I have felt as though I have been wrestling with the devil, a feeling that dissipated last night. I will be held accountable for this choice by God. I am trusting in Him that all of the comments made by older and wiser people than me, have been His way of telling me that Lilly was meant for the

McKinneys. By giving her up, I lay one burden down and pick up another. I will be leaving the farm the week after next. In the agreement I have made with Sarah, I can never come back. I am sorry, Pa. I know this will leave you short on help."

My Pa spoke before I had time to continue "Seems to me, this is too much to ask. I don't think Sarah had any right to make you give up your family." Having said that, Pa rose from the table without taking one bite of his breakfast and left the house. Ma gazed intently at her food. I doubted she would speak, but she surprised me.

"Ella Rea, don't you ever forget where you come from and that your family loves you."

Ma never addressed me by my full name. She had told me as a young child that I was nothing like my namesake, her mother. Grandma Ella was a kind and gentle soul, long suffering and unassuming. She felt to use that name for me, once she knew the kind of person that I was, would be somehow sacrilege. Ma said people marked names for better or for bad. She would remind me that no one ever named their child Judas. In her thinking, my obvious faults would taint the name that her Ma so wonderfully carried throughout her life. For her to use it now was life inspiring for me.

"Ma, you called me Ella!"

"I see my ma living in you today, Rea. She would have been very pleased with you, I have no doubt."

With that simple compliment, Ma gave me more than she would ever know. It was a wonderful thing for her to do and so unlike her. She left me sitting at the table, taking Lilly from the room as she went. The child was unaware of the changes going on around her. I could hear her laughing and babbling to Ma as they climbed the stairs.

CHAPTER NINE

Starting Over

Sarah did not come to the house to care for Lilly after my talk with Robert. Whatever the reason, I was thankful that she gave us the last few days with Lilly alone. Pa let work go for the remaining days of August. I could see him walking the fields and roaming the woods with Lilly on his shoulders. Ma often joined the happy pair as Pa explained the beauty of nature to the tiny child, who became ever more joyous with each new discovery. In the evenings, we gathered around her—the center of our universe—a bright sun in an otherwise grey world. None of us spoke of the coming day when she would cease to be a part of our lives. When bereft of the joy she had brought to our monotonous days, we would all face the future without her.

The Saturday following Robert's visit to the milk barn, I went to work at the clinic, mostly to see Sarah. She was literally spouting with excitement. She grabbed my hand as I came into the office and led me back to her kitchen. Before I could speak, she was hugging, crying, and laughing all at the same time. I had to admit that if I was in her place, my reaction would have been even more dramatic. Once she regained her composure, I took the opportunity to ask her for one more favor.

"I gather that Robert told you the news."

"Oh, Rea, I really never thought you would be able to give her up. I know that I never could."

"Somehow that doesn't speak well of me, but that is not important. I have a request to make of you."

"Anything, Rea, just ask."

"First, I know that you do not want Lilly to know who her grandparents are. My parents understand and will never tell her the truth. But could you please somehow work them into her life? They have broken my heart over and over the last few days. She is so very important to them and brings such joy to their lives that depriving them of her is becoming the hardest part of this whole situation."

"Oh, that would be easy. I will make certain that they see her every week. She may never know they are her real grandparents, but they will nevertheless be an important part of her life. You can trust me on this, Rea. Do not doubt that I am good for my word."

"I do not doubt it, Sarah. Also, Robert mentioned you would be going to Chattanooga to register me for high school in the next couple of days. I would like to go by my first name, Ella, from now on."

"What a beautiful name. I never knew."

"It was my grandmother's name. It seems right to use it now that I will be living a different life."

"Have you decided what you want to do with your life? Where you would like to attend college?"

"Actually I have. I want to go to medical school to become a doctor like Robert and help children born into misery and disease. Grandma Ella grew up in the Appalachian Mountains. I want to go there and set up a clinic somewhere deep in the hills. I can still remember her talking about the hardship her family went through in those mountains, especially the children."

"Are you sure, Rea? That would be an even harder life than you have here."

"I'm sure. Could you please ask Robert if he will send me to school for that long?"

"If that's what you want, Rea, it will be fine with him."

"Thank you, but I may not be able to get into medical school."

"Rea, I have no doubt that you can do anything you put your heart into. Now I know this is hard, but when do I get Lilly? We have the adoption papers ready for you to sign."

"I will bring her to you the day I leave Rock Island for good."

Sarah hugged me one more time before we returned to the office and faced a waiting room full of patients. She asked my permission to tell our neighbors about the adoption, and I gave my consent to start spreading the news. It did not take long for the word to filter out into the community. People began dropping by in the late afternoon to check on the truth of the rumor and share in the McKinneys' joy. As the day wore on and the crowd increased, it became apparent that Sarah had been confiding in many about her desire to adopt Lilly. By sunset, a full-fledged party was underway at the McKinney home. As Pa pulled up in the wagon to take me back to the farm, he became overwhelmed by friends in their attempt to show their support for my decision. I could not help but feel sorry for my pa. It was obviously painful for him. On the ride back, Pa had very little to say. He stared resolutely ahead and would not look in my direction. To try and lift his spirits, I told him of my talk with Sarah.

"I talked to Sarah today about you and Ma. She promised me that you would see Lilly at least once a week. Even though she will not know that you are her grandparents, she will be free to love you without interference from them."

"You have her word on this?"

"Yes and Robert's too. He caught me right before I left and told me he intends for you to be involved in Lilly's life. You have to take my place, Pa. Teach her all that you have taught us. Be there when I can't."

"We will do our best."

"I know you will, Pa, and that is all I can ask."

True to Pa's nature, no sentiment or affection was displayed, but there was trust and love. His love had never once failed me; it would never fail Lilly either.

The next week seemed to pass in the blink of an eye. The sadness that enveloped us even brought Lilly into a somber mood. She sat silent and intent in Ma's lap and took to patting my pa on the cheek for minutes at a time. She began to come to me as sleep called her away from the world of light. She would crawl into my arms and nestle until she almost became part of me once again. In those moments of silence, I said good-bye to Lilly in my heart. From now on, she might belong to someone else, but I would forever be able to feel her next to me as she was in those moments. On the morning we were to leave, Ma and Pa sat stone silent at the kitchen table. Lilly stared up at each in turn, waiting for them to notice she was there.

I finally couldn't take the sheer misery of the room any longer. "Lilly and I are going to wait on the porch." At first, they did not seem to hear me, but it wasn't long before they joined us to continue their silent vigil in the porch swing. In the soft breeze of the early morning, Lilly's curls danced playfully on her head. She was unusually calm, occupied by a small rag doll Ma had made her soon after we brought her home. Lilly's beauty in the early morning light was breathtaking, and my attention was so consumed I did not hear the approaching car. I would carry that vivid, mental image with me throughout my life.

"Rea, they're here."

Sarah had come with Robert and the instant Lilly saw her, a smile returned to her tiny face. Ma took her from my lap and hugged her good-bye, handing her over to Sarah as Robert helped me load my bags into the car. Pa never said good-bye to me that day. When I turned from the car, he had already disappeared into the house. I want to think that it was just too hard for him to face me leaving, but I knew it was Lilly he could not watch drive away.

Ma came down to the car and stood by the door as I climbed into the back seat. She bent over and handed me my Grandma Ella's ancient Bible through the back window. I protested, but she insisted, and I accepted it. As Robert drove us out of the yard, I turned and watched Ma still standing and staring in my direction, growing smaller and smaller as we made our way down the lane and onto the main road. To keep myself from becoming totally consumed in grief, I opened the Bible and began reading the list of Ma's family going back three generations. I knew then that Lilly would never have this link to the past. Just one more thing I had never considered when I accepted Sarah's offer. The knowledge of this caused the last of a girl named Rea to rise up and flow out the window in the breeze headed back toward our farm. I left her there that day and with her my heart.

We dropped Sarah and Lilly off at the McKinney home. Lilly watched us drive away, and I saw her wave. Pa had been trying to help her master this skill for some time. Apparently, he had succeeded. He would never know how much it meant to me to have my daughter wave good-bye.

The farther we drove from Rock Island, the less of me I could remember. By the time we reached the Chattanooga city limits, I realized that I had not spoken a word the entire journey and had no idea where I was going. It seemed pointless to ask. I soon learned that I would be living with an elderly couple, a retired doctor and his wife: Campbell and Flora Daniels. They seemed kind upon first impression and to my surprise, thoroughly excited to have me move into their home. At the dinner table that night, they spoke of their only son, killed recently in the war in the Pacific. They acted graciously toward me even though I was fairly certain they had heard the version of the story Sarah planned on telling her parents.

My final year in high school was difficult because the students at the school treated me even worse than the kids back home. At the private school, they did not realize my specific circumstances, but my accent and country ways made me an oddity. At least Robert had gotten permission for me to live off campus. While this made me even more of an outcast, it gave me a break from the school every night. Sarah supplied me with all the finest clothes, but, as Ma always said, you can't make a silk purse out of a sow's ear.

My grades remained high. At the end of the year, I was accepted into the University of Tennessee. Robert and Sarah stayed true to their word about paying for my education. Robert went beyond what I expected. Without Sarah's knowledge, he sent me information and pictures of Lilly. She had been adamant that I remain completely in the dark where Lilly was concerned. My parents even agreed not to mention her to me. In the few letters I did receive from home, not one contained any news about my daughter.

Through the waning years of the war, I struggled to adjust to college life. I had lost contact with the people in Rock Island. I suppose they all bowed to Sarah's wishes, and no one even wanted to know if I was still alive. The few friends I thought I had failed me in the end. To increase my pain, I heard no other word concerning Jinx. It was as if I had never lived on the farm. Eventually, I began not to consider it my home. The kindness of the Daniels kept me focused and sane throughout the long years I spent in Knoxville. I returned to their house for the breaks and holidays from school, mainly because they treated me with compassion and love. They became my family, and I decided to treat them as I would have treated my parents.

The day I graduated from UT dawned bright and sunny. With very few women in the line, it was not difficult to pick me out. I did not expect anyone to come to graduation that day, but I was surprised to hear my name called out once the exercises were completed. I turned toward the voices and immediately saw Robert McKinney standing beside the Daniels, all smiling profusely. Behind them stood a young man, very thin and tired looking. At first, I did not recognize him. But then he smiled, and I knew my friend in the person before me.

Jinx had been liberated from the prison camp and sent home. No one had bothered to let me know. His recovery from the harsh treatment he had endured was still ongoing. It did not take long for him to find out how I had spent the eighteen months after he left. Robert had explained to Jinx where I was and what I had been doing since giving Lilly to them. Robert said that Jinx was a very persistent person and he felt that I would not mind him knowing the details of my life. It was a great gift that day to be able to see my friend; it just didn't last long enough.

Robert managed to get me accepted into medical school in Atlanta. Once the admissions office determined that I really intended to practice deep in the Appalachians, they deemed my education not wasted. As a woman, I was expected to work harder and do more than the men in my class. It seemed as though my professors were just looking for a reason to fail me. I looked back on those years later and marveled that I had the stamina to endure the stress. When things reached a crisis point at school, somehow Robert would know and suddenly appear to encourage me, and he always shared pictures and stories of Lilly.

By the time I completed medical school, Lilly had grown into a lovely young girl. According to Robert, the entire community was still wrapped around her little finger. She spent many days on the farm with my rapidly aging parents and my brother Steve. Jeff had been killed in the war, a fact I heard only many months after his death. Steve had returned home after his discharge to run the farm. Ma wrote to tell me that he suffered nightmares and had grown very quiet since returning to Rock Island. It was sad to think an entire generation would be marked in some way by the horrors brought to life in that war.

Steve took it upon himself to end the silence on my family's part concerning Lilly. In his letters, he made it clear to me that he felt as though I had not been treated fairly. He begged me to return and visit at the very least. When I refused, he went to great effort to record every moment that Lilly spent at the farm with his camera. It felt odd to have my brother be so kind and insightful regarding my life.

Robert went beyond what he had agreed to and researched out a place to set up my clinic in the mountains. He made several trips to the site the year before I finished medical school. He sent me countless letters describing the people and place I would soon call home. He wanted me to be prepared for a very hard life. I would have to be self-sufficient since I would be many miles from the nearest road. He was concerned that the people would not be receptive of me. He said they were very wary of any strangers. I suspected that he wanted to paint a bleak picture so that I would not expect too much.

By the time I finished my boards and internship, I had developed an almost hysterical dread of walking into those moun-

Jan Kendall

tains. With the work Robert had already invested in my future, I could not back out on my decision. He had discovered Baptist missionaries working one ridge over from where he planned to build the clinic. They offered to let me rent a room until we could get a cabin built on the site selected. This thought calmed my nerves a bit. Nevertheless, the fear of the unknown took its toll, and my health declined that last year before I would leave on my journey to begin my new life.

I spent the last few weeks preceding my departure with the Daniels in Chattanooga. Flora cooked my favorite foods and tried her best to give me back my strength. They were supportive, as always, but sad that I would be so far away. I promised to return every Christmas to visit for two weeks. However, before the next Christmas, they had both passed into the next life.

I walked into the mountains with Robert on a crisp, fall day. The trees rippled with color and, try as I might to not allow it, my mind kept returning to the farm. We had a guide with us, a mountain man named Gus, and several heavily loaded pack mules. It was necessary to take all the medicines and equipment we anticipated I would need for at least eight months. Not wanting to be a burden on the missionaries I would be staying with, we also brought in the food I would consume. Gus said very little. It was painfully obvious that he was uncomfortable around me although he seemed to be less repulsed by Robert. As we made our way slowly into the hills, I had an uneasy feeling that we were being watched. However, there was never any evidence that backed up my suspicions.

The missionaries were kind and welcoming. Bev was a buxom woman with bright eyes and a stalwart spirit. She dwarfed her husband, Joshua, in size but not in determination. His single-minded passion to save the lost souls of those who dwelled nearby seemed to permeate every inch of the area the couple occupied. I could not walk within the house or stroll about the surrounding countryside without being aware any and all were welcome in the name of God by these lovely people.

Before Robert prepared to leave, the decision had been made to construct my clinic in the valley below the mission instead of over the next ridge. Knowing people would be close did much to alleviate my fears. However, I could not shake the uneasy feeling that had plagued me on the trip into this secluded hollow. Somewhere out in those woods, just like the night of the attack, someone or something was watching me. One cool fall afternoon, I decided that the only way to relieve my fears was to face them. After gathering my coat and walking stick, I made my way into the forest with the intent to make a wide circle around the mission.

It was only a short time before my suspicions of watching eyes took the form of two small, underfed children. They did not approach me but walked some distance behind with the look and movement of frightened animals. When I turned to face them, they disappeared briefly from sight and then reappeared at a different location. They were present the entire time I walked, never coming close enough for me to speak but always near enough to be seen. On my return, I went straight to find Bev.

"Well, Dr. Wilson, did you discover anything new on your walk?"

"Were you aware that there were children lurking out there in the woods?"

"No, but I am not surprised. Your appearance at the mission has not gone unnoticed. I'm sure Gus has spread the news across the ridges that a new doctor has arrived and a woman doctor at that. It might surprise you to know that being a woman will not be of any concern to these people. Their injuries and illnesses have always been treated by the older and wiser of their women. Old Gram Hannah is the local dispenser of home remedies in this area. She will, more than likely, do her best to prevent the locals from using your services. Do not get discouraged if you are not accepted by these people quickly. It will take a great deal of time for them to trust you."

I soon learned that Bev had told me the truth. During the winter that followed and into the next spring, I had only one opportunity to treat a patient. Early one morning, a gaunt woman stood on the porch of the mission holding a barely breathing baby. After much discussion between Bev and Joshua, they all turned to me.

"Ella, this baby is very near death. Ina says they have tried everything that Old Gram knew. Against the wishes of her husband, she has brought the little girl to you. Before you agree to treat her, you must understand that if you try and fail, her death will be blamed on you. Should that happen, I doubt anyone will ever come to ask for your help again."

I could see the child gasping in her mother's arms. The expression on the mother's face was one of torment. This could end my hopes of being a blessing in the lives of the mountain people.

"Bev, does she have any other children?"

"Several, but that does not matter to her. At the moment, only this one occupies her heart."

"Tell her to bring in the baby and place it on the table."

"Are you sure?"

"Yes. I know that whatever chance I have here is going to be someone in a desperate situation. This one is as good as any, and honestly, I came because of the children. I cannot turn her away."

After questioning the mother for a few minutes, I learned that the baby girl had come at least a month early and was now only a week old. I kept thinking about Lilly being so small at birth. During medical school, I had been very attentive to the treatment of premature babies. My supplies included as much as possible that would help under these conditions. The mother refused to speak to me directly, so I relayed my messages through Bev.

"Tell her I will make no promises, but she will have to leave her baby with us if there is any chance to save her. We will send Joshua after her if there is any change."

"Ella, this is dangerous. These people are apt to associate anything they don't understand with magic or evil spirits. It would be better if she stayed and watched whatever it is that you intend to do."

"Fine with me, but it is going to take several days before we know if she will pull through."

After much debate, Ina sent Joshua back to her home in search of her oldest daughter. Apparently, it would fall to the girl to monitor everything that happened to her baby sister. The mother was needed at home if for no other reason than to face her husband's wrath so that he would not take it out on the other children. My heart went out to the woman standing sentinel over her newborn. Was there no end to the misery this life inflicted upon the women living in this world?

The older daughter arrived—a miniature version of her mother. Even though she was probably no more than twelve or thirteen, she too already had a worn and tired appearance. Her eyes never stopped darting between me and the baby. Over a long couple of weeks, I never even knew the name of the child that shadowed my every move. With each change in treatment, she eyed me with suspicion and fear. It was a nerve-wracking and exhausting ordeal. I never slept more than a few hours at a time over the next several days. To my surprise, however, the baby born into such misery and hardship possessed a stubborn will to live. By the second week, it became fairly evident that she would have as good a chance as most to survive this harsh and unforgiving life before her. I sent her sister to bring the woman, named Ina, back to collect her baby.

Ina returned to my clinic quickly. Gathering her baby daughter up in her arms, she looked at me as she walked to the door. My only payment from her was a self-conscious smile of few teeth. As she walked away, I thanked God for answering the many prayers I had laid at His feet on the baby girl's behalf. I would have liked to think I saved her; I knew that was not the case. I did accept her survival as a sign that He approved of my choices so far and would bless the mountain population through my efforts.

During the early summer, Robert returned as promised. To my surprise, Jinx was with him. Since last seeing him, Jinx had recovered his health and strength. The man standing before me that day resembled the boy I remembered in only small ways. The first night after they arrived, we all found our way to the mission porch. As I sat on the steps, I was lulled into a contented state by the tone of the soft conversation behind me and the multitude of stars filling the sky above me. When I realized that

Jan Kendall

things had grown too quiet, I looked up to find that everyone had suddenly disappeared leaving me alone with Jinx.

"Gracious, where did everybody go? Is it time for bed already?"

"I think they just wanted to leave us alone."

"Why on earth would they want to do that?"

"You know, Rea, sometimes you are the densest person I know."

"I go by Ella now, remember?"

"You will always be Rea to me, no matter what name you go by. I've come a long way to talk to you. Now will you listen without getting your temper all stirred up?"

"Don't be silly, Jinx. I would never get mad at you."

"I have seen you get mad at me plenty in the past. However, you and I have a lot of unresolved history between us, and that is what I want to discuss. For starters, you were not honest with me about your circumstances after I left to join the navy. I blame myself for that. I couldn't bear being around you knowing I could have prevented what happened to you on that bridge. I ran away and left you, but I always intended to come back. If I knew your pa at all, I knew he would still be trying to find you a husband. I was hoping he would have a hard time marrying you off quickly after what happened. I intended to use the navy to help me figure out a way to support you and take you off that farm. The attack at Pearl Harbor and my capture prevented me from sending you the letter I intended to write. I wanted to tell you that I loved you and to wait for me until I could get back."

I was thankful for the darkness between us. The look on my face could only be disbelief and mortification. No man had ever spoken to me in such a manner. Before I could prevent him from speaking further, he continued without stopping to catch his breath.

"I know you have your reasons for leaving Rock Island. It took some doing, but I finally got the truth out of Robert. Why you chose to come to this godforsaken place, I will never understand, but you're here now and wherever you are is where I want to be. You may not feel the same about me, but you will have to admit that I could be a lot of help to you here. Maybe I could at least keep you from starving to death. I've come all this way to try and get you to marry me."

At first I could barely think, much less speak. There was no doubt I loved the man sitting behind me on the porch. It was just so unexpected that he loved me back. I may be a fool in many aspects of my life, but I recognize a blessing when it is talking to me. There was something though that I had to know.

"Are you asking me this to help ease the guilt you feel about the attack?"

"No, Rea. I have loved you for years. Your pa knew how I felt, but he knew I would take you away. You never realized you were his favorite. He wanted to tie you to the farm so that you would never leave. In the end, what happened that night on the bridge took you away from both of us."

"Do you know that I am damaged goods? I cannot have any more children, and I'm not very good at being loved and loving back." I kept my head down, afraid to look back at Jinx.

"Yes, I know there will be no children through us, but it doesn't matter to me. I have seen so much evil in this world that I would be fearful to bring a child to life. And as far as learning to love, well, I will be more than happy to teach you how."

If it is possible to hear the voices of heaven falling down from above, I heard them that night. My heart had never been filled with such joy and peace. In Jinx's offer came both release from old demons and redemption from my self-imposed isolation. Without turning from my position on the steps to face him, I gave Jinx the answer I prayed he wanted.

"Marrying you sounds good to me, Jinx. Should I plan a wedding?"

"I'd say let's do it right now, but I think the preacher is in bed, so in the morning will have to do. Robert plans to leave early. I want him to be a witness; he can take the news back to your parents."

"What about all your stuff back home?"

"I brought it all with me. It's stored at the railhead in Johnson City. I was kind of hoping you would say yes."

I turned, but I couldn't see his face. I could tell though by the tone of his voice that he was grinning. "You're awfully confident it seems to me."

"Yeah, or awfully stupid. But since it appears that it was worth the effort, let's just say that I was confident if anyone asks."

"Men, you're all about ego. I'm going to bed. I'll be up before dawn and ready. Apparently, we'll be making a trek through the mountains to the railhead after breakfast." I could hear Jinx laughing softly as I climbed the steps and went into the mission. Each step drew a prayer of thanksgiving from my heart. God had given me more in Jinx than I could have ever possibly imagined or hoped for.

No one seemed the least bit surprised by our request that Joshua marry us at first light the next morning. Robert was enthused with joy. Up until then, I had not considered the possibility that he had a great deal of influence in the outcome of Jinx's visit. I began to look at Robert differently. It was obvious that he had been working on this for a long time. He was trying to give me back what was taken away during the adoption. He was giving me back a sense of family.

The ceremony was short and to the point. Bev supplied a feast of a marriage breakfast. On that beautiful morning, the life of Rea and Ella blended into one identity. I was no longer the girl I had been in Rock Island or the one who had survived the disappointments and hardships of separation from my home. Jinx brought me back the best of what came before, and I chose to remember the best of what had come to me since then.

Over time, Jinx proved to be right about many things. He taught me a wonderful and approving love. More than once, he prevented me from starving to death; he became the source of my greatest strength. He could not quite fill the void left by the loss of Lilly, but he seemed to understand the burden that came with that loss and did his best to help me carry it.

Our start at married life, however, was less than enthusiastic. When we finished breakfast after our wedding, I left the table and returned to my room to gather my things for the long trip

Bridge Over Calm Water

to the railhead. As I walked off, Jinx and Joshua were in a deep discussion concerning what should be brought back and what should be stored until the cabin could be constructed. I had just entered my room when I heard someone come to the door. Turning around, I saw my husband staring in my direction with a look of determination on his face. I had seen that look before. He had his mind set on accomplishing something, and he was expecting opposition from me.

"Something wrong, Jinx?"

"Actually things would be perfect if I didn't have to go and collect my stuff. Joshua and I are about ready to leave, and I wanted one more kiss from my bride before I left."

Jinx had used this tactic on me before on the farm. If he wanted to avoid a fight with me over something, he would simply pass by my opinions and proceed without me. He knew I wanted to go with him, and he had already decided that was not going to happen. The ploy to distract me with a kiss was his way of avoiding a fight over me staying put. The old Rea would have jumped right into a full-blown argument without thinking twice. The new Ella Rea would avoid a fight at all cost.

"Oh, I assumed I would go back with you. I could be a lot of help loading up. It might make the trip quicker."

For just a brief instant, I saw something flicker in his eyes. I had surprised him with my answer. He had expected me to put up a fight, and now he was thrown off balance, just enough that he was not sure how to proceed.

"I guess you would make the trip more pleasant, but it will be a physically hard journey. I don't want you to have to do any more hard work as long as I am around. Robert is still concerned that you are not as strong as you once were."

At one time, I would have thought that he was being less than sincere and just using his concern for my welfare as a way to persuade me to his way of thinking. Trying to read his motives in his face, I could see only genuine concern for me. This was unfamiliar territory. No man had ever really considered my welfare when there was work to be done.

"Oh, all right, so come and give me my kiss."

The most wonderful of smiles slowly spread across his face. It seemed my new husband was happy with how I reacted to his directives. He was across the room in two strides. Grabbing me in a bear hug, he swung me around in circles before setting me on my feet and kissing me gently on the mouth. With his mission accomplished, he walked quickly to the door, turning to grin in my direction before he disappeared down the hall. I stood and thought for a moment. I was not a romantic person, but we definitely needed to work on our kissing when he got back.

I walked out onto the porch and watched as the men made their way across the meadow and out of sight into the woods. The strangest sensation started to build in my chest. I felt as if something had been sucked out and a part of me was missing. I knew then that I was going to like being married. We had not even had our honeymoon, and already Jinx had somehow found a way to move in to the deepest part of my being. As I stood staring at the place where he had disappeared from my sight, the pain of his leaving became mixed up with the excitement associated with his return. Yep, I was going to like being married a whole lot.

CHAPTER TEN

Jinx

Once I returned to my room, it did not take Bev long to come in search of me. I was trying to decide how to make room for Jinx in my small space when she knocked on the door casing.

"I like your young man, Ella. He has a soft and giving heart."

"I still can't believe we are married. This is going to take some getting used to."

"That's why I'm here. Jinx asked me to talk to you after he left."

"Something wrong?"

"No. He just wanted me to find out exactly how you felt about all this."

"I feel fine about it. I have always loved Jinx, but I will have to admit until yesterday, I never thought about Jinx as a possible husband. In fact, I really thought I would never marry."

"I believe he loves you very much. But he thinks that you might need time to get use to him again. He told me that you often just go along with something without standing up for yourself. He said you gave in awfully easily on making the trip with them to the railhead. He thinks something isn't quite right. He does not want to force you into something you're not ready for. When he returns, he is moving into the storage room in the back. He wants to court you for a while. He thinks a little romance would do you a world of good."

"Romance, has he lost his mind? This is the most unromantic place I have ever been. What a waste of human energy when it is so hard to just survive here."

"Ella, I don't ever want to pry in your private business. But I think that it's time you let someone show you that there's more to life than hard work and misery. I think Jinx is the man for the job. So I am telling you now that you will let this young man romance you—no matter how impractical you believe it to be." Bev stood stoic and determined in front of me, her soft arms folded across her generous bosom.

"Okay, I won't hurt his feelings."

"That's my girl. Now let's get into that storage room and make a place for that oh-so-handsome husband of yours to sleep, for a little while anyway."

"You think Jinx is handsome?"

"Child, are you blind? He is one of the most gorgeous creatures I have ever seen, but let's keep that between me and you. I wouldn't want to hurt Joshua's feelings, although I doubt he would care."

I followed Bev to the back room and commented, "I suppose we need to get started on the clinic as soon as possible, but I'm not sure if we can gather enough money to pay for the materials we need."

"Oh! Don't fret about that. Jinx is picking up the materials before he comes back. It will take them a day or so to get everything he and Joshua put on the list. I don't expect them back before day after tomorrow."

"Where did he get the money, Bev? Did Dr. McKinney give it to him?"

"No, I think Jinx is paying for all the things you will need. He considers it his duty to provide you a home and a place to work."

"Jinx is paying for all of the materials? I can't let him do that. He has worked too hard for his money."

"You're married now, child. What's his is yours and what's yours is his."

She showed me where to start with the clearing out and went to gather cleaning supplies. It took a full day just to create a place for a small cot and a dressing table. My conscience began to bother me when I thought of the soft feather bed I enjoyed and my husband's long frame on the short lumpy cot.

Jinx returned late in the evening on the third day, and good to his word, he moved into the cramped space in the back of the mission. The evening was hot and muggy, so Bev, Joshua, and I made our way out onto the porch to soak up the cool, mountain breezes. Jinx eventually joined us and sat by me on the steps. I was aware of Bev and Joshua slipping away as silently as they could from the porch and back into the house.

"Bev told me you were not exactly overly enthusiastic about us courting."

"Honestly Jinx, what purpose will it serve, except to give you terrible backaches from sleeping on that cot?"

"Rea, we have known each other for a very long time. I know you are fond of me, and we are really good friends. I want to know that you love me, the kind of love that invades your heart and your mind. A love that makes you long to be one with me the way a man and woman are supposed to be when they are married."

"I do love you, Jinx."

"Yes, but I don't really think you have given up the young boy that you grew up with and replaced him with the man that I've become. I'm not bragging, but I've never had a woman turn me down for a date. You have only seen me a couple of times since I left for the navy, and let's just say that you don't seem as impressed as most of the women I have met since I've been gone."

"Gracious, Jinx, sounds like you're mighty confident of the effect you have on women."

"Well, I am certainly interested in finding out if there is more to my wife than her physical beauty and great brains. Somewhere in there, I just know there's a fire and I intend to light it and keep it burning for all the days of our lives."

"You actually think I'm beautiful?"

"Why do you think your mother worried so much about you looking too good in those dresses? I don't like to talk about the prison camp, but the memory of you in those overalls working by my side every day kept me from losing my mind. Oh, you're beautiful all right, and everyone knew it back home but you."

Listening to someone talk to me in such a way made me squirmy, so I attempted to redirect the conversation. "I'm sorry you had to go through that during the war, Jinx."

"I hope the worst of our lives are behind us, Rea. Why don't we agree right now not to dredge up the past to spoil the joy we could cultivate from now on?"

"I will gladly agree to that."

"Wonderful, now it's late and we have a long day tomorrow, so we need to get some rest."

"I'll be in shortly. I like to sit out in the quiet for a while and listen to the sounds of the forest and stare at the stars."

"I'm not sure I like you sitting out here by yourself."

"Don't forget about Rufus; he never wanders out from underneath the porch at night." At the mention of his name, Joshua's old hound whimpered softly from beneath our feet.

"All right, but I will need you sharp tomorrow because we are going to start the cabin, so not too late." Jinx leaned over and gently placed a kiss on my forehead. The kiss created a sensation on my skin that spread down my neck and to my arms, causing goose bumps as it slowly made its way to my ankles. I found myself holding my breath and staring intently at his back as he walked into the mission.

The next morning, I woke to the sound of men milling around outside in the early morning fog. Looking out my window, I could see them blowing on their hands between the loads that they removed from a pack of mules lined up in the meadow. In the front yard, I saw several women preparing tables for a noon meal. It took only a few seconds to process that they were there to begin work on the cabin. Taking one last look, I noticed Joshua and Jinx bent over a large paper intently discussing some important detail before them.

Apparently, Jinx had done a great deal of work while he was gone. Decisions were obviously being made about my clinic and future home without my involvement. I should have anticipated that there would be no delay in beginning. Quickly, I dressed and walked out the front door to join the two men. So consumed by their conversation, they were unaware of my presence only a few feet away. Not wanting to interrupt, I stopped just short of where they stood but close enough that I could hear what they were discussing.

"So on the way back to the train, you talked to Dr. McKinney about the changes you wanted to make to his design?"

"He was very enthusiastic when I told him I wanted to build two structures connected by a hallway. That way we have a true home and not just a clinic with a bedroom attached at the back."

"Have you discussed any of this with Ella?"

"Not yet, but she will not object, I hope."

"Don't want to interfere in your marriage, but my experience with your wife so far makes me believe you might want to talk this over with her before we get too far along in the building process."

Joshua slapped Jinx on the back and turned to face me standing in the direction in which he intended to walk. "I'd say right about now would be a good time to have that talk." He continued on chuckling to himself as Jinx slowly turned to face me.

"Not nice to eavesdrop, Rea."

"It's not like I was hiding behind that old tree over there, and besides, I just caught the very end of your conversation. What do you need to talk to me about?"

"Well, the original plans for the clinic really didn't take into account that you would have a husband and that it would serve as a home for both of us."

"Yes, we tried to come up with the most efficient plan we could so that it wouldn't cost so much to build since it would be funded by donations."

"Well, I told Dr. McKinney that I wanted to be responsible for the cost of construction."

"Bev told me that. I don't want you to spend all of your hard-earned money for the clinic, Jinx."

"Dr. McKinney agreed with you on that point, so we came to a compromise on the way back out of the mountains. He has enough donations to build a small clinic similar to the original plan. I am going to build us a separate cabin beside it as a home."

Jinx stood before me grinning brightly and patiently waiting on my response. How could life contain in itself such capacity for extreme hurt and pain along with extreme joy and blessings? I was so blown over by his consideration that I stood dumbfounded before him. Time began to draw out; the smile slowly faded from his face.

"Are you not happy with my idea, Rea?"

"Oh . . . I'm sorry, Jinx. I am just so surprised by the kindness in your offer that I can't think of anything nearly adequate enough to tell how very happy I am at this moment."

The smile returned as he grabbed me once again to swing me in circles.

"Okay Jinx, you're making me seasick."

He put me down and looked at me with concern on his face. "Sorry, I just expected you to argue with me like you used to do on the farm almost every day."

"I've grown up too, Jinx. I know a gift from God even if it is embodied in a handsome man."

"You think I'm handsome?"

"You implied last night that you consider yourself handsome based on your experiences with other women. Am I not supposed to believe what my husband tells me is the truth? Now get back to your work—summer will be gone before you know it. Fall comes early this high up."

"Don't you want to see the plans?"

"No, I think I want to be surprised. I trust you, Jinx. Whatever you think is best, that will be just great with me."

I walked away with a smile, knowing that behind me Jinx was still staring in my direction trying to figure out if he really knew the woman he had married. The strange thing was that I did trust Jinx. I had thought I would never truly be able to trust any man to have my best interest at heart, but I had no doubt that it was true of Jinx.

Starting that day, I began an almost constant vigil of the progress being made on the cabin. Bev and Joshua insisted that our home be built first since the clinic was already set up at the mission. Many days, I sat on the front porch watching the men from surrounding hollers and ridges working to give us a home before winter returned to the mountains. Jinx was paying the laborers generous wages, and the men soon came to treat him as a friend. Those who had never spoken to me at least acknowledged my presence at the work site.

I could hear Jinx describing to the men the farm where I was raised and how we had spent so much time working hard side by side. It had never occurred to me that the men considered me a foreigner, not only because I came from the outside, but also because they assumed I had no idea of the trials faced in just surviving. Many times, Jinx over elaborated on the true difficulty we had faced. It finally occurred to me that he was trying to build a connection for me with this community. My admiration for his wisdom grew with each passing day.

Although he was constantly busy overseeing and building, Jinx did not forget his conviction that I needed to be courted. He insisted that the men take Saturdays and Sundays off to take care of their responsibilities at home. Joshua tried to persuade him to just let them off on Sundays, but Jinx was adamant. The first weekend after his return, I discovered the reason behind his weekdays-only schedule.

The sun came up brightly in a clear sky that particular Saturday morning, something not so very common in the Smokey Mountains. My small window faced the east and on these mornings, even I could not sleep past sunrise. Bev was already up and had breakfast on the table before I made it into the kitchen.

"I can never beat you in here no matter how early I get up."

"Honey child, we've been up for a couple of hours studying."

"Gosh Bev, I always feel like a poor example of a believer when I compare myself to you."

"You're young yet, and I've no doubt that your mind is occupied with other things right now."

"That's true, but it's no excuse."

"You just keep heading in the right direction. The Savior will make up the difference for you."

"Have I told you how thankful I am for everything you have done for me?"

"Yes, many times. Have you mentioned something along that line of thinking to Jinx?"

"Sort of, but I could do better. Have you seen him? Is he up yet?"

"As a matter of fact, he is already outside waiting on you. He said to make sure you ate something before you came out and that you put on your good walking shoes."

"What has he got in mind for today?"

"Can't say that I have any idea, but I wouldn't keep him waiting. I've been noticing all the young, pretty, single girls coming to the mission more than usual since your new husband arrived."

"Really?"

"Really!"

"Bev, you worry entirely too much."

I found Jinx sitting on the porch swing with a wicker basket at his feet.

"What's up and why the basket?"

"The workers have been talking all week about the beautiful lake in a valley several ridges over from here. Have you ever been there?"

"No, but I've seen it from a distance traveling around the area to check on sick patients. Why?"

"Well, I want us to hike over there today for a picnic. Before you say you have a couple of sick children to visit today, I know that they live on the way. We will stop to check on them as we go."

"Is this part of the courting?"

"Ahh . . . yes, you could say that."

"All right, I'll go and get my medical pack."

Jinx took my pack from me as I left the mission. I tried to protest, but he only gave me an exasperated look and began to lead me out into the meadow in the general direction of the lake.

"Jinx, do you even know exactly where we are going?"

"I know which path to take, and I am counting on you to correct me if we begin to stray from our destination."

"Okay."

The day began to warm as we made our way into the trees and started our climb up the first ridge. I was not accustomed to walking as fast as was necessary to keep up with Jinx's long strides. By the time we reached the top of the ridge, I was gasping for air.

"Something wrong, Rea?"

"No, just a little winded. You are setting quite a pace, considering I have to take two steps for each of yours."

"Do I need to carry you too?"

"No, you just keep going, I may fall behind, but I know the way; I'll catch up eventually."

He just smiled and dropped back to walk behind me. "Maybe you should lead for a while. I don't want you exhausted before we even get there."

"I suppose Dr. McKinney is right. I'm not as strong as I was before you joined the navy."

I heard him draw in a deep breath. Even though I didn't elaborate on the reason for my loss of stamina, Jinx knew why I no longer could keep up with him as I once had done. The cabin of my first patient was coming into view through the woods. We did not continue the conversation because the children of the family ran up the path to meet us. The little girl I had come to check on was in the middle of the pack. Once they reached us, I could tell that the cast I had applied to her arm a month before was dirty and worn but otherwise intact. "Lulu, how is the arm doing?"

"It be fine. Ya gonna take this har ol' thang off'n my arm?"

Before I could reply, Lulu's older brother, added, "Yeah, Doc Eller, ya gotta take that thar thang off'n her arm!"

"Now, Squirt, why do you care?"

"She done gone an' wupped us all, looks at Pepper's black patches!"

Without a doubt, Lulu, who was half the size of her brothers, had put the cast to good use over the last month. She had made them pay dearly for any past transgressions on their part. She didn't seem disappointed to find out she still had a couple of weeks left to torment her brothers. Her ma came out to meet us and assured me she would bring Lulu to the clinic in two weeks so that I could cut the cast off. Apparently, it had been a point of contention in the family the entire time she had been wearing it.

My next patient was two valleys and three ridges away. Jinx insisted on resting twice before we reached the cabin. I assured him that since we had slowed the pace, I was once again able to continue without stopping, but he was not about to be deterred. My final visit was a little more complicated and disturbing. The mother of the family had died from pneumonia the winter before, and now the youngest daughter was pregnant. We had no idea how old she was, but Bev had told me that she could not be any older than fifteen. A shy and timid child, she would say absolutely nothing about who was the father of the baby. She had been fainting regularly enough that her older brother had brought her to my clinic one day against the wishes of his father.

Her pregnancy was not progressing normally. She was not gaining weight, and the baby remained extremely small in size even though her brother assured me she would be having it within the next month. I pressed him on how he could be so certain, but he would say nothing else. I knew that my visit would not be welcomed, but this child about to be a mother tugged at my heart for all the obvious reasons. Her pa met us at the door. I could see the girl standing behind him in the doorway of the cabin. It was fairly evident that he did not want me treating his daughter.

"Ya ain't needed har. Ma boy should'n of nev'r mixed yous up in this. It ain't none of yourn' business."

"I just want to check her health, Mr. Day."

"She be fine, now git 'fer I sic my dawg on ya."

"Okay, sorry we bothered you."

I led Jinx away from the cabin and took the path toward the lake. We didn't speak for several minutes. Voices carry well in the quite mountain air. When we dropped down into the lake valley, Jinx ventured to ask me about the Day girl.

"You gave up on the poor girl awfully quick, Rea. Did you see her? She looks like a walking skeleton with a bloated belly."

"I have dealt with her father before when her mother was sick. He doesn't make false threats. His dog is one evil animal. I didn't expect him to be so stubborn today. Something is definitely not right about this situation."

"Have you dealt with his dog before?"

The tone in Jinx's voice made me stop and look back in his direction. He had stopped walking and seemed to be contemplating something as he stared off into the distance.

"No, but he brought him down to the clinic the day after his wife died. He had come the day before to demand I give him the medicine that he had heard could cure his wife. I refused to hand the antibiotics over to him; he refused to bring her down to the clinic or allow me to go near her. His visit after her death was one of the truly scarier moments of my time here. He stood on the mission porch and pronounced a mountain curse upon me for not saving his wife. Bev and Joshua handled the situation like pros. It seems that curses are spewed forth in abundance in these mountains. It is unnerving though when you are on the receiving end of those violent words."

"What was the curse?"

"Well, if it had been effective we would not be talking right now."

"I can't believe you went there after what he did."

"It isn't the girl's fault her father is cruel; besides the mountain people believe that if the curse doesn't stick on you it bounces back and sticks to them. In essence, they end up cursing themselves. Since his curse had no effect on me, he has been sitting around waiting on the ax to fall, so to speak. All he has left to threaten me with is the dog, which is enough."

"Well, you won't be making anymore trips into these mountains without me along. Do you understand?"

"Fine by me. But just so you know, Joshua has always come with me before. Now I'm getting hungry, so let's get down to the lake so we can eat. Oh, and by the way, we need to keep an eye out for bears."

"I have been warned about the bears—that's why I brought my pistol."

"I love a man who's prepared for any emergency."

"That sounded less than sincere."

The lake came into view just as Jinx finished his sentence, and I turned to point out the wild turkeys pecking around the meadow. "They'll let us know if there are any bears around. How about eating over under that big oak?"

Jinx stopped beneath the tree, took an old quilt out of the basket, and spread it on the ground. He built a small fire to warm up the leftover quail meat from our supper the prior night. While we greedily consumed the cornbread, goat cheese, and quail meat he had supplied for our lunch, we watched the wildlife move about the valley floor. A doe stepped out of the woods not far from us followed by a pair of fawns. Hawks circled above the trees trying to pick out small prey on the valley floor. The turkeys continued their pecking as they walked away from us, turning to look back in our direction occasionally.

"Wish I had brought my shotgun. We could have turkey for supper tonight."

"I can't believe you came this far away from the mission without it. I've grown accustomed to seeing you with it close by all the time."

"I thought that bringing a shotgun on our date would not be proper. Since the war, I have not gone far without a gun in tow. Remember I have a pistol in the basket. We are here to have fun though, so enough talk about guns. That lake is really beautiful. I've been sitting here thinking that as hot as it is a dip might make the day perfect."

"Be my guest, but I didn't bring my suit."

"Well, I was thinking we really don't need suits. My brothers and I went skinny dipping all the time back home."

"You want me to strip down naked and go swimming in broad daylight in front of God and everybody?"

"We are in the middle of nowhere, Rea."

"Actually we aren't. Do you see that ridge right there?"

Jinx turned to look in the direction I was pointing and answered, "Yes."

"There's a cabin on that ridge. And in the cabin lives a man by the name of Uncle Charlie Kates. Uncle Charlie has a pair of binoculars—a rarity in these hills. He considers what goes on in this valley as his personal entertainment. Now not many people know about those binoculars. I found out when we put him to sleep to clean out a wound that would not heal on his leg. As he came out from under the ether, he began to tell us what he had seen through those binoculars. His tales were so embarrassing to Bev she had to leave the room. I have no doubt that he has been watching us since we got here. As tempting as a swim would be, I really don't want him spreading a description of me naked around the mountain population."

"You're sure he's watching?"

"Positive."

"Okay, I will agree about the naked part, but I still want to go for a swim." Jinx jumped to his feet. Before I could resist, he easily swept me up and across his shoulders, turned and began walking toward the lake.

"Jinx, please don't! The water is freezing."

"I need a nice cold swim, and you're going in with me."

Within seconds, he tossed me back first into the frigid lake. The extremely cold water sucked the breath out of me. It took a few seconds for my muscles to work. I knew Jinx followed me in because I heard and felt the splash nearby. When I came up for air, he was nowhere in sight. Waiting on him to grab me from beneath, I began to work my way toward the bank. As the seconds dragged by, I started to panic. I felt my foot brush something soft, but it did not move. I dove beneath the surface and found him lying motionless on the floor of the lake. Without thinking, I grabbed him by the shoulders and began to drag him out of the lake. Once I reached a few inches of water, I could move him no farther. I flipped him on his back and checked to see if he was still breathing. When I could feel no breath, I tilted his head back to begin giving him air. I was in such a panic that I forgot to feel for his pulse. Mine, however, was racing, and I was so cold that I had a hard time concentrating. When I bent down to blow air into his mouth, his arms came up around my neck, and he kissed me with more passion than he had exhibited before. Under other circumstances, I would have been blown away by that kiss, but I was too scared, cold, and angry to consider the tenderness contained in that moment. I scrambled to my feet and stomped out of the water leaving him laughing in the wake.

"Rea, don't be mad. I just couldn't resist."

I bit the side of my mouth trying to restrain the tears I could feel in my eyes. I was shaking from cold and fear. I realized that I cared for Jinx much more deeply than I had ever thought possible. I remembered the many times he had frightened me while we worked together and tried to calm myself down before I said something I would regret. I finally made it to the quilt and drug it out into the sunshine to sit in the sun. Jinx was right behind me by the time I lowered myself onto the blanket.

"I'm sorry, Rea. I didn't mean to scare you. I thought you would remember that I could hold my breath a really long time. It just seemed like an excellent opportunity to steal a kiss." As he spoke Jinx placed his arms around me and tried to rub warmth back into my arms.

"I'm not mad, Jinx. But I was scared; please don't ever do anything like that again. You don't have to go to such lengths for a kiss."

"I don't. Really?"

This time, Jinx took his finger to raise my face to his and placed his lips right up to mine and said, "You're sure Uncle Charlie is watching?"

"Uh huh, but don't pay him no mind."

This time, the kiss warmed even my purple toes and fingers. Before I could think straight, Jinx jumped to his feet and proclaimed it was time to head back to the mission so we could get out of the wet clothes. I sat completely still, soaking in the sun and letting the love in that kiss fill up empty places in my heart. It occurred to me that Jinx was the first person to ever really kiss me.

"Jinx, do you know that you are the first person to kiss me?"

Bridge Over Calm Water

"I don't believe that! You cannot tell me that considering all those men you met at the university, not one ever kissed you."

"No, I really paid very little attention to guys unless I had to work with them in some class. I believe that the majority of them weren't impressed by the country hick in overalls."

"So you took your overalls to Knoxville? I was under the impression that Sarah sent you clothes on a regular basis."

"Oh she did, but I donated the majority of them to charities. I would never want to hurt her feelings, but the clothes she sent made me feel very uncomfortable."

"Well, that explains why someone didn't steal you away before I could get back home."

"I thought you said something once about remembering me in my overalls while you were in the prison camp?"

"I had the advantage of seeing you in your swimsuit every once and awhile."

"I don't recall us ever going swimming together."

"Oh, we didn't. Your pa would have never allowed you to swim with anyone but your brothers. I happened to be doing some squirrel hunting one day and heard y'all laughing down at the river. After I discovered where you went to swim, I planned my hunting trips for the days when I caught wind of the fact you were going there to cool off after work."

"Jinx Cummings, you spied on me!"

"Guilty as charged and not sorry one bit that I did."

The trip back to the mission did not seem nearly as long as the trip out had been. We walked hand and hand talking continuously as Jinx questioned me about what I would like to have for our new cabin. The rest of the afternoon a strange sort of calm and peace wrapped around me like a warm blanket. I wondered if people who had the opportunity to court for a while before they married felt like I did on that day. I wished I could make the feeling last forever.

CHAPTER ELEVEN

Sorrow

During the last week of August, the humidity rose to an almost unbearable level. The cabin walls were up, and the men had begun setting the heavy beams for the roof. Something seemed odd about the design of the beams, but Jinx just ignored my questions when I could get his attention long enough to ask him about it. I have to admit I made several attempts at getting him to repeat the kiss in the meadow, but he always seemed to be unaware of the opportunity before him. At first, I chalked it up to the pressure and pace of the building. Fall was looming, and I knew he wanted the cabin to be completed by the time the temperature dropped below a comfortable level.

As the weeks passed, my confidence in his love had begun to waver, and I feared that he didn't want to kiss me. That fear began to consume my every waking moment and my dreams. I was short-tempered with my patients and slow in thought and deed. It became increasingly difficult to concentrate, and watching Jinx at work did nothing to help my mood.

I woke the morning of the last day of August with a severe headache brought on by disturbing dreams and a lack of sleep. Bev sent me to the porch with a glass of herbal tea and instructions to stay out of the sun. I did not like being idle; my mind always wandered back in time and across the miles between me and Rock Island, and I would begin to think about Lilly. I still received short reports from Robert when he sent me supplies for the clinic, but it was never enough to give me a sense of the person Lilly was becoming. To my annoyance, he never elaborated beyond her health and apparent contentment in their home. I was still haunted by the decision to give her up—even though I kept trying to convince myself it was the right one.

Sitting in the porch swing that morning, I had an easy view of all the work going on across the fifty or so yards to the cabin. Several daughters of the men working at the site had begun showing up with the excuse of bringing their fathers' lunches. Bev had been right about their obvious infatuation with my husband. More often than not, the women of these mountains began as true natural beauties before hard work had a chance to destroy their looks. Of the eight or so standing around the cabin that morning, most were quite pretty. One was absolutely gorgeous and demonstrated an ever-increasing interest in Jinx.

Sally Karin was one of those women other women longed to see when they gazed into their mirrors. Long, auburn hair fell in waves down Sally's back. Her complexion was the color of whipped cream, and her figure was flawless. She knew she had the attention of every man, young or old, and she relished in her power to make them turn and stare in her direction as she swayed by.

To Jinx's credit, I never actually saw him make a deliberate effort to take in her beauty as the other men did. She was a determined young woman, however, and took every opportunity to corner him and start a conversation. Bev assured me she was no threat, but I just couldn't seem to accept the truth of that statement. Especially on this unusually hot day. In the heat it did not take long for the men to begin shedding their shirts. Jinx kept his on until the sweat poured off of him like water. Heatstroke was a real possibility, and I began to worry.

Pushing myself up from the porch swing, I went to the well and lowered the water bucket down into the dark coolness for some of the spring water. Once it was full, I cranked it to the top and reached to unhook it. Before I could grab the handle, an arm reached beyond me to take hold on the bucket.

"Bev says you have one of your headaches. You do not need to be out in this sun carrying water."

"Bev has a tendency to talk too much. Besides, you and the men are the ones needing to be careful. I really don't feel like treating you all for heatstroke."

"We're used to hard work, but I am about to call for a break."

"I noticed lunch seems to be getting delivered earlier and earlier." The remark sounded sour, but I felt sour at the moment.

"Yep, we are attracting quite a crowd these days."

"Not we, you."

Jinx rolled his eyes, shook his head, and planted a kiss on the top of my head.

"I have a mouth you know." The words came out before I could stop them.

Jinx bent down and whispered in my ear, "I am painfully aware of your mouth." He turned and headed back toward the cabin.

When I recovered my senses, I yelled in his direction to cool off before he went back to work. He turned and smiled at me, set down the bucket, and stripped off his sweat-soaked shirt. I could not be so dumb as to miss the message he sent me across that yard. I also could not miss the look on Sally Karin's face. If she kept it up, I would be forced to yank that pretty auburn hair right out of her head one day, and I might really enjoy doing it.

The headache stayed with me all week. Jinx began to watch me whenever I came out of the mission. Several patients had shown up with various injuries. A few were in need of stitches and a couple had broken bones. One of the boys who came in that week was the youngest son of Mr. Day. I tried not to ask about the welfare of his sister, for fear of the father, but I could not resist. Her situation tugged at my heart. Right before he walked out, I let the question slip from my lips, "How is your sister doing—has she had her baby yet?"

"Na, she be hurt'n' today, Pa say it come soon."

I knew that I could not go to help her and that made my headache jump into my stomach. I ran out the back door and grabbed the first tree to keep from passing out. I slid down the trunk, bark cutting into my back, and dropped my head between my knees. The noise from the cabin construction was not so intense behind the mission, and the air was cooler coming out of the trees. Knowing I would be covered in chiggers and ticks did not keep me from lying down on the mossy ground and drifting off into a painful, hazy sleep. Time passed; I suddenly felt myself being carried in strong arms and laid gently on a bed. Opening my eyes increased the nausea, but I needed to see Jinx before I faced the night.

"What time is it?"

"It's not late, the sun is still up. Now close your eyes and rest."

"Will you wake me up in a little while?"

"Maybe, depends on how you sleep."

"Jinx?"

"Yes, Rea."

"Thanks for bringing me in. I love you."

"You're welcome. I love you too." Words are so powerful, that I already knew, but his words helped lull me into a peaceful pain-free sleep.

Jinx did not have to return to wake me. A faint cry from outside drew me back to face the pain in my head. At first, I thought I had dreamed the sound into existence, but I heard the pitiful cry again. I eased myself up to keep from making myself sick and walked into the main part of the mission. Bev was busy cooking the evening meal. I could see Joshua and Jinx standing on the front porch of our cabin talking to some of the workers.

"Bev, did you hear that crying somewhere outside?"

She turned to me with an unreadable expression on her face. "Where did it sound like it was coming from?"

"Somewhere out back."

"Come on—we need to check on this right now."

I followed her out the back door and around to the side of the mission where the woods ran almost up to the wall. There in the tall grass was a small bundle of dirty rags. Bev stopped me before I reached to pick it up.

"Ella, this is not going to be easy for you to accept, but sometimes death is more merciful than life. If this is what I think it is, this is one of those times."

She reached past me and gently lifted the rag bundle out of the weeds. A strange mewing sound began to seep out from inside. Bev led me back into the mission toward the room that served as my clinic. Very gently, she laid the bundle on the examination table and carefully unfolded the rags to reveal the tiny creature inside.

I had never seen a baby so badly deformed. All of the limbs were malformed, and the head was larger on one side than the other. Bev went to warm some water over the fire to wash the child off, and I began to examine the little boy more closely. Turning him over caused the child to wail in pain. To my horror, I discovered that the lower half of his spine was open. By the time Bev returned, I had dissolved into hysteria and was sitting by the table rocking in rhythm with the baby's cries. I managed to tell her about his spine but was no help in cleaning him up. She wrapped him in soft flannel cloth and laid him on a large, feather pillow.

"We can only try to keep him comfortable. As you know, most of these babies do not live very long."

"There have been others like this?"

"Unfortunately, yes, but we will talk about that later. I am going to get Joshua to start on a casket. You stay here and keep him company. I know it's hard, but I think the babies know when someone is close. They seem to calm some. He needs a name, Ella. Could you come up with one please?"

She left me sitting there weighed down with sorrow and something close to fury. I knew without a doubt the mother of this child was Mr. Day's daughter. This was his grandchild, and by the looks of things, maybe his child. I had heard of this sort of thing in medical school. I knew that it happened in remote places. I had just never seen it for myself. I tried to focus on the baby and give him whatever comfort I could manage. I could not sing, but I did try to hum. His wails turned to mews and, eventually, he ceased to cry at all. The small struggled gasps of a child fighting to survive overpowered the silence in that room.

Jinx walked in and drew up a chair beside me. We sat in a silent vigil deep into the night. Sometime near midnight, the tiny forlorn and deserted child gasped for one final breath; his time on this earth had passed. Jinx helped me wrap him in clean flannel once more.

"There isn't anything else we can do, Rea. We'll help Joshua and Bev bury him in the morning."

"But I still don't have a name for him Jinx."

"Once you've had some rest, you'll think of one."

Taking the oil lamp in his hand, he led me out of the room and away from the pitiful little baby. My headache had intensified, and I could no longer focus. It never occurred to me to wonder at the fact that Jinx led me to my room and gently undressed me, helping me into my gown. He lifted me into bed and climbed in beside me fully clothed. He remained there until I awoke in his arms the next morning. I still felt the sorrow from the death of the baby, but the pain of the headache was gone. The name for the child came to me in that thought. I would name him Sorrow because he was the embodiment of human sorrow.

I was unsuccessful at removing myself from Jinx's arms without waking him. He tightened his hold and spoke softly into my neck.

"Are you so anxious to get away from me this morning, Rea?"

"No, I just thought I would go and see if Bev needed my help with breakfast. I'm sure she's tired of being our maid."

"She'll understand if you don't show up early this morning. We are all concerned that this headache you've been having has gone on for too long. I am considering taking you to a doctor outside of these mountains and have you checked."

"It's gone, not a sign of it this morning."

"I am still going to leave the option open in case it comes back. Now, lie back down and try to rest. I will go and offer to help Bev. I will bring you something back to eat in a little while."

I tried to obey, but the image of baby Sorrow kept coming back into my mind. Finally, I climbed out of bed and dressed for the day. After breakfast, we placed the baby in the tiny casket Joshua had completed during the night and carried it out behind the mission to a small, cleared opening several yards into the woods. I had never been to this spot before. What I saw before me was a tragedy. Rows of tiny crosses stood at various angles to the ground. Sorrow would not lie alone but in the company of many. A tiny grave was already dug in the ground.

"Joshua, did you dig this out since last night?"

"No, someone from the family of the child dug the grave during the late of night. We never hear or see anyone, but the grave is always ready the morning after a child like this one dies. Some have lived for days, yet the grave is never dug until after the death."

Joshua said a few simple words over Sorrow. Then, he and Jinx placed the casket in the grave. Just as they finished, we could hear men gathering in the front to begin work.

I looked to Jinx and Joshua, "Go on and get started on the cabin. I can fill in the grave."

"Are you sure you want to do that, Rea?"

"I'll be fine." Joshua handed me the shovel and left with Jinx. Bev hesitated, but I nodded her away with an attempt at a smile. Then I turned to face the open grave. I had been feeling the same odd sensation that I felt the night I walked the deserted road to the bridge. Someone was out in the woods watching all of this. I began to deliberately fill the dirt in over the grave. I prayed that God placed Sorrow in the care of angels and that he know only love and happiness. As I finished patting the dirt down, I heard a small noise off to my left. Standing several feet back in the trees was the emaciated girl that had given birth only the day before. She was crying softly and staring at the grave that held her baby.

"Just so you'll know, I named him Sorrow."

She nodded that she understood, and I turned and left her to grieve in private. Several more of these deformed babies would find their way to the mission while I lived in the mountains. With each one, my soul once again knew devastation, but none were as difficult to bear as Sorrow.

Lilly occupied my mind for several days after the death and burial of Sorrow. I kept comparing myself to the mother who had

Bridge Over Calm Water

hidden in the trees. We were both young and had to bear children against our will. She grieved for a child so badly deformed that he would seem almost unlovable. I grieved for a child so very beautiful she could make my heart leap in my chest. Maybe our grief was not bound to just our children. Maybe we grieved for our chance to live a normal life or for the sheer misery of being unable to choose for ourselves when and who would father our children. The last was becoming increasingly hard not to dwell on, considering how much I was growing to love Jinx and how very badly I would love to have carried his children within me.

Try as I might, I could not keep my spirits up, and Jinx eventually noticed. Late one afternoon, I was checking a perfectly healthy baby girl that a young mother had delivered the day before. Because of Ina's faith in my abilities with newborns, nearly all the new mothers brought their children to be examined right after birth. No matter how perfect these children might be, the mothers seemed to all be very nervous until I told them their babies were healthy. I began to suspect that the babies buried in the back might be offspring of more of the women in the area than Bev thought was possible. She considered the practice of incest to be limited to a few families that isolated themselves on far away ridges and hollers. I wasn't so sure she was right.

As I finished up the examination and led the mother out onto the porch, Jinx walked up the steps and stopped to stand by me and compliment the new mom on her beautiful little girl. The mother and baby left in happy spirits, and I turned to thank Jinx for his kindness. He spoke before I could.

"Rea, I was thinking that a stroll down to the creek would be nice after we finish. Before we leave, I want to give you a tour of the cabin. It's almost finished."

"Really? I had no idea you were so far along. I would love a tour and wading in the creek sounds refreshing. I can leave anytime, just come and get me."

"Wonderful! It won't be long before we finish for the day."

Knowing that the cabin would soon be ready to move into raised my sagging spirits. Jinx had begun avoiding close contact with me. He confided in Joshua, who went straight to Bev that it was becoming increasingly difficult not to start the honeymoon phase of our marriage before the cabin was completed. He and Joshua also had been building a bed in the back shed, a surprise I was not allowed to see. Bev took me aside one day and encouraged me not to make the wait any more difficult for Jinx than it already was. Apparently, the men had somehow picked up on the fact that Jinx and I were married in word only and had begun making remarks. Jinx was taking quite a bit of ribbing from all of the married men. Some of the unmarried ones had begun to suggest I might get tired of waiting on him and decide to choose one of them. I had lost interest days ago in watching the progress on the cabin. Day after day, I was forced to watch the young women flirting with my husband while I had to keep my distance. This whole idea of a courtship had begun to give me a bitter taste in my mouth.

Jinx returned within the hour and led me by the hand to the cabin that I had not entered since the walls were raised. He had built us a small entry room so that we did not walk directly into the main living area from the outside. Although he had taken a great deal of criticism from the men working for him, this would help keep the cabin warmer during the winter. Stepping across the threshold into the heart of the structure felt oddly comforting. The main room was large and the hearth had been laid out of beautiful limestone. The walls were tightly sealed. No wind would find its way in during the cold months. Jinx smiled as I ran my hand along a beautifully carved mantel.

"Did you make this?"

"Yes, I had that wood shipped in from home. The tree came from your father's farm."

I turned and promptly threw my arms around Jinx's neck. "Thank you Jinx, what a sweet surprise!"

"I thought you might like it."

"I love it."

Slowly he unwound my arms with a sheepish smile on his face. "We aren't finished touring."

"Oh, right, sorry."

Taking my hand again, he walked me back to the bedroom, but to my utter disappointment there was no bed. "Where's the bed?"

"I didn't think you were that anxious for me to finish the bed."

"Are you kidding me? I honestly don't know how much longer I can tolerate this courting."

Jinx swept me up into his arms and crushed me in a fierce hug. Then he kissed me, and it was a kiss to remember. I completely forgot we were standing in the cabin. I forgot we were in the mountains. I forgot we were just courting. I forgot my promise to Bev, but unfortunately, Jinx didn't forget. He gently placed me back on my feet and waited for me to come back to my senses.

"We have waited so long now I refuse to spoil the surprise I have planned for the first night in this cabin. I have one more thing to show you, and then we'll go down to the creek and cool off in the water."

He led me to a small storage room behind the bedroom. To my left was a narrow steep stairway. Looking back at Jinx I waited for an explanation, but he pointed me up the stairs. Once I reached the top, I stepped onto a platform that had been built above the roof of the back porch.

"I don't understand. What is this for?"

"This is for you to sit out on and gaze at the stars without me worrying about you being outside alone. I know that you sneak out at all times of the night and lay on your back in the yard staring up at the sky. I don't want you out there when I am asleep and can't protect you."

"I doubt there is any danger that you need to worry about, but I appreciate you going to the trouble to build me an observation deck."

"We didn't think you would be hurt on the bridge, but you were. I don't intend to take any more chances."

"How long have you known about my star gazing?"

Jan Kendall

"Since right after we married. I heard a noise one night and went to investigate. Do Bev and Joshua know about your late night activities?"

"I never thought about telling them."

"I'm pretty sure they wouldn't approve, they feel very protective of you."

"Really, it was not my intention to worry anyone. I just feel so peaceful staring up at all those thousands of stars. It also keeps me humble knowing how really small and insignificant I am compared to the universe."

"You're not insignificant to me. So once we move in, you'll be doing your star gazing from here."

"Once we move in."

"Yes, and from now on, if you get the urge to sneak out you are going to have my company. I sleep very lightly, and I hear you when you tiptoe out. Up until now, I have watched you through the window; from now on, I will be out there with you."

"Really, I think you are being way too protective, but the thought makes me love you even more."

"There are some mean people in these mountains, Rea. I can never be too careful."

"Okay, can we go to the creek now? This heat is unbearable."

"Lead the way, my lady."

We did not have the creek to ourselves. Apparently half of the mountain population had the same idea. Men and women, young and old, sat along the banks and on the rocks above the slow moving water. Children of all ages splashed and swam in the shallow pools. We were greeted warmly by most and stared at by others.

To my dismay, Sally and a few of the other young unmarried women were gathered in a cluster not far down the bank by a popular swimming hole. They were watching several young men show off their skills at diving from the high, rocky bank. On occasion, they would surface close to the girls and splash them with the water or grab one and pull her in. Once they were wet, the lightweight cotton dresses clung like a second skin to the women's bodies, leaving absolutely nothing to

Bridge Over Calm Water

the imagination of the men in the water or on the bank. These young women showed little shame, if any, and even the old men could not keep their eyes off of the antics taking place only a few yards away.

Jinx seated himself with his back to the women and began to chatter happily about the few things that he had left to do on the cabin. Materials had already been ordered to begin the clinic; he was confident that it too would be finished by Thanksgiving. I listened contentedly to his plans and watched the creek minnows darting in and out of the rocks beneath my feet. At first, I did not hear my name being called until Jinx stopped in mid sentence and took my arm.

"Doc Ella, did ya har me?"

I followed Jinx's gaze down the riverbank to a flat rock where Sally Karin stood, hands on her hips and her dress not only wet and clinging, but nearly sheer in the afternoon sun.

"I says ta ya that people round har been saying that thar purty fellar of yourn ain't ner bedded ya. That so Doc Ella? Cause I be mor'n happy to takes car' of that fer ya."

Jinx tightened his grip on my arm and turned to face me. "Pay no attention to her, Rea. She is uneducated and not very popular even among her own people."

"They's a saying sumpun' be wrong with ya. Tha' ya cain't be no real wife."

Jinx jumped to his feet to head in her direction, but I stopped him before he could take a step. What could I say, for I was the one who had to speak? The answer to the first question was yes and everyone along this bank knew it. The second statement could also be true. Robert had been honest with me and Jinx the morning of our wedding. He was not sure how my injuries would affect my physical relationship with Jinx. I'm sure that Jinx worried about what would happen during the fast approaching honeymoon night. Jinx was staring deep into my eyes. The pain for me was evident in his face.

I leaned in close so only he could hear me. "It matters not one bit to me what these people think about us, but I want you to know that I wouldn't have started our marriage any other way.

It's been hard, I hope as hard for you as for me, but it was the best thing for us."

I stepped around him and faced Sally. I spoke in a loud enough voice to be heard by everyone. "You are right Sally, my husband hasn't, how did you put it, bedded me yet." Turning, I looked at Jinx and smiled. "And in a way, I'm not a whole woman. Dr. McKinney had to take what is most precious to a woman, my ability to have children, in order to save my life when I was not as old as you. We aren't sure how that will affect my ability to be a real wife to Jinx. But know this. I love him with all that I have left within me. When he breathes, I breathe; when he hurts, I hurt. From now on, where he goes I will follow. I may not be a real wife, by your standards, but your standards are not very noble ones. I would prefer that if anyone has any other questions about me, instead of gossiping behind our backs, that you just come and ask me to my face."

Jinx stepped to my side and placed his arm around my waist, looked over the crowd, and then turned and guided me away from the creek back toward the mission. As we began to walk away, he said very clearly and quite loudly, "I am devoted to you, just in case anyone is wondering how I feel."

"Thank you for clearing that up for me."

After that day at the creek, Sally Karin never showed her face at the mission again. Four years later, her body was found naked and floating face down in that swimming hole, her head bashed in by a bloody rock lying on the shore.

The only thing I ever heard concerning her death came from my friend Ina. Late one night, she came to take me with her to help save a woman who was trying to deliver a baby in the breach position. The poor woman kept mumbling about being punished for something. When we were successful in turning the child and saving her life, she kept thanking me and assuring me justice had been delivered on our enemy by her hand. On the way back down the mountain, I asked Ina what she could have meant.

"She be a talkin' bout that thar Karin she devil."

I stopped dead in my tracks and grabbed Ina's shoulder to turn her back in my direction. "Do you mean she was telling me she was the one that bashed in her head?"

"Reckon so."

"Does anyone else know she did it?"

"Thar's been talk."

"What will happen to her when everyone finds out?"

"Mountain justis, it be old Bible justis. Eye fer a eye, twont' be nothn' done. That thar she devil tried ta kill the love of a man fer his woman. Sa it be his woman's right ta take her'n life in return. You be quik ta forgiv', Ella. You be lucky that thar husban' of yourn' sa faithful."

The years that separated that day on the bank and Ina's explanation of Sally's death had proven to me the worth of a faithful husband. But as Jinx and I walked back from the creek that day, I was not so confident in myself or my husband.

CHAPTER TWELVE

Home at Last

The episode at the creek haunted my dreams for the next few days. I began to quiz Jinx daily as to the progress on our home. He took it all in good humor telling me we were so close he could move us in right then, but he was waiting on Gus to return from the railway with one last addition to the cabin. The workers broke ground for the clinic as I continued to treat the few patients I had coming to see me at the mission. Ina came to visit me not long after the embarrassing incident with Sally and before I had time to completely recover. She brought a bag of herbs that she said would help relieve the pain I had been having in my head.

"I don't suppose you'll tell me how you knew my head had been hurting again. I haven't told a soul."

"Tain't hard ta figur seein' you had that thar run-in with that thar wild cat woman."

"Apparently, we have been the topic of much conversation among our neighbors."

"Yous different that fer sure, tain't no way to keeps peoples from a talkin'. Best jest to turn a deaf ear. Jest wondern' though, I gots me a mountain potion sure ta bring that thar man around. If you be needn' it, I gots it in this har pouch, only gots to mix it in hisn coffee ever mornin."

"That's sweet of you to offer Ina, but I prefer to let things come about naturally if you know what I mean."

Bridge Over Calm Water

"Tain't wise ta ignor them thar women like that thar Karin girl. Theys don't gives up."

"I hope that we pass out of the courting phase and on to the honeymoon in a few days."

"Humph . . . . That thar husband of yourn' don't seem right in da head."

"Like you said, we're different."

"I's keeps it made up if youn' change yourn mind."

"Thanks, Ina, I won't forget."

I walked Ina outside. To my relief, I saw Gus standing in the yard with a pack mule. Jinx was in the process of unloading something rather bulky. "Ina, my salvation has arrived."

"Gus ain't nevar saved nobody."

"Not Gus, whatever Jinx is unloading off that mule."

"What evers on that thar mule gonna get your'n husband in da mood?"

"As a matter of fact, yes."

Ina turned and looked at me oddly. I suppose the conversation had taken on bizarre nature, but I was so excited to see the delivery I didn't really care to explain. She left me standing on the porch. As she walked away, she shook her head and laughed.

As soon as Gus took his mule and left, I expected Jinx to come and get me, but he didn't. I sat down on the porch to wait, but he never came back out of the cabin. Darkness started to fall, and even though I had every right to walk the short distance to the cabin door and see what was in the box, I didn't. I sat there on the porch and stewed. I stewed about how frustrating it had been to be married to Jinx but not be treated like a real wife. I stewed about the gossip going around the mountains that implied that my husband had no interest in me physically. I stewed about having to air my most horrible past to the general public. I stewed until the sun fell and I had a headache so severe I could barely open my eyes. When I saw a lamp being lit inside the cabin, I knew he would not come out anytime soon, so I went to bed with a pounding head. Bev tried in vain to get me to eat, but I could not bear the thought of food.

"You need to let Jinx take you to see a doctor, Rea. These headaches aren't normal."

"I've had them off and on all my life. Besides, Jinx is the reason for this one."

Bev didn't pry into the exact cause and left me in peace to stomp myself off to bed. Eventually, I must have fallen asleep because I awoke with a start sometime deep in the night. The room was pitch black. The headache had abandoned me but had left me little strength. Unfortunately, I was still upset with Jinx. I reasoned it was childish on my part, but it didn't make the whole situation any easier to bear. I had fallen asleep on top of the bed still dressed in my work clothes. Deciding to take advantage of the dark, starry night, I grabbed my quilt and carried it to the yard. The air was cool and refreshing; I found my favorite spot to stretch out with little effort. As I scanned the sky searching out the constellations, I realized someone was standing very close to me at my head.

"I told you, I don't like you coming out here without bringing me along."

"Honestly, it didn't occur to me to wake you up."

"I came to get you earlier, but you were already in your room with a headache, according to Bev."

"Yep, it was pretty bad, but it's gone now. I have found in the past that the night air always helps clear the cobwebs that are left behind."

"Are you mad at me, Rea?"

"Bev tell you that?"

"No, but I know you so well I can tell by the tone of your voice."

"All right since you asked. I saw Gus in the yard this afternoon. His delivery was the last excuse you had to keep us out of the cabin. Do you know that Ina came here today to offer me some kind of love potion? Seems everyone believes that you are not the least bit attracted to me, and now I need help to inspire you so to speak."

Jinx started laughing. He dropped down on the quilt and picked me up into his arms. "Don't say another word, Rea.

Just listen to me for a minute. I'm not laughing at you, just at how stupid all of these people are. You're the most beautiful woman in these mountains, and you're my wife. I made you wait because I wanted to give you a chance to love me as much as I love you. Now you lie here and stare at those stars, and I'll go light a lamp in the cabin and come back and get you."

"Let me go with you!"

"Can you please just do what I ask?"

"Yes."

"Thanks, my love."

My heart pounded hard enough to bruise my chest. I began to hyperventilate; lying still to look at the stars was impossible. It occurred to me I was reacting like some lovesick school girl. To be honest, I liked it. I had never in my life felt so alive and so out of control. I was so wrapped up in all my emotions that I didn't hear Jinx walk back. He pulled me up off the quilt and threw it over his shoulder. Then he swept me up into his arms and carried me across the yard into the cabin. He sat me down inside the living area and closed and latched both the doors. "That's just in case you try to make a run for it. Come with me."

Taking me by the hand, he led me through the house to the back storage room, walking quickly past the large bed in the back. I tried to grab at the huge carved post to stop his progress but missed and left all of my wonderful emotions that screamed for attention clinging to the post. He never looked back to notice my confusion as we climbed the little staircase to the observation platform. Once we reached the top, Jinx stepped from in front of me so that I could look past him. I gasped at the sight of a fully assembled telescope.

"This is your wedding gift. You won't believe what you can see through this thing. Our commander had one set up on the ship, and we all learned how to use it. I remembered you telling me how you would sneak outside at night when you were still on the farm. Your pa would talk about how crazy he thought you were. I already had it ordered when I came here to try and get you to marry me. I watched you for several nights before I caught you sneaking out. Then I knew you were still enchanted by the stars and would like my gift."

To say the least, I struggled at that moment to comprehend all the love pouring into me. "It's wonderful. Will you teach me how to use it?"

"Take a look, I have it set up. It's what took so long to get back to the mission this afternoon. I had to wait until after dark to finish."

He didn't have to ask me twice. I had already forgotten that I was now on my honeymoon. Once I took my first look into the heavens through Jinx's gift, I was frozen by the incredible view the telescope presented. As I stared in amazement, Jinx moved behind me and slid his arms around my waist. He began to kiss me very lightly on the back of my neck. With each kiss, my concentration deteriorated and my knees began to turn to mush.

"At the risk of interrupting your star gazing, I have decided to demand my rights as your husband."

I made an attempt at a feeble protest, but my heart wasn't in it and Jinx knew it. As we descended the steps, the attack on the bridge flashed across my mind causing me to gasp. Jinx stopped and turned back to face me.

"What?"

"Nothing, keep going."

"I don't believe you. You're pale as a ghost."

"Just a flashback of that night on the bridge. I'm sorry, Jinx. It just popped into my mind. But it's gone now. Really, it's no big deal."

"Oh, Rea, I would never hurt you."

I took his face in my hands and kissed away the worry from between his eyes. "That thought has never entered my mind. But I do worry that this might not be as wonderful as it would have been had that night never happened. Will you leave me if I am not able to be a whole woman for you?"

"Do you remember the night I slept next to you in your bed when Sorrow died?"

"Yes."

"I knew then that whatever happened on this night would only add more stars to my heaven."

He lifted me into his arms and carried me into the bedroom and, literally, into another world. My fears and his were unfounded. I don't know how other women feel the first time they are loved. But for me, it was as if I had been seeing everything in black and white. After that night, my life was full of the brightest most wonderful colors. I was not prepared for the feelings that consumed my mind and captured my heart. I did not know that I could be possessed by another human being in such a way. I craved his touch and the sound of his voice. I suffered when we were separated by great distance or time. I was constantly worried about his welfare and ever vigilant to be attentive to his health. What I had said that day at the creek became truly real; my breath and heartbeat were connected directly to his.

I suppose a wise woman might wonder if she is loved as much as she loves. I did not care. For after that night, my life became one and the same as his; I was devoted to Jinx. Whatever the future would throw our way, I had no intention of ever letting him face it alone. I say all this as though other people could see the change in me as much as I could feel it. In all honesty, I doubt they had any idea. I continued my life pretty much as before. I wanted to keep what we had sequestered and hidden away. Jinx seemed to understand, or maybe he felt the same way. It was as if we had discovered some hidden treasure, so immense and precious, that to protect it we had to keep it out of the sight of those who might want to steal it from us.

The mountain people quickly became aware that we lived together in the cabin, and it was assumed we had taken up the normal activities associated with man and wife. They inferred upon us their own experiences and never realized we had transformed like two worms emerging from cocoons as butterflies. I never knew of Jinx discussing our personal relationship with anyone else, but his happiness was as evident as mine.

Bev remarked that we seemed to radiate energy between us, one feeding off of the other and then sending it back twofold. It was an accurate description. I could work for hours as long as he was close. He would come and find me to be near him if he needed the strength or will to finish a job. We were one and the same, two halves of a whole. The problem with being so very close to a person is that when the suffering comes to the one you love, and it will always come, your suffering is beyond all comprehension. It did not take long for me to discover just how much I could be made to suffer because I loved Jinx.

As fall weather settled in and the air took on a sharp bite at night, the atmosphere cleared up and I took every opportunity to use Jinx's gift. Many nights, he would drag me downstairs citing how bad I would feel the next day from lack of sleep and how much he missed his wife in his bed. At times, he got so irritated that he lamented ever having bought the telescope. I assured him that eventually I would become accustomed to having it around and not be drawn up to the observation tower so often. It was something I said just to appease him. I doubted I would ever lose my obsession with the heavens.

Winter lagged just out of reach until after Christmas, making a gale-like entrance the last day of the year. Sleet beat against the side of the cabin all day. We sat around the fire warm and cozy. Thanks to Jinx's meticulous care with the cabin's construction, no cold drafts made it into the cabin from the vicious wind. The temperature dropped steadily all day, making it increasingly difficult to walk outside to retrieve firewood from the shed. Late in the afternoon, I jumped at a loud banging on the outside door. Jinx quickly went to the entrance area, shutting the inside door behind him. The loud noise from the wind made it impossible to hear the conversation taking place beyond the inside door. Stepping to the window I watched Joshua run back toward the mission, as Jinx returned to stand before me.

"Rea, little Lulu Templeton and her oldest brother are lost out in this storm somewhere between here and their cabin. Mr. Templeton came looking for them when they did not return home by dark."

"What were they doing out in this weather?"

"Lulu is really sick, and her pa refused to let her mother bring her in until her fever got so high she became unresponsive and had to be carried. They sent her with her brother. They are hoping he has taken her to Limpers Cave. We are going to hike up there and see if we can find them and bring her back to you here."

"I need to go if she is that sick. I will get my pack and coat."

Jinx grabbed my shoulder and stopped me in my tracks.

"You aren't going anywhere. It is too cold and dangerous. We can't afford for you to get hurt or sick. Joshua is afraid this might be the mumps from what her father described. We need you ready to treat her and others if it spreads around the ridges. You can go over to the mission with me, but then you will just have to sit tight until we can find them. Don't give me that stubborn look of yours either. I don't relish throwing around my authority as your husband. But this time, I don't have any choice. We are going to do this my way, whether you like it or not."

I was speechless. In all the time I had known Jinx, he had never been so adamant about anything. The normally gentle man before me looked more like a lion than my lamb. I knew without a doubt there was no way to change his mind. He was even more stubborn than I was. I nodded in agreement and he smiled and kissed me on the top of my head.

"That's my girl. Now run and get your warmest coat and boots. We need to get to the mission."

Looking back on my life, I wonder how I sometimes missed obviously important things, stuff that normally screamed for attention, but went unnoticed during stressful situations. It never once occurred to me to ask the men before they left if they had the mumps as children. I vividly remembered having them although I was only three at the time and had them just on one side. It was by far the most painful of the childhood diseases I experienced. I could only hope, once they left to find the missing children, that it was not the mumps she was suffering from or that all of the searchers were already immune, especially my Jinx.

Bev and I made a large pot of coffee and sat down to wait on the return of our husbands, hopefully with the Templetons. The winds continued to howl. The sleet turned from ice to snow and began to pile up on the ground and trees around the mission. The cave was only about a mile away, it should not take them very long to return if the children were sheltering there. It kept nagging at me that I couldn't remember Jinx ever talking about any of his childhood diseases. I had allowed the men to go in search of a desperately ill child with no instructions to prevent them from becoming infected as well. I had failed at my job.

To my relief, they returned quicker than I had hoped for. The child's fever still raged, and it did not take more than a brief exam to confirm Joshua's suspicions. We got her settled into a bed and warmed up her father and brother by the fire. After questioning them, I found out that they, as well as the majority of her family, had had this particular illness. They left her with me and returned to their cabin within the next couple of hours.

Jinx sat quietly by the table and listened. The entire time I questioned them, he did not say one word until they had left and I turned to face him.

"You want to know if I had the mumps?"

"Yes."

"I don't remember."

"You don't remember—do you remember anyone in your family having them?"

"No, can't say that I do."

"How close did you get to her?"

"I carried her quite a ways. It's not a fatal disease, Rea, don't worry."

"True, but it would be much harder on you, and it's the fever that bothers me."

"Have you had the mumps, Rea?"

"Yes. And so have Bev and Joshua. So you are the only one we need to worry about right now."

"I'm not too concerned. Don't you worry either."

"I have to stay here tonight. Go back to the cabin and get some sleep. You need to keep yourself strong. Don't argue with me either."

Jinx kissed me softly and stood to leave me at Lulu's bedside. Before he walked through the door, he turned to look back and smiled in a way that normally melted my heart. I managed to smile back, but my soul was weighed down with concern for him. It took days for signs of the mumps to show. It would be many days before I would know if he had contracted the disease. I would not rest well until the time had passed that would prove him to be clear of infection.

Lulu began to gain back her strength over the next few days, and Jinx remained symptom free. I tried not to worry, but it was nearly impossible to keep my eyes off my husband when he came anywhere near me. Eventually, he began to be irritated by my constant surveillance and avoided me as much as possible during the day. At night he said little, and I spent as many nights as the weather would allow on the observation deck, trying to ignore the nagging feeling deep in my stomach. A little under two weeks after the search and rescue, I knew the incubation period was nearing an end. My hopes and fears grew, mingling inside of me until my head began to pound beyond all reason.

I climbed the ridge early one morning and met Ina on her way down toward the clinic. Not that it was any surprise, but she was headed down to bring me herbs for my head. She handed me her bundle without comment, turned, and walked back toward the relative warmth of her cabin.

When I returned to our home, I found Jinx lying across the bed. His head was turned away from me, but I could see the swollen glands on the side of his neck. He had contracted the mumps. I walked to the side of the bed and bent down to feel his forehead. The fever was already building in his body. I moved his head and discovered that both sides of his neck were swollen. It was as bad as I had feared. He looked weakly in my direction and started to say something. I placed my finger over his lips and smiled.

"Don't try to talk. I'm here. I won't leave you until you are better." He nodded and closed his eyes.

Over the next days, I regretted not letting him speak. I wondered a thousand times what he wanted to say to me. His fever continued to rise at an alarming rate all night long; by the next day, he was writhing in pain. The fever had surpassed what I thought was possible. I did not sleep for days trying to keep his high temperature from killing him. Bev and Joshua brought me snow packed until it was almost ice, which I placed around his motionless body on our bed. I began to worry that if he survived, he would not be the Jinx that I had known all my life. The fever lagged so long that Bev and Joshua began to take turns sitting with him while I took short naps on a pallet at the foot of the bed.

The bad weather had returned. As the snow piled up to the windows, the cabin began to feel like a tomb. I prayed and begged God to intervene and save Jinx because I could not. Late into the fifth day, the fever began to ease somewhat, but Jinx still lay limp on the damp bed. I could barely stand from exhaustion, but I could not leave his side. I told my friends to return to their home now that the worst was over, and I lay down beside him to try and sleep.

The sleep was fitful, but I did not wake until morning. When I opened my eyes, Jinx lay facing me. His eyes were weak but clear, and he had a smile on his face. I waited on him to speak, but he said nothing as he stared at me intently.

"You scared me. Are you feeling any better?"

He nodded but still did not speak to me. I thought at first that he might be too tired to say anything, but then panic filtered into my awareness.

"Do you know who I am?" I held my breath. What if my husband no longer recognized me and was staying quiet while he tried to figure out who the strange woman was lying in his bed. To my relief, he grinned and nodded, but still no words.

"Jinx, can you talk?"

Now the smile faded from his face; he slowly shook his head. As he did, a tear dropped from his eye and slid down his check. I should have been prepared for something like this, but it was nevertheless difficult to accept. Not wanting him to see

Bridge Over Calm Water

the fear in my eyes, I leaped to my feet and made my way around the bed to his side.

"I know that it's scary Jinx, but this will pass in time I am sure. Now let me go and get Joshua so he can help me get you up. We need to check you over. You lie there and rest. I will be back as quickly as I can."

I grabbed my coat and boots and headed over to the mission. The snow lay in waist-deep drifts along the path from our cabin. As I struggled slowly through the snow, it gave me the chance to get control of my emotions and try to look at this only from a medical prospective. I had to keep my heart out of this, or it would be harder to help Jinx. Once I had explained the situation to the Eatons, Joshua returned to the cabin with me. Bev headed into her bedroom to pray. At the moment, I felt that Jinx needed God's involvement in this situation more than he needed me.

Joshua and I got Jinx into a sitting position, but his muscles could not keep him upright for long. I feared he could not walk, but he was too weak to confirm my fears. Over the next couple of days, we slowly began to nourish him with liquids. During the next few weeks, he began to regain his strength and could remain sitting in a chair by himself. He had some control of his legs, but not the strength yet to hold himself in a standing position. Our attempts at getting his speech back did not progress as well as his physical improvements. He struggled to say even the simplest of words to no avail. He seemed to grow more frustrated by the day.

One morning, Bev came to me with a request. "Now, I know I'm no doctor, but would you let me take over helping Jinx regain his speech?"

"Thanks for offering, but I'm not that busy, and I really want to do this for him."

"There's something you need to know. Before I tell you, you have to promise me you won't say anything to Jinx."

"Sure, what's it about?"

"Jinx has been able to talk all along, but he struggles and there are long pauses between his words."

"How do you know this and I don't?"

"This is difficult for him, and struggling in front of you makes it especially hard. He has been talking quite a bit to me, mostly when you are out on rounds and working in the clinic."

I was speechless. I had been beyond worry about Jinx. Yet he had been able to talk all along.

Bev could see the anger beginning to build up in me. She took my arm before I could turn and storm out of the mission to confront Jinx.

"You said you would not say anything to Jinx about this. I know you're mad, and I would be too. But there is no understanding the pride of men. He's afraid that you will think less of him because it takes him so long to express himself now."

"That is absurd!"

"Maybe, but it doesn't change the way he feels about it. He tried to wake you that first morning. When the sentence took him a while to get out, he decided not to talk to you at all. Now will you let me help him get his self-esteem back, or are you going to be stubborn and make him suffer even more?"

Every fiber of my body wanted to go over to our cabin and shake Jinx until his teeth rattled. Did he not understand that I was so thankful to have him alive that I did not care if he ever talked again? As I stood there, I slowly began to realize that I had really never told him that. I had tried to treat Jinx as I would a patient. I should have been treating him as my husband and someone I loved.

"I will gladly turn Jinx over into your care. I will not tell him we have talked, but I need to go and tell him something else that you have just made me realize."

I ran to our cabin as fast as three feet of snow would allow. I found Jinx sitting by the fire staring into the flames with a sad and forsaken expression on his face. It was heart crushing. He turned and smiled in my direction. I stripped off my wet clothing and grabbed a wool blanket hanging by the door. Wrapping myself up as I walked in his direction, I could see the old Jinx dancing in his eyes. I would not let myself get sidetracked until I had said my piece. I knelt down at his feet, laying my head on his lap. He began to stroke the top of my head, which made concentrating on what I wanted to say even more difficult.

"Something just occurred to me, and I had to run over here to tell you. I am so thankful just to have you alive and here in this rocker at this moment that the joy I feel right now seems to be oozing out of every pore in my body. When I thought that you were going to die, and there was nothing I could do, it was the absolute worst moment of my life. Nothing else has even come close, not even that night on the bridge. I honestly don't know what I would have done if you had died. I don't believe I could have faced the rest of my life without you."

I raised my face to look at my husband and was rewarded with his most heart-melting smile. That was more than enough for me.

CHAPTER THIRTEEN

Grace Arrives

By the time Robert returned in the late spring, Jinx had recovered to the point that his speech was almost back to normal. Bev had worked wonders. Within weeks of our conversation in the mission, Jinx was talking to me. Even though he spoke mostly in short sentences, it was music to my ears. Eventually, the only recognizable effect of the fever was an uneven gait. His right side never fully recovered its agility, but it was noticeable only to me.

Once the new clinic was completed, our lives settled into a pattern. We had a few years of peaceful happiness. Over time, the void left by the loss of Lilly began to heal. It never filled in, just became less oppressive and much less painful when I remembered her. Robert continued his visits and had new tales of my daughter and her achievements. I noticed his stories had a sort of detached feel to them as if he were only an observer and not really intimately involved in her life. I mentioned this to Jinx one day after an especially detailed description of her first driving lesson. Robert had not been the one to give her the lesson—Sarah had. This made no sense to me considering I had never seen Sarah drive a car the entire time I had known her. Once Robert left the next morning, to return to Rock Island, he did not take the trepidation I felt about his relationship with Lilly along with him. I finally decided to talk to Jinx about my fears as we sat in our cabin one afternoon.

"Jinx, do you not think it is odd that Sarah would give Lilly her driving lesson and not Robert?"

"Not really. Sarah was not like your ma. She drove us to the train the last day I was in Rock Island."

"I just get the feeling that he doesn't have very much to do with Lilly."

"Don't start reading things into his stories, Rea. He loves her very much."

"I know he does. It's just that I really wanted her to be close to Robert. He is such a good man."

"I'm sure she is. He just has that doctor way of talking."

"Doctor's way of talking?"

"You know, sort of detached and business like."

"Do I talk that way?"

"Always with your patients; sometimes with me."

"I do not feel detached when I talk to them or you."

"It's all right, Rea. Sometimes it's best not to get too close to people, especially if you're their doctor. When you talk to me that way, you're mad at me about something. I know that you're trying not to lose control of your temper. Since I have seen you lose control before, I am perfectly content with the alternative."

I started to argue that he was wrong, but the more I thought about it the more I had to admit he probably wasn't. Even though what he said made sense at the time, I still could not rid myself of the feeling that something was not quite right within the McKinney family. It was not any of my business legally. But I couldn't let it go, and it took up root in the back of my mind. From that day on, I began to pay close attention to anything that Robert had to say about his daughter and mine.

The close call with Jinx's fever and the enduring cold of several harsh winters changed me. I began to long for a place of less hardship and more warmth. I mentioned my weariness with the mountains late one night as Jinx sat by me while I scanned the sky through my telescope.

"I know just the place to go if you seek warmth and a laid back lifestyle."

"Where might that be, oh dear one?"

"Hawaii or one of the South Sea Islands."

"That's an awfully long way from here."

"Well, it would have to be a one-way trip, and we would have to travel light. But I know that they need doctors all over the Southern Pacific—especially since the horrible things that happened during the war. It would be an entirely different type of medicine with all of the malaria and tropical diseases."

"Are you serious? You would leave your family behind and go back to a place that caused you so much pain?"

"I loved the islands, Rea. The weather was beautiful, and each island is unique. The war had nothing to do with how I felt about the place or the people."

"This is such a surprise."

"One last thing, the stars look different in the southern hemisphere. We would have to take the telescope even if we could not take anything else."

"I have to admit it's tempting."

"You would love it there. I think you've spent enough time cloistered away in these mountains. Before we get too old, let's pack up and move to a tropical paradise."

"You've been thinking about this for a while, haven't you?"

"Every time I chop wood for the winter and every time the first frost falls, I remember those soft humid island nights. I only came back to the mainland to find you. I intended to take you back as soon as I could, but you already had all of this planned with Robert. I just never said anything about what I had hoped for us."

"You've spent all these years up here with me and all along you wanted to be in the South Pacific?"

"I wouldn't be anywhere without you, but let me just say that I would prefer to be with you in a warmer, more joyful place. These mountains drain the happiness right out of you over time."

"I agree with that, and since you were sick, I have begun to fear what might happen next. I will think about this."

"You think about it for a long time, Rea. I don't want you making any hasty decision that you will regret later."

"All right, but you make it sound really wonderful."

I returned to the telescope. Although we did not discuss Jinx's dream any longer, tropical islands began to float lazily across my imagination. I knew very little about that region of the world. As for the practice of medicine there, diseases associated with the tropics had not captured much of my attention at medical school. I would have to do quite a bit of studying before I could make any kind of intelligent decision.

The sun rose the next morning, awakening me after a long and pleasant dream of swaying palm trees and bright blue water. Jinx's suggestion had gone deeper into my subconscious than I had realized. Dragging my body out of bed was an effort, but the sun was already up and life in the mountains starts very early. I had just finished dressing when I heard a loud knock on our front door. Jinx answered it before I could walk out of the bedroom. When I joined him at the door, I saw Joshua with a sad expression on his face.

"Dr. Ella, could you come to the mission? Someone left another baby at the door, and Bev needs your help."

Nothing in this world robbed the peace from my day like an abandoned baby. This was the sixth one since the birth of the baby Sorrow. Those babies now lay buried in the woods behind the mission. During the past winter, I found myself drawn to the little graveyard to sweep away the snow. Each time, I would remember seeing Sarah doing the same thing to the graves of her children, and my heart would ache for Lilly who was as dead to me as those small human beings lying beneath the cold hard ground. This was one of the many things that I would not miss about the mountains. Jinx had assured me that all children were considered a blessing by the island people, no matter the circumstances of their births.

Bev was bent over her kitchen table cleaning up the baby that lay squirming beneath her slowly moving hands. I walked to her side and discovered that the child was outwardly perfect, quite beautiful actually. Large, coal-black eyes stared out of a delicate oval face. Her skin was an olive tone and, unlike most newborns, almost blemish free. After taking a closer look, it was apparent that she was actually not newly born.

"Bev, I don't think this is a newborn."

"I know it's not a newborn. I saw her mother place her on the porch from my bedroom window. She had her about a month ago. Her mother's name is Bess Talbert. Her husband is due back today from the coal mine where he has been working for the past year in West Virginia. No one has any idea who this baby's father might be, but it's definitely not Roy Talbert's. Everyone here knows about her, but no one will dare tell Roy when he gets back. It would be the death of Bess for sure. She is loved by her neighbors, who, in turn, despise her cruel husband."

"So she just abandoned the baby here to protect herself from him?"

Bev turned to look me directly in the eye. I knew what she was thinking before she continued. "You of all people should understand that sometimes you have to sacrifice being a mother for the good of the child. Roy wouldn't stop with Bess. The baby would not be allowed to live and remind him of his wife's unfaithfulness. Folks around here, especially the men, do not abide in adultery. I know that seems hypocritical considering those babies out back, but it's just one of the many contradictions wrapped up in life here. No one would stand up for Bess if her husband found out. I suspect that Ina had something to do with her decision to bring the baby here. It may seem strange to you, but these people feel sorry for you and Jinx because you will never have children. Family means everything to them; nothing is as important as blood kin."

"Are you trying to tell me that she brought this child here for me?"

"Without a doubt, the mother means for you to have this baby. I saw her face as she walked away. She loves this little girl as I suspect she loves its father."

I stood speechless and rather numb. As I was so well aware, life sometimes knocks you to your knees. This was one of those times, and I didn't know whether I wanted to laugh or cry. I had become accustomed to the fact that I would never be a mother. It had become so ingrained in my thinking that I never considered any other alternatives. Jinx and I had simply assumed it would always be just us. Now, before me on the table, lay a baby; I could see the potential for much joy and heartache. I struggled to maintain my composure when I felt an arm come around my shoulder. I turned expecting to see Bev, but it was Jinx.

"Joshua filled me in on the situation after you left. I thought I needed to come and see our new daughter. She is our new daughter isn't she, Rea?"

"I don't want to sound selfish, but I like having you all to myself. This would change us, Jinx."

"I know, but we have so much love between us, don't you think we have enough to share with her?"

"So you don't mind adding to our family?"

"Actually, I think this is a gift from God. I know she can't take the place of Lilly, but she would be awfully lucky to have you for a mother."

"Do you really believe that is true?"

"I know it's the truth. So what do you say? We've both been through some hard stuff. Let's see if we can give this little girl a good home so she won't have to suffer like we did."

"Okay, but you are going to have to help out a lot more than these men around here help their women."

"Fine by me, I've always been a sucker for dark-haired females. I can already tell that she's gonna be a heartbreaker with those big eyes of hers."

Bev chose that moment to step into the conversation. "I have heard through Ina that her mother did not call her by any name. So I guess your first job as her parents will be to name her."

"I suspect that her arrival at the mission was not a surprise to you, Bev. I beginning to think that you and Ina set this whole thing up. Am I right?"

"I truly had nothing to do with this, but I did suspect Ina was up to something when she dropped by a week or so ago asking questions." Bev then launched into a detailed account of Ina's visit.

I turned to look from her to the baby while she talked and caught Jinx bending over the child gently and rubbing the top of her head. She had a death grip on Jinx's finger and looked intently toward his face. If I had ever witnessed love at first sight, it was embodied in my husband at that very moment. I did not have the heart to voice any reservations I might feel about this baby to Jinx. I would give him anything within my power, and this was within my power.

"So she needs a name?"

"How about Grace?" Jinx said softly without turning away from her.

"Grace, I like that name. But I think maybe you have a reason for wanting to name her that."

"God's grace can be found in many forms, Rea."

"You think this unexpected child is His grace come to us?"

"Of course, she is a gift. One we didn't know we wanted or needed."

"Well, it's crystal clear that you want her, but I am warning both of you now that she will have to grow on me."

Jinx rose up and laughed. He walked around to my side of the table and took me in his arms. "Don't worry Sweetie. She'll win you over, I have no doubt."

"I trust you with my love, but what if she doesn't love us back?"

"Have some faith, Rea. God wouldn't have put her here if it wasn't meant to be."

"All right, Grace it is, but I want to add a middle name please. I think it needs to be Grace Hope Cummings."

"Hope?" Jinx said with a smile.

"Yes, because with grace comes hope."

Jinx kissed me lightly and hugged me until I could barely get my breath. As we sat down by our new daughter to discuss the many things we would need to care for her, Bev left the room. Grace came to us with only the dirty rags in which she was wrapped. At least the weather was becoming warmer by the day so that the need for clothes was not as pressing as it would have been during the winter months. We had no cradle or a cow for milk. Jinx took a piece of paper from Joshua's desk and began to make notes. We knew that Robert would be returning within the next month. If we could get word to him, he would bring us some supplies when he came. The cow became the most important item on the list because Grace would no longer have the benefit of her mother's breast milk.

As though she understood our conversation, Grace began to cry. Jinx left immediately to purchase a cow from one of the few families that owned more than one. Bev returned with sugar water in a bottle to pacify her until Jinx could get back. She also wrapped Grace in a beautiful soft blanket that I had never seen before.

"This is lovely, Bev. Where did you get it?"

"This belonged to my Betsy."

"I didn't know you had a daughter."

"She died many years ago from polio. The fever took her late one night when she was three."

"I am so sorry, Bev."

"She was a little angel, sweet and kind with such a gentle spirit. I still miss her even after all these years. It's why I never speak of her; it still hurts to remember how she suffered. Anyway, I can't think of a better use for her things than to give them to your Grace. I have all her clothes and shoes. Some of them may be moth-eaten or dry-rotted, but I think we can find enough to get you through for a while."

"I don't know what to say."

"Say yes, you silly goose, and let's get this little girl dressed up before her daddy gets back with that cow."

I couldn't speak. Tears were choking me, tears for Bev's loss and her kindness. I hugged her instead, and she smiled and wiped away tears of her own. By the time Jinx returned with the cow, Grace was clean and wearing a simple white gown with tiny pink roses embroidered around the neckline. She was demanding something more substantial than sugar water. The cow supplied warm, creamy milk to calm her rather nerve-shattering wails.

Jinx insisted on giving her the bottle. I settled in the rocker across from him and enjoyed watching how such a large man could be so delicate in his movements. Suddenly, I found that I could not bear the fact that I was depriving him of natural offspring. The thought that such a wonderful man would not be able to pass along his kindness and compassion through his own children made me nauseous, and my stomach began to draw in knots. As quietly as I could, I rose from the rocker and left the mission to walk back to our cabin. I doubt that Jinx even realized that I had left. He was so absorbed with Grace that I did not worry about my leaving disturbing him.

I walked into our cabin and back to our bedroom. It would now have to serve as Grace's room too. I tried to calm my stomach and decide how we would fit even a small crib in the tight space around our bed. Lost in thought, I did not hear the door open. I felt him behind me before I heard him. Turning to look at my husband, I knew that he had noticed my hasty departure and had come to find out the cause.

"I just got overwhelmed by how perfectly you seemed to be suited at being a father. I can't help but feel bad that you can't have your own children because of me."

"Rea, all my life I wanted nothing more than to have a family with you. When I found out the option had been taken away from us, I was sad for a while. Eventually, I was just so thankful that you survived and I could still have you that I never thought about having kids again. Try to remember how you felt after my bout with the mumps. Don't you see that Grace gives us the chance to have that family? I know she's not ours. But if we love her, it won't make any difference, and we can show her that family is about more than just blood."

"You're right. I am being self-absorbed, sorry."

"You don't have anything to be sorry for. Bev has just informed me that if we can be adoptive parents, she and Joshua can be adoptive grandparents. Joshua is already out in his workshop constructing a cradle for Grace."

"That's something else that bothers me. Will we be able to adopt this baby legally since it's such a secret about her mother and father?"

"I don't know how we'll manage it, but I intend to make it legal."

Bridge Over Calm Water

Trusting Jinx to follow up on the legal part, I began to tackle the many little tasks involved in taking care of a baby. I located a wooden crate behind the cabin and cleaned it and lined it with empty flour sacks. Ina showed up later that afternoon with a small, goose feather pillow. The pillow fit perfectly inside the crate and would make a soft bed for Grace until Joshua could finish the cradle. Ina never ceased to amaze me with her ability to always know what was needed and produce it.

The first few weeks were difficult. It was obvious that Grace missed her mother in many ways. She was never quite satisfied with the cow's milk and would never settle until someone sang her to sleep. Bev said that her mother could sing like a nightingale, which would explain why she loved to be sung to. The days and nights became calmer over time, but she still was not an easy child to deal with. Her small delicate body contained a spirit of great determination. She seemed to be struggling against some unseen force, one that she longed to free herself from. In this one way, she bore so much resemblance to Lilly that I found myself overcome with sadness as I watched her squirm.

I mentioned this to Ina on one of her many visits since Grace arrived. She said a very odd thing. According to Ina, some souls are not comfortable contained in a human body. They struggle from birth to free themselves and return to the realm we cannot see. Ina said that Grace would never truly be happy in this life. Her soul yearned to be free and would never allow her peace for all the days that she lived.

Jinx would have laughed and said that Ina was crazier every year, but I couldn't quite make myself disregard her words. I kept them within my heart and worried that Ina might be right. Grace could be one of the tortured souls, people who struggle their entire lives against something not apparent to anyone but themselves. If Grace could be that way then so might Lilly.

As the summer wore on, it was this struggle in the small child that eventually captivated my heart. The few times her face would light up in a smile, it was like seeing a rainbow after the worst of storms. My love for her grew, and I began to think she

Jan Kendall

would be what finally filled the void left by Lilly. Jinx adored the child. Even I had to admit I understood why she tugged so strongly at his heart strings. Jinx was naturally drawn to less than perfect people, or he wouldn't be here with me. Grace gave him someone else to protect and lavish with love. He relished every moment he spent with her.

As always happened, summer slowly faded into fall. To let Grace enjoy the sunshine late one Indian summer day, we carried a blanket to the meadow and spread it under a red oak tree. Grace had learned to sit upright and was finding delight in a dark red leaf. Jinx and I sat leaned against the enormous tree, watching her in one of her rare moments of happiness. As Jinx talked softly to her about the leaf, my eyes began to wander around the meadow. As I scanned the tree line, I made out the form of a woman standing just inside the trees. When I tried to focus on her features, she stepped farther back into the darkness of the forest. I did not think I knew her from my brief glance. But nevertheless, it was unnerving that she did not want me to see who she was.

"Jinx, have you had any luck getting in touch with Bess about the adoption?"

"Not yet, but Roy just went back to the mine a week ago. He won't be back until Christmas so we have time to work out the details."

"Would you do me a favor and try to get it all settled as soon as you can? I've been seriously considering your suggestion to move to the tropics. I want to take Grace out of these mountains—maybe then she will be more calm and happy."

"Are you serious? You are ready to leave?"

"Yes, I am more than ready for a change."

Jinx swept Grace up and began to dance around the tree swinging her in his arms. This gave me a chance to watch him and scan the trees again for the woman. Once she stepped into the sun to keep Jinx in her sight, and I got a good look. I had never seen the woman, but I knew without a doubt who watched us from across the meadow. Only a mother separated from her child could have such intense grief written across her features.

The afternoon wore away. As the sun dropped lower in the sky, the temperature began to fall. We gathered up the blanket and headed back across the meadow toward our cabin. I could not see her, but I knew the woman still followed us along the edge of the woods. When we climbed the porch steps, I hung back and turned to look in her direction. She did not try to hide and was close enough for me to see her face clearly. I felt myself return to that day when I had handed Lilly over for the last time. I knew what she was feeling and that scared me. She now had a desperate look on her face, and a desperate woman might do anything to keep her child.

I rose earlier than usual the next morning. My excuse to Jinx was that I needed to visit an expectant mother high up in the hills. It was not a lie. I did plan to check on the Baker woman briefly on my way to see Ina. Normally, Jinx would have insisted on accompanying me, but he was already occupied with Grace. I slipped out practically unnoticed. Ina would know, if anyone did, what Bess might be thinking about the adoption. The climb up the steep ridge gave me a chance to remember how I had felt in Bess's place. She had left her baby with us to protect her from Roy. She would have to be told we planned to leave the mountains and take her baby out of her reach forever. I would not take her child if she was not aware that she would never see her again.

Ina was rocking on the porch when I arrived and invited me in for a cup of herbal tea. "So what brings ya up ta da top of this har ridge?"

"I need your advice. I think we may have a problem with adopting Grace. We can't get Bess to meet us even though we know that Roy has already gone back to the mine."

"She be hurtn' I suppose, she love that thar baby more'n life itself."

"Do you think she has changed her mind? I mean does she have any other choice than to give her up?"

"Tain't nothn' changed. As long as that thar devil live, she got no choice."

"Do you think she might be hoping he might not come out of that mine one day? If that happened, she would be able to get Grace back."

"You be a smart woman. What da ya think?"

"I think I would be hoping just that very thing if I were her. I'm afraid that things are going to go badly for someone in this situation."

"Why's ya thinkin' dat?"

"Bess watched us yesterday while we were in the meadow with Grace. I wasn't completely sure it was her until Bev asked me if I saw her out in the woods. She had a painful and desperate expression on her face. I can't imagine what Jinx will do if she comes to take that baby back."

"Maybe it be best ifn' you goes an' talks ta her perty soon."

"Will you go with me? So far, she has been avoiding Jinx's efforts to contact her."

"Wes best be a leavn' if'n we gonna get thar and back by sundown."

The hike through the woods toward Bess's cabin was long and difficult. There was not a trail leading down into the valley where her cabin was located. Following along after Ina, I began to think about what I might say to Bess once we found her. I had asked as many questions about the Talberts as my patients were willing to answer. Privacy was a sacred privilege in those mountains. What happened in a family remained private to the family. I did manage to find out, from a couple of my expectant mothers, that Bess had suffered much at the hands of her husband. Roy was an extremely jealous man, and Bess's beauty, which was one of the few things everyone would freely discuss, only fueled his suspicions of his wife. Apparently, there was some truth to what Roy suspected his wife to be guilty of, considering Grace was not his child.

Ina turned and pointed across a long, narrow meadow with a small stream along one side. The cabin nestled back against a hill was one of the nicest I had seen. As we drew closer, I noticed an older woman churning butter under a tree several yards from the front door. Ina dropped back to fall in step with me and began to talk in very soft tones, never taking her eyes off of the path ahead.

"That be Roy's ma, she most likely har to keeps an eye on Bess. I knows her. Her mind be sharp likes a parin' knife. You gonna needs ta gives her a cause ta talks ta Bess. She be like a mean ol' cur dog."

"Wonderful, what is this old watch dog's name?"

"Those that still speaks ta er calls er Ma Minnie."

"I gather she has not had an easy life."

"Roy's a man likes his pa; that makes fer a mean woman."

"Thanks for the warning. Let's just make this a social call. I never made it this far on my original visits to the surrounding homesteads."

We were forced to end our conversation because we were drawing close and didn't want her to hear us. Ma Minnie glanced in our direction once but did not look back up from her churning until we had drawn to a stop in front of her.

"What brings ya sa far from your'n ridge, Ina?"

"This be Doc Ella, we be a workin' our ways around checkn' on folks before winter set in."

Ma Minnie turned to eye me. I suppose I expected her to bite my head off. Instead, she leaned over onto the paddle of the churn and smiled at me. "Seems ya been in dese har mountains fer a while. Took yous a spell to git har."

"Sorry about that, Ma Minnie. But you live a long way from the clinic. I have to say that this is a beautiful homestead."

"My Roy, he be a good provider. Bess be blessed to hav' him fer a husbin."

"Oh, this isn't your cabin? Where do you live then?"

"Up yonder on that thar ridge. I be har keepn' Bess a company."

"Oh, well, that saves me from having to climb that ridge. Is your husband still living?"

"He be stout as yonder oak."

"Well, you seem to be fine. Do you have any problems I might help you with?"

"Naw, I be ta stubborn ta die and ta mean ta abide with a achin'."

"Apparently, this may have been a wasted trip. Is your daughter-in-law here? Could I see her before we begin the climb back out?"

"Bess be inside. She don't needs no doctor neither."

"Would you mind if I met her? To be honest Ma Minnie, I want to see her beauty that everyone talks about."

"These peoples in these har a hills theys talks ta much. Go's on in thar seein' yous come all this way, but be quick, ya hear?"

"Thank you, I will be quick."

Ina stepped to Minnie's side and proceeded to distract her in conversation. I walked up to the open cabin door and peered inside toward the woman standing with her back to me, staring out the window toward her mother-in-law.

"Excuse me, Bess, could I come in for a short visit?"

"You be here to talks about ma baby I's guess."

"Yes, I am here to talk about your daughter. I am confused about one thing now that I have met Ma Minnie. She has to be aware that you gave birth to a baby. How is it that she has not told her son about her?"

"She not wantn' to go back up on top of da ridge with Pappy. Ifn' Roy git rid of me she hafta go backs an' face Pappy ever day."

"I don't have much time. I need to tell you that we will have the papers for the adoption in a couple of weeks. We plan to leave the mountains soon, and we will be taking your daughter away from here. Considering this situation she will be much better off out of this area."

Bess turned to face me now. The tears rolling down her face brought my own pain back sharply into memory. I knew she was in a horrible position. "You ever lost some'un you love so much it make you sick down deep in your'n soul?"

"Yes, I had a child and I can understand your loss. You need to decide if giving this baby up is something you can live with, but do it soon. My husband is very attached to her and only grows more so every day. I will have Ina get you word when the papers are here." I turned slowly and walked out of the cabin and back across the space separating me from Minnie and Ina. Minnie turned to face me as I stopped.

"Don't ya be a worryn' about that thar girl backin' out of this. She be thar to sign them thar papers Ina been telln' me about. I ain't about ta go backs to a livn' with Pappy."

"Thank you, Ma Minnie."

"Humph."

She went back to churning and Ina led me away from the cabin and back into the hills toward my clinic. It was late when I finally made my way back down the steep slope to our cabin. Jinx did not ask me any questions, but more than likely, he knew where I had gone. The next couple of weeks went by slowly for me. Jinx grew more anxious as the days wore on. We expected Robert to arrive with the papers at any time. To our relief, he showed up with supplies early one afternoon. I sent word to Ina that we needed Bess to come to the mission; then we settled in to wait on her arrival.

As the days passed by, and Bess did not come, the weather turned gloomy right along with our dispositions. Jinx fell into a melancholy spirit and, strangely, so did Grace. He wandered around the cabin with her in his arms, saying little. Late one afternoon, as rain slashed across the meadow and beat on our windows, we heard a soft knock on the outer door. Jinx handed me Grace and walked into the small front room. He opened the door to Bess and a man who had helped Jinx with the construction of our cabin. Both were soaking wet. The man hovered protectively behind Bess. I knew without a doubt this had to be Grace's father. Jinx stepped back to allow them to enter the cabin, and I drew chairs close to the fire. Giving Grace back to Jinx, I went for blankets to wrap them in and coffee to warm them up.

The couple sat before our fire and said nothing for many minutes. I could tell by the look on Jinx's face that he knew that this would be the end of our hopes to adopt Grace. He rocked her softly back and forth in his arms and waited for Bess to speak.

"I be har to gits my girl. This har is her'n pa. We be gonna leave these cursed hills and takes her'n with us. I knows yous had it in yourn' heart to be her ma and pa, I be sorry you gonna be sad, but I don't reckon I be able to live apart from her."

At that moment, I didn't have the words to fill the massive gulf that had opened up to consume our hopes. Jinx held tightly to Grace who was staring intently toward her mother. It was obvious that she had some memory of the woman before her. Jinx finally found his tongue and spoke in a low and strained voice.

"What about Roy? Won't he hunt you down? Aren't you putting Grace in danger?"

"Roy ain't gonna hurt nobody. He be dead."

"Dead, are you sure?"

"Yes um'. He be dead fer sure."

Bess did all the talking; the handsome young man beside her just stared ahead into the fire. I would never know exactly how Roy Talbert died, even Ina could not find out what happened to him. With Bess's announcement, Jinx lost his strength and sat down at our table. Bess fell silent as time ticked off slowly on the old mantel clock. Finally, I got control of my emotions and turned to face Bess. "So now you expect us to just hand her over to you without considering what it will do to her?"

"She be ta little ta 'member any of this."

"You are right, she won't remember us. That doesn't mean that we won't remember her or that we don't love her. I may not have a right to this baby, but there is no way I'm going to let you take her out in this weather. The two of you will have to stay here or at the mission tonight. If the weather is better in the morning, we will make a decision as to what needs to be done to help you get on your way."

Bess thought about what I had said and nodded in agreement.

Jinx let out an exasperated sigh. He turned and addressed the man directly, never looking at me. "Ben, do you want me to walk you over to the mission? Bess can stay here with Grace tonight."

Ben slowly rose from the chair and left without saying a word to Bess. It occurred to me that Jinx might have in mind the idea of divide and conquer. He probably hoped to convince Ben not to go along with Bess's plans, and he left Bess with me to work on.

Unfortunately for Jinx, he had no idea how much I could relate to Bess and her pitiful situation. Once the men had forged into the rain, I turned to hand Grace to her mother. Bess's face eased into a beautiful smile as she held her daughter for the first time in many months. She began to sing to her softly, and I watched as Grace's face took on an almost angelic glow. I had never seen her look so at peace and so happy. All my common sense told me that Grace would have an easier life with us, but would she ever be happy in that life? The bond between the mother and daughter was evident as one sang and the other listened.

I could not deprive Grace of what I saw taking place before me at that moment. I wanted to believe that there was something special between a mother and her child, something that exists only between them, unexplainable and eternal. It was foolish of me, but I imagined myself and Lilly in this situation and wanted to believe that Lilly would be able to recognize me even after all these years.

Wrapped up in my thoughts, I did not hear Jinx when he returned. Bess was still singing as he walked up beside me and laid his arm across my shoulder. He leaned in and whispered in my ear, "My heart is breaking, but look at how happy she is with Bess."

"I know." We watched in silence and listened to the mountain lullaby Bess was singing in a soft voice. Slowly Grace's eyes began to droop. In a very short time, she fell into a deep sleep. Bess turned toward us and whispered. "Do ya mind ifn' I puts her'n in da cradle?"

"Not at all, just bring her into the bedroom."

"Grace be her'n only name?"

"Grace Hope."

Once Grace was settled and breathing steadily, I led Bess to the cot in the back storage room. "Sorry, but this is all I have to offer."

"Be fine with me."

I closed the door behind me as I left, joining Jinx at Grace's bedside. We kept watch over the sleeping child all night. Morning dawned bright, the sun burning away our hopes of being Grace's parents. Bess helped me pack up Grace's few worldly belongings in a burlap potato sack. Not long afterward, Jinx and I stood on our porch, and watched the young couple carry their child away from our cabin and out of our lives. Once they were out of sight, Jinx turned to me. "Is this what it was like when you had to leave Lilly in Rock Island?"

"I'd imagine what you feel is very close."

"I'm so sorry, Rea, I had no idea. Do you think we made the right decision?"

"We can only pray that God spares us the torment of doubting ourselves and wondering throughout our lives if what we did now was right for her."

"Have you been tormented by the decision to give up Lilly?"

"Not constantly, but at times."

Jinx and I spent the rest of the day and many afterwards in a haze of misery. He grieved the loss of Grace. For me, the situation was just too much like losing Lilly all over again. As the days shortened into winter, we talked more seriously about leaving the mountains. One night after many hours of discussion, we finally decided that the next summer would be the last we spent there. The idea of a new life appealed to me, and I began to prepare for my departure from the clinic.

One cold winter morning, I sat by the window composing a letter to Robert to inform him of our decision and ask for his help. When I looked up from my paper and out the window, I saw the doctor slowly coming up the hill. As I watched him walk toward the cabin, I noticed that he wore an exhausted expression.

CHAPTER FOURTEEN

A Hard Truth

Robert's sudden appearance, during the coldest part of winter, sent dread traveling from my mind to my heart. Robert never showed up unexpectedly. Jinx heard me gasp when I saw him coming toward the cabin and walked to the window to investigate. He quickly went to the door to open it for our friend. We watched as Robert made his way to the nearest chair and sat down.

In the few months since his last visit, he looked as though he had aged many years. While Jinx stoked up the fire, I quickly put the kettle on to make Robert's favorite tea that we kept just for his visits. He sat silently before our fire while Jinx and I exchanged quick anxious glances above his head. As the morning wore into afternoon, Robert continued to stare forlornly into the fire but said nothing. Jinx and I waited patiently on our friend to bring up the point of his sudden visit. The day continued. Most of the afternoon, we sat around the fire in silence. Occasionally, Jinx added more wood to the fire and I refilled the tea cups. Just as the sun was about to set, Robert straightened up in his chair and turned to face me. My heart almost stopped with dread of what he was about to say.

"I am sorry to come unannounced like this, but I needed to talk to you, Rea. Just a few days after I returned home from my last visit, Sarah became ill. At first, she ran a low-grade fever. Then her energy level dropped, and she began spending a great deal of time in bed. I begged her to go to Nashville and see a specialist, but she refused. The pain began about a week after the fever and grew steadily worse over the next month or so. I watched as my beautiful wife wasted away before my eyes. When she finally consented to go and see the doctor, it was too late."

Robert paused to take a long ragged breath. His pain was evident but there was little we could do to ease it for him. Once again we sat listening to the sounds of the fire and waited. Finally he found the strength to continue.

"Cancer had spread throughout her body. She died the first of last month."

"Robert, I'm so very sorry. I can't imagine how hard this has been for you and Lilly."

He turned to me with an understanding smile and shook his head with weariness. "I will admit to you that there have been times that I did not want to wake up and face the next day. Lilly was away at school during most of her mother's illness. I made a terrible mistake by not telling her how sick Sarah really was." Robert paused for a moment and cast an apologetic look in my direction before adding, "She was the only mother she remembers."

"I know, Robert, and that is how it was supposed to be."

He dropped his gaze to the floor. "You have always been very understanding about Sarah's demands concerning Lilly. Sadly, in the end, her determination to be a mother could not save her. She went from bad to worse very quickly. I called Lilly to come home, but she did not make it back to Rock Island before Sarah died. She blames me for not giving her the chance to say good-bye to her mother. She left home to stay with Sarah's parents the day of the funeral. I have not talked to her since. Lilly is a very stubborn child, always has been. I fear she will never be able to forgive me."

Jinx stood up and walked out of the room, leaving me to face the sad doctor alone. I suppose he felt too much of an outsider to the tragedy playing out around my daughter.

"I know she will come around in time Robert. She loves you dearly, I have no doubt. Just give her room, she will grieve and then she will come back to you."

"After the funeral, I took out all of the pictures of her since you let us have her. I've thought about the blessings we have received by having her as our daughter. The more I remembered, the more I felt that I had to come and talk to you. It was never my wish that you leave Rock Island. Sarah was adamant though, and I let her have her way. I loved her too much and had seen her suffer terribly when we lost our two babies. She wanted Lilly to be loyal to her as her mother. I hope you can understand why she felt the way she did."

"I understand, Robert. Please do not feel bad about me staying away. I believed it was best for Lilly."

Robert sighed before continuing, "Because I know you have tried to do what was right for Lilly, I am here to ask for your help. No, it is better to say I have come to beg you to do something for me. If you refuse, I will understand and not mention this again. Please listen to what I have to say. Then think about it for a while before you give me your answer."

My inner heart suddenly felt heavy with fear, but I nodded for him to continue.

"In the weeks since Sarah's death, I have thought a great deal about what it means to be part of a family. Sarah was determined to give Lilly the perfect life, no mattered who suffered because of her ambitions. I ended up as an intimate spectator, not really a participant. You were not the only one to be pushed away from Lilly. Sarah made sure that I never had the chance at a close relationship with our daughter. As a result, when Lilly lost her mother, she lost her center of balance."

This only confirmed to me what I had long suspected and added to the heaviness pressing down on my soul.

"I blame myself for this. I could have reined in Sarah's obsession with monopolizing Lilly at the expense of anything or anyone in her way. When you still had Lilly, I knew Sarah had enlisted the help of the women at your church and throughout the community in trying to persuade you to give her up. I have tried to justify the fact that she forced you away from your home and everyone you knew for the good of Lilly. I have tried, but I can only see a young girl manipulated by all of us into a decision that altered her life. I know that you would argue that we gave you great opportunities. But in truth, it was cruel and self-centered on our part."

Robert leaned back in the chair and closed his eyes as he continued.

"The result of Sarah's obsession is that Lilly has grown up believing that one person in this world loved her beyond the capacity of all others. She and her mother existed in a world created by Sarah. Now that Sarah is no longer here, Lilly's world has vanished. When Sarah died, Lilly stood alone, bereft of the one thing that gave her life meaning. She's lost, Rea, and she is sinking deeper and deeper into a state of apathy. I talked to Sarah's mother just before I came here. Lilly has not left her room since returning from the funeral. They bring her food, but she eats very little, if at all. It's as though she has given up on life."

At that moment I began to spiral back down into the uncertainty that had plagued me so very long ago. Had I made the wrong decision after all? Robert continued unaware of his effect on me.

"I tell you all of this because you do not know the person your daughter has become. The once joyous child has grown into a self-absorbed young adult. I think it is past time that Lilly understands just how many people loved her throughout her life and the kind of sacrifices that were made for her. Until she knows, she will not realize that we are loved by many people in many different ways. I want her to understand that family is not just defined by those of our immediate association but by layers of people extending out in waves like the ripples on your pa's pond."

As Robert talked, air became more difficult to pull into my lungs. I struggled just to focus on what he was saying. He kept his eyes closed and his head back, unaware of the effect his words were having on me.

"She needs to know that an entire community came together to help because her young mother had the courage to ask for their assistance. She is totally unaware of the extent of the love given freely on her behalf. Once the adoption was final, Sarah made sure she was Lilly's only caregiver. Lilly lost close contact with almost everyone who had been such an intricate part of her life up until that time. Your parents did their best, but, to a certain extent, their hands were tied. Sarah had rules, ones that you were unaware of. Your parents were forced to abide by those rules if they were to continue seeing Lilly."

Robert's voice grew more and more agitated as I sunk lower into despair. I suddenly noticed that Jinx had come back into the room and stood behind Robert staring at me.

"Lilly grew to love the farm and your parents. I have seen her go to great lengths to keep Sarah from finding out how she felt for fear that she would not be allowed to return. Once Sarah was able to enroll Lilly in boarding school, the trips to the farm ceased."

Robert finally raised his head and looked at me as he took the tea cup that Jinx offered him. I couldn't move from my chair. I could tell Jinx was still watching me, but I could not take my eyes off of Robert. It was that obvious he had every intention of telling Lilly about me if I would give him my permission. By the tone of resolution in his voice, I wasn't sure he even cared if I gave him my permission. Before I could work myself up into a full-blown panic, Jinx came to stand behind me, placing his hand on my shoulder. Robert smiled at Jinx and then continued.

"I have had several opportunities during the years to tell Lilly the truth and break the stranglehold Sarah had on her emotions. My fear of losing Sarah's love stopped me. That is why I am here now. When I get back, I want to tell her about her real mother. No, that's not right. I want you to tell her the story."

I jumped to my feet even with Jinx trying to hold me in my chair. He stepped to my side and wrapped his arm around my waist, leaning in close. Robert could see the panic in my eyes, and he stopped me before I could speak.

"I stated that poorly, I don't want you to tell her personally. I would never put you through that. I want you to write it down in story form and from your perspective. I want you to start just before Collin raped you on that bridge and end with the conversation we are having now. I want our daughter, yours and mine, to know the truth. I want to give her the opportunity to reach back and hold onto the love she received from you, your family, and all of our neighbors. I want her to know the sacrifices made on her behalf. Please think before you say anything. Think about it hard, Rea."

Robert ended there without giving me a chance to speak. He took his bag and walked out of the cabin in the direction of the mission. I could see Bev and Joshua come to the porch and welcome him in as though they had been watching for him all along. When I turned to look at Jinx, he shook his head and bent to kiss me tenderly. Without saying a word, he left to do chores that should have been completed by now. He knew that as much as he loved me, nothing he could do would make any of this easier for me. I was left alone in the cabin with Robert's words twisting my heart until I could barely breathe.

The past had returned to haunt me. The cabin felt colder as I stared out the window in the direction Robert had walked. This was the first time in my life that I found myself not liking Robert McKinney. I spent the next several hours pacing and wearing away the floor beneath my feet. Finally exhausted and overwhelmed, I crawled weak and shaking into the soft folds of our old feather mattress. It barely registered when Jinx joined me. By then my head felt as though it was packed with sharp daggers, each fighting to free itself from my skull.

The first rays of light woke me from a dream-ridden sleep, and the nervous energy of the night before returned with the sun. Jinx was already up and gone—perhaps to avoid being witness to the hysteria brewing within me. I quickly dressed in my warmest clothes. I needed space and fresh air to clear my mind and help me think coherently. Many footpaths led away from the clinic into the surrounding hills. I strode quickly across the meadow and took the first path that fell into my line of sight.

I began to recall all the years I had lived in those beautiful and harsh mountains. Having walked many miles, treating and visiting the patients brave enough to come to me for help, I knew the landscape by heart.

The number of my patients had increased slightly every year. However, when Old Gram Hannah died a few years back, the mountain community began to beat a path to Ina's cabin door before they would venture down to my clinic. By bringing her baby to me, her courage had won the respect of the people who could not bring themselves to trust an outsider. Ina had been a great help to those who lived there in the years I had known her. She had brought many people to me who would have died otherwise. During all the long nights and days, she had served me as much as I served her neighbors. We were friends, Ina and I, even with the many differences we had. I had developed a great respect for her as I hope she had for me.

I had also learned over the course of time that the religion practiced in those hills was an odd combination of superstition and fear. Life was so very hard and uncertain that mercy could find no foothold. Therefore, a God of mercy had no common ground with the people who walked the wooded ridges and valleys near my clinic. They were a group of souls wandering in a desert of despair and solitude. So cut off from civilization, the world moved on and left them behind. They believed in God but worked into their belief was the assumption He had no interest or involvement in their everyday lives. They stood alone to fight the enemies they could and couldn't see: hunger, disease, drought, and a host of demons they believed inhabited the dark and foreboding places. Ina served not only as a healer but often as a spiritual guide for those who knocked on her door.

On that morning of confusion and despondency, I walked north along the well-worn path leading to Ina's family cabin. I understood then why so many sought her out. On the way up the ridge, it occurred to me that I should be trying to work this out through prayer, considering the strong evidence of its power that I had witnessed throughout the years. However, I feared God was not happy with me. So I followed the path to the sympathetic ear of my friend and not my God.

The climb was hard and helped to alleviate my frustrated feeling of being pushed into a corner with nowhere to go. It was not surprising, but nevertheless disconcerting, that Ina walked out onto her porch as I climbed the last of the hill leading up to

Jan Kendall

her door. She stood confident, with her arms crossed against the cold as I paced myself coming up the steep rise.

"Seems a might cold ta be out on a walk fer pleasure today, Ella. What brings ya up ta da top of this har ridge?"

"I come in search of advice today, Ina. Could you spare some time for me?"

"I ain't got much ta spare but time. Come inside and gits warm by da fire."

Ina lived alone on a wind-buffeted rock. Her husband had died shortly after I arrived at the mission. A victim of an easily cured infection, he was too stubborn to follow his wife's lead to my doorstep. The nine children, of her short but productive marriage, had died or moved on to other similar hard-fought outcroppings of mountain survival. Like all the cabins, Ina's place had many cracks that let in the brutal mountain wind. Her small fire struggled against the overpowering assault of winter cold, and, in truth, barely kept the temperature inside above freezing. Ina added more wood to the fire, a generous gesture on her part. Two rockers sat opposite each other and very close to the hearth. I chose one and Ina seated herself in the other.

"I have come to ask your opinion on a decision I have to make. Are you up to listening to a very long story?"

"Winter's da best time fer stories."

That said, she took her pipe from the mantel and began to smoke and rock in her chair. She stared into the flames, waiting on me to begin. So I settled in before her fire and told her what had brought me into her mountains. I didn't tell her everything but enough that she would understand why I had left my daughter behind. Then I told her about Robert's visit, his request, and the reason behind it.

For a very long time, Ina sat rocking and smoking across from me, deep in thought. Finally, she stopped the chair and looked me in the eye. "I ain't never been outside of these har hills. All my days been spent just a trying ta makes it through da time I been given. I knows there's life beyond these ol' ridges and hollers. Always thought it was sort of like da promised land, plenty of food and not sa many dying babies. I'm a guessin' I'm a wrong. Mankind, they ain't nothing but evil all their'n days. There ain't no real place of rest on this har earth for us women folk. Always wondered what brung ya har. Now I knows ya was just a looking for a place ta forget. Problem is there ain't no forgetting da past. It gives birth ta da future just like thar little youngn' yous left behind. Yous aferd of telling her about her pa, spreading that thar evil visited on ya into da now?"

I nodded as I said, "I suppose you could say that. I feel as though this will only hurt her. I keep remembering something I read in the Bible about not dwelling on the past and to only look ahead. Wouldn't I be dragging up the past and laying the burden of it firmly in the lap of a young woman who has no idea of the misery that is buried there? I cannot justify that in my mind. Tell me, Ina. Can you see any reason to tell her about her father and add this to the grief she is already suffering?"

"Ya place great store in da words of that thar holy book. I don't need no book ta tell me aboutn' God. He lives in these har hills. His'n glory I see any which ways I looks. He give that thar book ta men, and I suspectn' men be a usen' it more ta serve themselves than da Almighty. Wish I could read them words in thar, maybes I could helps ya more. Who were it that wrote them thar words anyhow?"

"A man called Paul."

"I's remembers hearing that thar traveling preacher man talk about a Paul feller. That Paul, he weren't no woman, and as such weren't a partaker in da sufferings of woman. I don't see nair a thang in that thar writin' t'would bear up ta a woman's struggles. A woman ain't free ta forget, our'n past be bound up in ours childurn."

"But why should my past cause Lilly pain when it can be avoided by not telling her?"

"What I knows is life be hard, ain't no way ta keep pain from findin' us all. You be da one told me da Good Book calls it'n trial bys fire, God's way of riddin' us of da bad, leaving only da good. This Lilly, she needs ta walk through her'n trials too. If'n you think yous gonna protect her from all that thar bad, you is wrong. We's either gonna suffer da fire whiles we's a walkn' this ol' earth, or we's a gonna suffer um when we's passed and tain't no way out. God put da world turnin' a certain way and you'all tried to change it for that thar child. Living in these har mountains, it be hard ta bear, but we's sure about where we's come from and sure whar we's a going at da end of ourn days. It's da betrix and between where'n da fat hits the fire as my pappy always was a sayin'. There ain't nothing good ever happen in this har ol' life which ain't somehows wrapped ups in mis'ry."

Ina stopped and returned to her pipe and her rocking.

There was truth in all she said, but it didn't give me the answer I was so desperately seeking. Ina often reminded me of a politician side stepping the questions and never giving a definite answer. I looked at her and said, "I sacrificed my life so that she could have better than me. I made the best decision I knew how to make, not perfect, but the best I could make at the time. Now I feel as though all my choices were wrong. Robert tells me that Lilly has grown into a person very different than I had hoped she would be."

"T'weren't wrong ta try and give her'n a better life, but it were wrapped up in a lie. Tain't nothing good ever come dressed in no lie."

Ina turned her attention back to the fire, and I wearily tried to resign myself to the truth of her words. Well meaning as my and Sarah's intentions had been to give Lilly a better life, we lied to her in the process. But wasn't a lie in this case better than knowing the truth? Ina was right that I could never really forget the past, not as long as I walked among the living on this earth. Silence enveloped the cabin and the crackle of the fire began to soothe and slow my thoughts.

The light coming through the only window had grown dim, and I knew that it was time to begin my trek back to the clinic. I bid farewell to my friend and started the long walk into the trees. In a very short time, darkness began to envelop the forest. I squinted to see the roots and dead undergrowth that could cause me to fall and tumble headlong down the steep hillside. Ina had not made a protest at my late start even though she knew how difficult the mountains were to traverse in the dark.

As I began to contemplate returning to her cabin, I caught sight of the glow of a lantern coming toward me through the trees. I stopped to wait on the approaching traveler and heard Jinx call my name. He did not scold me for being caught out without a light; he only smiled and took my hand to lead me home to safety. Jinx said nothing on the way back to the cabin. I didn't break the silence. As we walked the last yards through the meadow toward the welcoming light coming from our home, he suddenly stopped and drew me to a halt.

"Rea, this thing that Robert has asked you to do, you know you're not beholden to him?"

"I know that, Jinx. Honestly, I don't know that I have the strength to do this, but I still feel like I can't tell him no after all he's done for me."

"I'll tell him for you if you want."

"Thank you for offering, but this is something I have to do on my own. But tell me how you knew where to find me tonight?"

"I followed you this morning. When you didn't come back by late afternoon, I knew you'd need a light. Robert's in there waiting on your answer; do you have one for him?"

"I have a question for him first."

Jinx wrapped his arm around my shoulders and led me the last few steps to the cabin door. Robert stood with his back to the fire holding a large bundle wrapped in brown paper in his arms.

"What's that, Robert?"

"I thought you might need supplies for writing and an envelope to send it back. The postage is already attached to it. Did you make up your mind while you were gone? Are you going to write down the story for Lilly?"

"Well, I went to visit a wise woman today. I've grown to appreciate the straightforward way of looking at things the people have here. I was hoping that by talking to Ina I could wash away all of this doubt and confusion so that I could make the right decision. Yet, I find myself in the same position I was in nineteen years ago. There is really no way of knowing if telling

Lilly the truth about her father and me will be beneficial to her. You think she has the right to know, Ina thinks that telling her a lie in the first place was bad, and I have a horrible feeling that this is the wrong thing to do."

"I can tell her without your help, Rea. I was there, remember? I patched you up and watched you fight for your life the morning after the attack. I delivered Lilly and then had to tell you she would be your only child. I saw how the community pitched in to help. I will tell her myself if I have to. She deserves the truth, all of it, and only you can give her the whole truth."

"If I were her, I would not want to know my father raped my mother and I was the result of his actions."

"It will not be easy for Lilly to hear, but she needs to hear it anyway. Lilly is not a bad person, just a misguided one. She has such potential in her abilities as a scholar with the resources she will have at her disposal. I believe she could use her gifts to make a true difference in the world. Unfortunately, she will never have the self-discipline to do that until she realizes what it took to put her where she is today. Honestly looking at our past can be a soul-altering experience, and it will take that to pull Lilly out of her self-absorbed lifestyle. Please, Rea, don't follow Sarah in her determination to protect Lilly from all that's hard in this world. My respect for you has been one of true admiration for your strong spirit. Don't let me down now. Lilly so desperately needs someone to show her the way into a promising future."

"You have to understand, Robert. I bear little resemblance to the girl you knew so many years ago. The tragedy and heartache so pervasive in the lives of these people I have worked with here have tempered my faith in our ability to influence the outcome of a life or the right to even try. I am just beginning to understand that this world is so awash in evil that our puny attempts to make a difference have very little effect at all. The very first baby I saved here, Ina's daughter, died late last summer in childbirth. Her husband will remarry, but what will become of the little girl she left behind? There is a tradition in this area that stepchildren are not treated with kindness. I hold myself accountable for the position that child will have in this world. If I had not saved her mother, she would never have been born. It is disheartening to see your best intended efforts end in such a sad way. This is the fear I have for Lilly. Maybe I have done enough damage to her already."

I stopped to take a deep breath.

"Maybe Pa was right about the curse on women. Maybe I committed the same sin with my decisions for Lilly as Eve did by grasping at forbidden fruit. I overstepped my authority trying to choose the direction Lilly's life would take. By telling her the truth now, will I set things back on their original path, or will I commit the same mistake all over again? Can you answer that question for me, Robert? How can anything good come out of the evil and heartache that is in the story you want me to tell? Would she really want to know the truth about her father? Would she even believe me, considering the picture that I know Sarah has given her of Collin over the years?"

Robert let his head drop and heaved a heavy sigh. I could tell by looking at his expression that he had already considered these questions and really had no answer for me. As we stood staring at each other's feet, I had to make a decision.

"Robert, I am perfectly content that she never knows anything about me. However, I have grown weary of battling the demons embedded in this secret that have tormented me for so long. Out of respect for you, I will do as you ask. I pray you are right and that I am wrong for Lilly's sake. Maybe in the end, you will choose not to show her my story."

Robert hugged me warmly and gathered his things to leave. Jinx offered to escort him back to the train station at morning's first light.

Robert left me with the stack of blank pages lying conspicuously on the table. I stared at the paper and began to think about those days in the spring of 1941. As I stood transfixed, going back over the misery of those months, my body began to shake. Jinx brought an old quilt to wrap around my shoulders and did not question my decision to shun the bed and sit down in the old creaky chair before our fire. It was a feeble attempt to shield myself from the bitter cold of the winter and the overpowering dread of what I was about to face. Jinx and I had never discussed in detail what had happened to me after he left to join the navy. He knew that it was not something that I relished remembering.

Bev came early the next morning bearing breakfast and moral support. The night had been long and depressing. During the little amount of time I slept while sitting up in the chair, I dreamed of the bridge again with brutal clarity. Time after time, I would wake with a start and dwell on the events of that life-changing summer. I truly believed that I had climbed out of the horrible pit that had entrapped me and would never have to face it again. However, once more, I felt the void pulling me down into deep despair. Maybe Robert was right. Perhaps the only way back through the mire of misdirected steps was to tell Lilly the truth.

Bev volunteered to serve as my secretary. In part, I suspected, to be able to hear the whole story. I knew she was curious about what had brought me to the mountains, but she had respected my privacy. During all of the years we had known each other, she never asked me questions about my past.

I gladly accepted her offer. The thought of writing all of it down was a bit overwhelming for someone who seldom wrote anything at all. We settled in at the kitchen table and began to discuss how to approach my task in order to complete it as quickly as possible. Before long, we heard a knock at the door. Walking across the room to answer the summons, I expected to find someone in need of medical attention. Instead, Ina stood before me holding a sack and wearing a smile.

"Thought you's might needs a little company while's you's a writin' that thar stuff down fer yourn' friend."

"Ina, how did you know I would decide to do this?" She only smiled again then walked over to the table and sat down. "I believe you and Bev might just be the only two people who could help me finish this. What's in the sack?"

"Tea and herbs to calm that thar headache of your'n."

"You're a great friend, Ina."

That day we began a ritual that continued for several months. I spent the days remembering and the nights in restless sleep haunted by dreams and visions. We took every weekend off, and often I didn't have the strength to continue through the weekdays. For some reason, very few people came to the clinic. It was as though the entire community stood vigil, waiting on me to pass through what became a terrible ordeal. Ina's mountain remedies kept my energy up and my nerves from fraying at the ends. Bev said very little as she wrote silently at the table. Both women served as instigators with questions and observations as we proceeded through each long, soul-wrenching day. As we drew toward the completion late in June, I was still tormented by doubts and fears for Lilly, so I decided to try once more to obtain Ina's opinion.

"Ina, have you thought about what we discussed that day in your cabin? Do you think I am doing the right thing?"

"Writin' all this har misery down, it be good fer your'n soul. It be cleaning all that thar sourness out, and leavin' room fer better thangs ta grow, likes cleaning out a festerin' wound."

"You're very good at not answering a question. You remind me of Pa. When he wanted me to decide for myself, he would always give me something to think about and avoid the answer. I've been dreaming a lot about Pa these last few days. Dreams about the few times we would do things together. When I was little, he used to take me fishing at the lake. We would see schools of minnows swimming at the surface, feeding. It seemed like they were all fighting for the same spot.

"I keep thinking we're all just like those minnows, striving to get to the surface for something. Some of us are reaching for peace beyond this life, some for riches, and others for the love of another person, like Sarah was with Lilly. The problem is that we are knocking each other around and pushing each other down away from the air and light above. Most people never realize the effect their actions have on other people. I have no doubt that this will change Lilly's life, but how? I still think I am making a mistake."

"Don't make no difference now. You's done give yourn' word ta that thar doctor ta send him this har story."

"I know, Ina, but that doesn't make me feel any better about what I'm doing."

"Maybe he's a gonna change his'n mind not give it ta her a'tall."

"Maybe."

Bev sat quietly as she listened to my conversation with Ina. Her tendency to always be optimistic and her ability to always find the good in every situation had prevented me from seeking her advice. Some people in this life seem to live on a higher plane of existence. Bev and Joshua both resided there. After she heard the story, I feared that she disapproved of my decision because of the pain it would cause Lilly. She spoke up at that moment.

"Would you like my opinion on this, Rea? I don't want to pry, but I have been thinking about this a lot."

"Please tell me, Bev. I just assumed you did not approve of me doing this for Robert since you have said nothing before."

"This is what I think. Lilly has lived a pampered life enveloped in darkness. This will give her a chance to see the light so to speak. It will not be pleasant, but everyone deserves to know the truth that lives beyond a lie. If you feel uncomfortable with the idea, then turn your worries over to God. Let him guide Robert in his handling of the story once you send it to him."

"Thanks, Bev. That actually makes me feel some better."

After that conversation with my friends, I pushed myself to finish as quickly as I could. I felt lighter and freer with every day and word that brought me closer to the end. Today, I am sitting on the front porch of a rustic medical clinic, buried deep in the mountains, staring down at the last page I will be adding to the story Robert has asked for. The facts, as I remember them, are all here, every painful and unforgettable event that led me to this place. I have done all he has asked, but I struggle to consider this complete without saying something to the daughter I left behind so many years ago.

To Lilly:

What do I say to you? You owe me no loyalty. I gave up my right to have any influence in your life when I handed you to Sarah. You could not have had a better mother than Sarah McKinney. Robert feels she was too protective of you. I cannot find fault in her labor of love on your behalf.

I only ask that when thinking of Collin and what happened between us that you remember you are not defined by the mistakes of your parents, only by your own decisions. If you doubt the validity of this statement, look at the direction my life took after that one night on the bridge.

Your destiny spreads out before you with great promise. But the true treasure of your life lies buried outside your retrievable memories. As a very small child, you were able to unite a community to rise above their prejudice and come together in a common purpose. Without doing anything beyond being yourself, you gave people joy and happiness when there was very little to be found in the world. The war raging at that time left people torn and empty of hope. The families that cared for you at my request found hope in your smiles and laughter and peace in your gentle, kind spirit.

We are strangers, you and I; yet half of what makes you the person you are comes through me. I can tell you that you come from a strong and determined people. I know that you have within you the ability to weather any storm your life will produce, even the sadness in the story of your beginnings. Forgive me if you find this a burden to your soul, but I could not find it in my heart to tell your father no.

I will be leaving these mountains very soon. Jinx and I will travel to the South Pacific to work at several missionary outposts spread among the various islands. We have decided to stop in Rock Island on our way to San Francisco. I want to say good-bye to my family since we plan to spend the remainder of our days serving the native South Sea Island people. Jinx says they are a proud people with a deep sense of community.

I am going to deliver this story to Robert, although I will make sure to respect your mother's wishes. She

made me vow before God to never contact you, even after her death. She wanted you to only think of her when you thought of your mother, and well you should. My prayer for you is that you have a long and happy life, full of love and joy, absent of evil and pain. A wise woman has taught me that this is an impossible request of God on my part, but I will make it on your behalf anyway. Be kind to your father; he was always kind to me.
Rea

I laid the pen down on the swing beside me and took a deep breath of clean mountain air. In the yard before me, Jinx and Joshua struggled to load the few worldly possessions we would take with us on the back of the mission's cantankerous old mule. The two men were trying to balance the telescope on the top of the pile. The mission had located a new doctor who would arrive within the week. To help him and his young wife adjust to life here, we left everything in the cabin except our clothes, the telescope, and some mountain crafts I intended to give my brother and his family on our final visit.

Glancing across the meadow, I could see Ina and several of the mountain families coming toward the clinic. I expected a visit from my friend but not the people who trailed behind her. In the few minutes it took for the visitors to cross the meadow, I ran back through my mind all the times I had treated the families who were following her. I could see many children walking with their mothers. Until then, I had not realized how many times I had delivered the mother and later her child. Ina carried a bundle in her arms. At first, I thought she might be bringing a newborn for me to check before I left. But as she walked up the last part of the path, I could tell it was an unusually large quilt. I rose to meet her in the yard; our porch was way too small for such a group. She stopped me before I could descend the steps.

"Wait right thar, Ella. We's brought ya sumpun and everbody wants ta see ya when I's a telling ya about how it come ta be."

I stopped and waited for her to join me on the porch. Jinx, Bev, and Joshua came to stand with the group that gathered around the steps below me. Once everyone had found a spot, Ina asked Bev to help her hold out the quilt and positioned me so I, and the people in the yard, could see it clearly.

"You's remember that vary first time I's ever come ta da clinic? When I was a toting my baby Cassie and her's so sick?"

"I remember it very well, Ina."

"Wells, that vary next week, I's takes a small piece of that thar dress that Cassie was a wearing and I's puts it in a sack. Den ever time yous helps birth a new childs, I gots a scrap of'n cloth from thar ma and puts it in da sack too. Perty soon, grown peoples finds out about my sack and they be bring'n me scraps from whatever they be wearing when you's helps pull dem from da fires of sickness. Den these har women folk start coming up ta da cabin a helping me put them scraps together ta make this har quilt. Since you's a leaving, we's had ta stop a making it and we's come ta gives it ta yous."

Ina stopped and a wonderful heartwarming smile spread across her face. I glanced at the women and children below me; they too were grinning shyly in my direction. I turned back to look at the quilt. In the center, I saw a little cotton patch of tiny flowers on a faded, yellow background. I remembered the badly worn little dress that hung loosely from Ina's tiny infant's frame that very first time I saw her. This was a priceless gift; it embodied all the years of work that I had put into helping these people. I could literally reach out and touch a part of each person who had walked or been carried through the door of my clinic. Looking at it brought back the memory of the quilt I had received so many years ago as a gift for Lilly.

"Oh, Ina, this is the most magnificent thing I have ever seen. You do not know how much this means to me. I will carry this with me whereever I go for the rest of my life."

"Guess that means we be a going with ya on that thar journey you's about ta takes."

"You'll be there every step of the way."

Ina stepped forward and hugged me. The women and children followed suit and there was much laughing and reminiscing. Not long after, the men of the mountains began arriving carrying various instruments and jugs of cider and homemade spirits. Apparently a party had been planned in our honor without my knowledge. Bev and Joshua supplied a feast that was rarely seen by the people here and did not protest at the obvious alcohol-induced joy of most of the husbands. It did my heart good to see my neighbors and patients enjoy themselves even if it took my leaving to present them the excuse to do so.

    The party postponed our departure until early the next morning, but I didn't mind. I was leaving the mountains as an accepted member of the community, something that had seemed impossible so many years ago. I took with me their gift into which were sewn the memories of all that had been my life in that cradle of human suffering.

CHAPTER FIFTEEN

A New Beginning

The next morning, we walked out of the mountains under a soft blue sky. The air was heavy with a musty smell stirred up from the forest floor as the animals made their way through the trees. I was enveloped with sorrow as we wound our way down the mountain trail and away from my friends and the home we had made there. Jinx and I had not traveled often together and had no official honeymoon. We took the train into Chattanooga, a detour of some distance, but it gave us the opportunity to see the beauty of our home state one last time before we left the mainland for good.

We spent a week in Chattanooga gathering supplies to be shipped to the mission in Hawaii where we would have a base of operations. We would travel great distances from the Hawaiian Islands, but we needed a place to filter supplies to the different islands on which we would set up small clinics.

Through correspondence, Bev had enlisted the help of a missionary family on the big island of Hawaii she had worked with before in southern Georgia. They were excited to be involved and proved to have a valuable network of acquaintances spread out among the islands south of Hawaii. It was to their small missionary outpost that I sent the medical supplies with instructions for their storage until we would arrive in about a month.

On the day the train pulled into the small station outside of Rock Island, my brother Steve met us at the depot and loaded our bags into the back of his car to take us to the farm. He told me that he had not seen Lilly since Sarah's death and did not think she had returned to live with Robert. Over the next few days, we reconnected with my brother and got to know his wife and their children. Steve was already a grandfather and had grown to value the life he lived on our family farm. He was warm and loving with his family. The joy was evident in the house that had once endured so much heartache. I visited the graves of my parents. Not being able to attend their funerals had been one of the many things I had missed while away from my home. Standing by their tombstone, I was reminded of the graves of the small babies at the back of the cemetery. Turning to seek them out, I was sad to discover that they were so buried by leaves and debris that the markers were barely visible. In memory of Sarah, I carefully cleared away the graves and wiped off the markers with my jacket.

  The afternoon before our departure, Jinx's family gathered at his parents' home for a reunion. I felt the need to leave him in peace to say good-bye and yet was too restless to stay at the farmhouse without him there. Knowing I would never again see the place of my birth, I walked the lanes and woody paths around the farm tying to memorize the landscape so that I could recall it later.

  I had not thought out my route or really paid attention to the direction I took since the compulsion to cover as much territory as possible occupied my mind. As the sun began to sink behind the trees, I realized I was walking down a path that ran beside the road leading to Rock Island. I could already see the bridge through the foliage; my old instincts pulled at my determination to proceed further. Maybe I knew this would be my last chance to prove to myself that I had conquered my fears. Or maybe I just wanted to force myself to face it one more time. Whichever, I continued along the path to the edge of the lake and stared at the metal structure before me. It took several minutes, but I managed to walk with calm resolve out onto the center where I stopped to stare down at the calm, deep, green water below.

While peering into the water's silent, glass smooth surface, memories from all the years that lay behind me drifted back. Clear memories of my childhood flooded into the present, pleasant thoughts of the many times I had spent with family and friends swimming and fishing in this lake. As my daydreaming continued, I did not hear the footsteps of the person who came to stand beside me. I raised my head up when I felt the railing give because of the added weight.

I was not prepared to see the person that turned and smiled in my direction. The years melted away; I saw a face I could never forget and tried never to remember. The silver blond curls framed her head like a halo. I could see her father staring back through her amber-colored eyes and feel his presence in the way she stood and reached toward me with her hand extended in greeting. I tried to control my facial features, but I knew by her expression she could tell I had recognized her.

"I am sorry to startle you. My name is Lilly McKinney. You look like you have just seen a ghost."

She laughed nervously as I took her hand to shake it, trying to harness my overwhelmed emotions and search out the proper path to take through this minefield of a potential disaster.

"Hello, Lilly. My name is Ella Cummings. I'm sorry to seem a little taken aback, but I have not seen you since you were a baby. You have grown into such a lovely young woman."

"Ella Cummings, are you the Dr. Ella Cummings from the clinic in the Appalachians that my father has talked about all my life?"

"I had no idea that he spoke of me. I guess it never occurred to me that he would discuss the clinic with anyone from the outside."

"Oh, we heard in great detail about all the things that had happened between his visits. My mother was not especially interested, but I was always fascinated by the stories he would bring back and relive for me at night at our dinner table."

"It is a very interesting place. The people are extremely independent and self-reliant. Your father was a great help to me

Jan Kendall

throughout the years. I will miss working with him. He is such a caring and understanding physician."

"You are not working at the clinic any longer?"

"No, I needed a change. Jinx, my husband, and I are leaving tomorrow to work with the native people of the South Pacific Islands."

"Does my father know? I have not been at home much since my mother's funeral, but I can't imagine that he would not have mentioned it to me had he known."

"I wrote him about it a couple of months ago. I have not heard back from him. The doctor taking my place is hoping Robert will continue to come for at least a while to help him with the difficult process of winning the trust of the people there."

Lilly turned to look out over the lake, which gave me a chance to appreciate the beauty of the young woman before me. She truly bore a remarkable resemblance to Collin. I could see very little of me in her physical appearance, yet there was something about the way she stood leaning on the rail that was familiar.

"Dad and I have never been as close as Mother and I were. It's been really difficult talking to him after she died. I just came back this morning from my grandparent's home in Chattanooga Dad is gone to a medical meeting in Atlanta and won't be back until tomorrow. I wanted to surprise him when he returned. I am afraid that I have not treated him very well over the last few months. I walked down here to the bridge today because it is one of my favorite places to think. My mother did almost everything for me. I guess you could say that she spoiled me. I'm not comfortable trying to work things out on my own. I know Dad did not approve of how she protected me and gave me anything I wanted, but you can't blame me for enjoying the attention. Did you know I was adopted? Mama told me on my last visit here before she died. She said that she felt like I needed to know the truth now that I was older. My dad doesn't know she told me though. Her brother, Collin, was my father."

"Yes, I knew your parents before you came along. I used to see your mother out in the graveyard caring for the graves of the little babies she lost. It was one of the saddest things I have ever seen, and I have seen some very pitiful human tragedies in the mountains over the years."

"Did you know Collin? He was killed in the war before I was born." Her voice took on the quality of a small child, wistful and expectant.

"I met him a couple of times although I did not really know him. You look very much like him though."

"Did you know my real mother? All Mama would say about her was that she was very young and unable to care for me properly. I have asked everyone I know in Rock Island, and they are all very vague about her. I can't even get anyone to tell me her name."

"I'm sorry, Lilly. I made a promise to Sarah many years ago not to ever tell you about your mother. I knew I would not be around here, and I didn't ever think that we would be having this conversation. If it makes you feel any better, she was very young and not prepared for motherhood. She felt you were meant to fill the void in Sarah's life, but it was very difficult for her to give you up. Now please don't ask me anymore because I don't want to be unfaithful to my promise."

I quickly added, "I am sorry that I will miss Robert. We are leaving very early in the morning. Would you please tell him he has a beautiful daughter and that I have left him the information he requested from me on his last visit with my brother. You have a wonderful father, Lilly. Don't ever take him for granted. He is a very wise man and always has your best interest at heart."

Turning without saying goodbye I left the bridge. I did not look back for fear that Lilly would see the tears I could no longer hold back. I did not find the self-centered child in the young woman I had just met on the bridge, but the encounter was brief and I doubt I would ever be a true judge of Lilly's character. Apparently a mother will always see the best in her own child, even when she has been no mother at all.

The night was long and torturous. I was more than ready to set out at dawn's first light. It felt as though the hounds of hell nipped at my heels as I made my way down the steps and climbed into the waiting car. The unexpected meeting on the bridge had been dangerously close to breaking my promise to Sarah. I needed to once more put distance between myself and the daughter who now was more than just an apparition inhabiting the dark and painful corners of my memories. I could only hope that once Robert returned and saw his daughter, he would no longer feel the need to show Lilly my written words.

As we drove to the depot and loaded our belongings on the train, Jinx and I were absorbed in our own thoughts. Once the train moved out and picked up speed, I began to tell him about seeing Lilly, and he listened quietly. As the train slowly made its way across the breath of our home state, passing farms and small towns, I attempted to once again let go of the past and embrace a future as unfamiliar to me as the young woman I had left standing alone on the bridge the day before. I found solace in the fact that she had people to love and care for her. I tried to accept that I would never know if the decisions I had made concerning Lilly had been the right ones.

The train came into the Memphis station late on a Sunday afternoon. I watched people arriving and departing, all going in different directions, each with their own trials to face and fears to overcome. I thought of those I left in the mountains who struggled just to survive. I wanted to believe that God had led me into those mighty hills and that now he was leading me away. I wanted to believe. But deep within my heart there was still doubt. I could see nothing wrong in our decision to seek out a new life. But could the great distance cut the ties that bound me so tightly to my past and free me to live the rest of my life in peace?

The train began to move, heading ever farther from what lay behind. Trying to clear my thoughts, I closed my eyes and lay my head back against the seat. The rhythm of the wheels running along the tracks slowly lulled me to sleep. I began to dream again. Not of collapsing bridges or abandoned babies but of long white beaches and soft, lapping water. In the distance, I could see the outline of a beautiful woman walking away from me. There was something strangely familiar about her so I tried to draw closer. The faster I walked the more stiff the sea wind blew. Just as she turned to face me, I awoke with a start. I found Jinx eyeing me with concern.

"Somethin' wrong, Rea?"

"No, I was just having a dream."

"What kind of dream?"

"Oh, a dream about a wonderful, glistening beach on a warm tropical island." Jinx stared me down with a worrisome look.

"It was just a dream, Jinx, a dream that meant nothing."

I said this with lightness in my voice so that it would cover the heaviness I felt in my heart. I knew my dreams would haunt me the rest of my life, and I guess they would haunt Jinx too.

Out the window I could see the train was heading into an ominous storm. Raindrops splattered across the window and were pushed along by the wind. I began to imagine they were the fears wrapped up so tightly in my life. As each drop was ripped back into the storm, I began to let go of the doubts that had been my companions for so long. By the time the deluge began to wash a solid sheet of water past by gaze, my soul felt clean and light.

I would ride that train across many miles, but I had already completed the hardest journey I would ever take. Over the years and through all the trials, peace had somehow managed to find its way into my heart. I lay my head back against the seat and closed my eyes, allowing that peace to grow and fill my mind, sending me back to dream again of blue waters and sandy beaches.

CPSIA information can be obtained at www.ICGtesting.com
Printed in the USA
LVOW061248020612

284362LV00003B/2/P